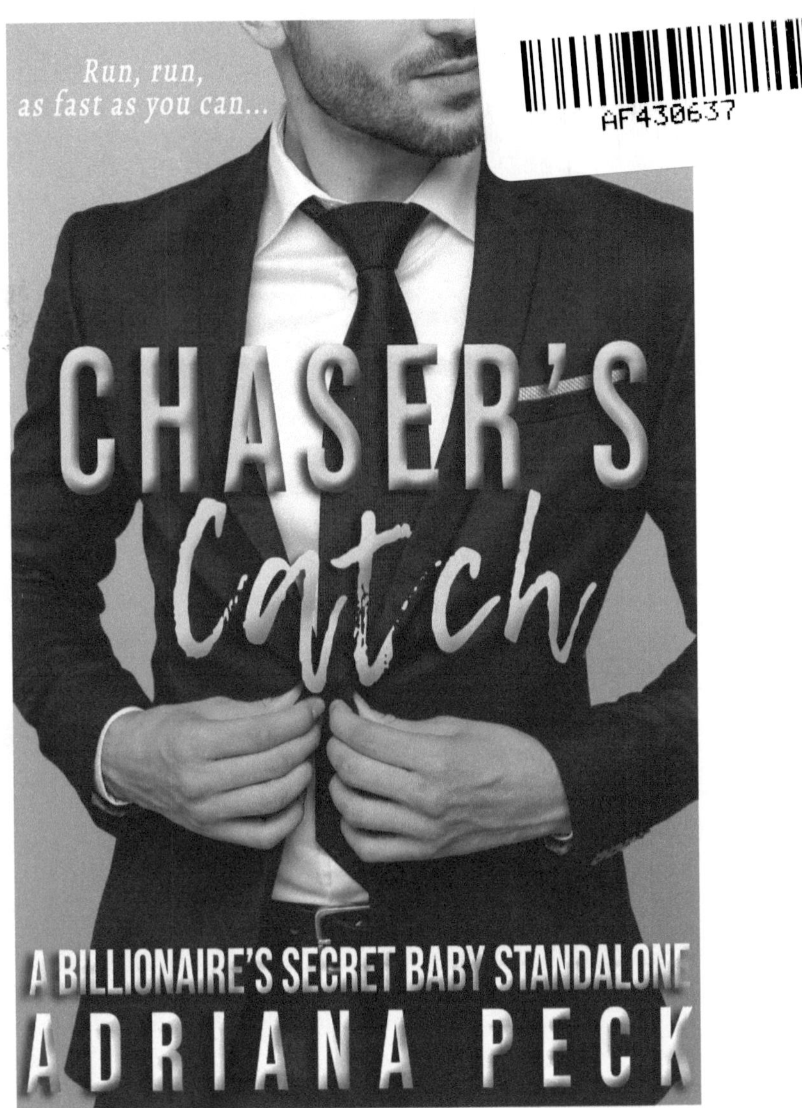

Run, run,
as fast as you can...
CHASER'S
Catch
A BILLIONAIRE'S SECRET BABY STANDALONE
ADRIANA PECK

I

CHASER'S CATCH

A Billionaire's Secret Baby Standalone

Adriana Peck

PREFACE

My life came to a screeching halt in that Moroccan bathroom.

Two pink lines. And this test doesn't lie.

I'm pregnant, and I know just the man responsible.

Alistair Jensen, the billionaire playboy CEO who's always on the move. I couldn't resist him back when we first met in Paris. Those dark hazelnut eyes, that powerful stare, that cheeky smirk of his in the soft light of the evening.

Irresistible.

Even if I was technically at work, I knew I had to have him.

And it looks like our one night in Paris came with a stipulation in its contract.

I'm nervous. Terrified. I don't even know where to begin.

I have no clue where I can find Alistair. He could be anywhere in the world, and I don't know if I'm even on his mind anymore.

But I have to find him. Before this pregnancy becomes the center of my life, before my supervisor overseas pulls me back home.

Before I lose Alistair forever.

And before it's too late.

ISBN-13: 9798642044858
ISBN-10: 1477123456

Cover design by: Adriana Peck
Library of Congress Control Number: 2018675309
Printed in the United States of America

For Amber

CONTENTS

ONE
Samantha

My life just came to a screeching halt in a Moroccan hotel bathroom. Seated there, hunched over on the toilet seat, I sit face-to-face with a life sentence. The plastic test in my shaking hand isn't lying. The two lines are on the left side of the stick, and the pidgin-English instructions on the box make things fairly clear. It's the third test I've taken so far today, and the results have all been the same.

I'm pregnant.

Oh my god.

How did this happen to me? I mean, seriously. My mind's racing, a million thoughts flying past me every moment. I rack my brain, collecting my thoughts as I re-trace every step I've taken this past month.

I've been in Morocco on work assignment this week, chasing down Terrence Malstrom, the US government's number one most wanted fugitive. He's a bad guy, I'll put it that way. Nothing's above him: financial crimes, bomb threats. Nada. Last week I was in Switzerland, the week before, France, just trying to track this guy down. Working as a field agent for the CIA keeps you busy, and my career's been nothing short of hectic ever since I started work as an intern six years ago. Life comes at you fast, promotions come even faster when you've got the work ethic I do.

I've been a field agent for the past two years, chasing down the US government's most-wanted criminals. They usually run abroad, and when that happens, I chase after them. Uncle Sam foots the bills—hotels, busses, planes, you name it. If I can find who they're looking for, the government doesn't particularly care what kind of bills I rack up. I've brought in three of the FBI's top ten most wanted since I took the field agent position. If I'm on the clock, they can count on me to get the job done. No matter the cost.

Until, that is, you wake up one morning, sick to your stomach. You have to call your boss, and your boss's boss, explaining to them both separately that you must've eaten something raw at dinner last night. I still haven't done that, and I know exactly how the conversation's going to go. They'll sound sympathetic enough, but everyone knows the longer you're sick in a hotel, the more it's going to cost them in travel fare. Hospital bills. Days and days of waiting for me to get better. It's a money pit, getting sick in the field as an agent. And it's usually followed by a performance review when you're well enough to fly home, if you're still able to finish the job, that is.

Except I don't have food poisoning.

This is worse. Much, *much* worse.

And before long, it's going to require my complete and undivided attention.

As I sit on the toilet seat, the bathroom door cracked open to the hotel room outside, I can feel my life passing in seconds. Every moment I sit here, unable to move, frozen in fear, is another moment gone.

I shake my head, trying to dust the cobwebs out from my frontal lobe.

Seriously, how did this happen?

When I'm out in the field, sometimes you get to have a little fun. Hey, no need to judge. I don't have a boyfriend back home, so nobody's waiting for me stateside. And it's not like I'm James —*Janet?*—Bond or anything. I'm not sleeping with every guy who flings themselves at me.

But there was one.

And I remember everything.

I run my fingers through my blonde hair, trying to get a grip on my reality.

It's all starting to come back to me now.

Paris, France. I was following a lead on the Malstrom case, staying in an inconspicuous hotel just a few blocks south of the Eiffel Tower.

There was a man in the lobby. I was tired, exhausted after a long day of reviewing the local police's case files in the lobby. I'd been sitting, burnt out, my head resting in my hand when I decided to head to the bar for a tall glass of ice-cold water.

And that's when I met him.

Tall, dark, handsome. He wore a suit, shook my hand casually when he sat down next to me. We hit it off, he bought me a drink. Charming. Funny banter, I remember that. And the night we shared wasn't half bad, either.

What was his name? I shake my head for the umpteenth time, bunching my hair up as I try to rack my brain. I can't believe I'd forgotten—

And then it hits me.

I remember his name. It was a famous one, one I'd heard somewhere before. When I recognized who he was, I was dumbstruck. Smitten. I honestly couldn't believe it then, and I certainly can't believe it now.

Alistair Jensen.

The world-famous CEO of Pemberton Computers, one of the most influential and well-known businessmen in the entire world. A billionaire, easily. And he was charming to boot, too.

How in the world could I forget *that?*

TWO
Alistair

The view from the top of the world isn't half-bad.

As I stand next to the contractor I've spend the last two hours negotiating with, staring out the massive plate-glass window in front of us, I can't help but feel like I've found my next office space. This contractor, Robertson, represents the Imar Family who owns this building, and it's been one hell of a deal getting this lined up.

The Burj Khalifa. The tallest building in the world, almost three-thousand feet tall, nearly a mile high. I'm renting out an office on the hundredth floor, which is no small task in and of itself. And I'm not *just* renting an office; I'm trying to get the whole floor. After all, the CEO doesn't usually have to be present when negotiations such as this take place. But when you're asking to rent out an entire floor of the tallest building in the world, heads turn. Questions get asked. And someone has to answer them.

The city below looks like a play-set for children, people walking about like ants, and I can see the desert bordering Dubai for miles in every direction. A sandstorm rages on the horizon, and I turn and face Robertson as I point out the storm.

"Should we be worried about that?"

Robertson chuckles. He's an older gentleman, someone who knows the ins-and-outs of high-value real estate. His suit's loose, tie fat, like the eighties never went out of style. And that fat ugly tie of his makes me want to gag, but I wouldn't dare think of doing so. He'll be the one who hands me the contract to sign, so I've done my best to butter him up these past few days. Now it looks like things are finally wrapping up between us, and the sooner the better. Time to get this show on the road.

"No," Robertson says. "The Burj is built to last, Mr. Jensen. Your staff'll be perfectly safe up here, guaranteed. This thing can weather any storm God hurls at it. It has so far."

I nod, raising my eyebrows. "You've got me convinced. I believe I've made it perfectly clear that I want in. How much?"

The old man chuckles again. "You can't win us over that easily, Mr. Jensen. We still have to run things by the Imar group, double-check your paperwork—"

I wave a hand dismissively, turning to face the old contractor next to me.

"How about we skip the formalities, just between you and me?"

The office is empty behind us, nobody's in earshot. The entire floor is empty, as far as I know. There'll be nobody here to eavesdrop.

Outside, the sandstorm rages, miles away from Dubai's city walls.

"Formalities?" Robertson asks.

I nod. "Formalities. You pretend there's more red tape than there has to be, and I sit on my hands while I wait for you and the family to decide if I can rent out the floor. We know it's the question of money between us."

Robertson nods. "That's usually how it goes. Why? Are you suggesting an alternative to…money?"

I grin. I'm practically working the old man in my hands like putty already. "Not different, still just money. But faster. And a bigger cut than you're used to. A little extra for all the trouble we're going to skip."

Robertson looks intrigued, and the old man cocks a bushy eyebrow as I purse my lips.

"What was your initial price? A billion for the floor?"

Robertson nods slowly.

"How about I double that? No, wait. I'll triple it. Pemberton

Computers needs this space, no doubt in my mind. And just for the fun of it, I'll throw in a little extra for good measure. How about…three-point-five billion?"

The contractor coughs suddenly, thrown completely off-guard by my offer. "W-what? You're serious?"

I nod. "I don't kid. Three-point-five bill, and I can have the money *today*. If the offer's acceptable to you, of course. As well as the Imar group."

Robertson turns and stares back out the window. The sandstorm's getting close, inching its way across the desert to storm Dubai's border. But I'll be fine. And I know I'm only moments away from getting exactly what I came here for.

"Let me make a few phone calls," Robertson says suddenly. I nod, and he leaves the room a moment later as he dials a number on his cell.

The solitude gives me peace, and I take a moment to clear my head. Meditation's one of the best ways to stay in shape, and a man of my being needs every moment of clarity he can afford.

I've been the CEO of Pemberton Computers for ten years, and not a day's gone by that I've regretted so far. The work's been nothing more than ten-minute brainstorming meetings with the higher-ups every day, and I'm able to play the big-picture role I've always dreamed of. I'm not a grunt or a slave to any system. I don't piece together the motherboards, I'm not the one who decides if our latest model comes with stainless-steel aluminum or clear over white plastic. I decide where the company goes, where we expand, how we expect to double our earnings ever year. This Dubai meeting's my brainchild, and I'll take all the credit when we're able to finally move a regional branch in here. It'll be good for business, good for internal development.

Ambition always comes with a cost, and I'm the only one who can afford to foot the bill.

My first wife always said I was deadly ambitious, and I always heard the second word over the first. Over time, I've found that the first word's more applicable. I take what I want. This floor space, my company, all the money I've managed to accrue over the years. I get what I want, and anybody who tells me no is dead to me. Sure, I've been rejected before, but living your best life is the most applicable revenge in this scenario. So when that first wife found me too deadly and sickeningly ambitious, we called it quits. *She* called it quits, to put it aptly. And ever since then, I've never slept alone, never been isolated in a bedroom unless I absolutely want to.

And I *never* want to.

But I digress.

It looks like we're about to make that deal after all.

Robertson enters the room, walking over to me, fat tie flopping about as he hangs up the phone. He's grinning from ear to ear, and I know I've got this meeting in the bag.

"So, Mr. Jensen, the Imar Family's come to an agreement. We'll give you the floor space for a little more than your newly minted offer; three-point-six billion for the hundredth floor of the Burj Khalifa should be more than appropriate, given the circumstances. And we'll have that money today, by sundown. Then we'll have a deal."

I check my watch. Two-oh-seven in the afternoon. Three hours, give or take, to amass three point six billion dollars in—

"Cash? Or do you take card?" I ask Robertson, grinning.

He returns the smile. "The Imar group prefers check. More secure that way."

I nod. "Even better."

I pull out my checkbook from my suit breast pocket, ripping off a blank check as Robertson hands me a pen. I write out the amount in full, three-point-six billion in total, not a penny more. I sign my name, handing the check over to Robertson.

"Mr. Jensen, I believe we have ourselves a deal," he says, extending his hand to me.

I shake it. "And one hell of a deal it is," I reply.

Three-point-six billion dollars. *Meh.*

It's not even the most money I've moved today.

Robertson shows me around the office space, pointing out the features that the hundredth floor offers. As he walks me past a corner office, as big as my first apartment back in college, I can't help but stare out the window.

The sandstorm outside reaches Dubai's city walls, and I peer outside as the storm ravages the city below. Ant-sized pedestrians scatter, cars swerving to the side of the road as the sand overtakes them. I'm safe and sound up here, away from the dangers of the world outside. And it *is* a dangerous world.

Sand buffets the glass floors below us, and I grin as the Burj Khalifa stands tall, weathering any force that dares push upon it.

The view from up here's never looked better.

THREE
Samantha

I've finally managed to calm myself, having spent the last hour and a half retracing my steps back in Paris. I open the window to the balcony and step outside, the cold Moroccan air stinging me as I wrap my bathrobe tight around me. Reality's set in, and I have to accept the truth the universe has just bestowed upon me.

I'm pregnant.

And I know who the father is. There's not a doubt in my mind.

The cold air buffets up against me as I stand out on the balcony, staring out into the soft evening glow of Morocco.

Alistair Jensen, the billionaire CEO of Pemberton Computers, Inc. Yeah, seriously. The philanthropist, the mega-donor. The man who single-handedly revolutionized the modern computing industry, who's won hundreds of awards in his field and even funded the cure for some viral diseases in the third world.

And he's the father of my child.

Now I remember everything that happened between us.

One night in Paris. That was all it took. He talked to me first, sitting down the length of the bar. I recognized him a little while after, and things escalated from there. We went upstairs to my room, spent the night together. He was charming, protective, sweet. The night was well worth it, that much I'll admit. When I had to leave in the morning, he told me some platitude about our story not being over, then handed me his business card with his secretary's phone number printed on it. I knew those were just hollow words as soon as he said them to me, the business card just a formality after a one-night-stand. But now it's my only hope.

I know that business card is floating around here somewhere.

I sigh, taking a deep breath of the cool night air as I gaze out into the city of Marrakesh, Morocco. I check out the view from down below, I'm only a few stories up off the ground. I can see a market closing down for the day, customers scattering into the street like leaves in the fall wind. Taxis honk, car brakes squeak. Marrakesh is busy, I'll give it that. I've spent the past week here in Morocco, trying to hunt down more details on Terrence Malstrom. And it's been nothing short of dead-ends after dead-ends.

Now I've lost all focus. I can't stop thinking about this baby. My life's come to a screeching halt, and my career's about to take a nose-dive into the shallow end of the kiddie pool. I still have to call my supervisors, tell them I'm 'sick'. Which is only partly true, I suppose, but still. I'm lost, utterly confused, drawing a blank on what to do.

Alistair's the father of my child.

There's no way I'll be able to get in touch with Alistair. And even if I could, I doubt he'd believe me. I'm sure his company gets thousands of calls a day from women claiming to be carrying his child. I don't know how many of them would be true, and I'm honestly scared to know that real-life number.

Alright, it's decided.

I can't tell Alistair about the baby.

Not yet, at least.

First, I have to find him. And then I have to see if he remembers me, because right now I'm terrified he won't. And I know how much that'll hurt.

From there I'll improvise the rest of the plan, because this is positively too much to handle right now. Somewhere down I'll tell him about the baby.

Maybe. I honestly don't know what I'm going to do.

But I do know what I have to do first.

I pull my phone out of my bathrobe pocket, scroll to my supervisor's contact. I dial his office number, holding my phone up to my ear as I pray to an unseen God that I'll be sent to voicemail.

Unfortunately my prayers go unanswered.

"Talk to me, Sam," I hear a voice crackling through the phone line.

It's Alan, my supervisor. He's always curt, to the point. Never lets a word go to waste. There's never a moment of small-talk with him, and for that I'm eternally grateful.

"Alan, I've got bad news. I'm sick. It's bad."

"How bad? Like, ate raw chicken with dinner, bad? Or something worse?"

I take a deep breath. I can't lie to him. I trust him too much to do that.

"Pregnant bad."

There's an awkward pause that hangs in the air as Alan collects his thoughts.

"*Shit*," I hear Alan mutter under his breath, and I want to call him out for his sexist undertones I can hear behind his word. But I stifle the feeling, telling myself it'll only stir up more trouble than it's worth. "How far along?"

"No more than two weeks."

"...So you were on assignment when it happened?"

No use beating around the bush. "Yeah, Alan, I was. Don't pretend the rest of the office isn't filled with a bunch of James Bond wannabes. I'm not the first to do something like this on assignment."

"Yes, but our male agents don't tend to bring the baby home."

I want to scream. But I hold it in, channeling my anger into something more productive. "Alan, I've still got some time before I need to come back home. Don't make me come back early. I can finish this. I can find Malstrom."

"Can you? With a baby on the way, I highly doubt your usefulness in the field is still the same as it was before."

There's a pause that hangs in the air, and I feel a sob creeping up the back of my throat. I never expected Alan to turn on me, not like this. He'd always held faith in me, recommending me for the field agent position after my internship ended. But by the feeling of this conversation, I have a hard time believing this is the same Alan Parker who'd taken me under his wing all those years ago.

"Alan, do you trust me?"

"I do. But right now, just barely."

"Then let me finish the job. I'll do it. I can find Malstrom, or at the very least enough information for the next agent to finish the job. You can trust me on that, Alan. I swear."

Alan sighs. "Okay, Sam, you win. One month. You have one month to find Malstrom, either bringing him in or enough information for someone else to finally finish the job. After that, we put you in a desk for the next few months. Someone in Human Resources'll contact you, explain maternity leave privileges the CIA can offer you."

"Thank you, Alan."

"I'm not finished. One month, Sam, and no more personal business. No side trips, no more using Uncle Sam's money for personal sideshows. Got it?"

I put the phone against my chest, taking a deep breath as I collect my thoughts.

I've never lied to Alan before, but there's always a first time for everything.

"Got it. No more personal business."

"Get to it, Sam. Don't make me regret this."

And with that, Alan hangs up.

I'm left standing on the hotel balcony, staring out into the cold settling night of Marrakesh. It's beautiful here, the city lights are all aglow as the people here get ready for an evening to unwind. The markets are still open, fryers and grills coming to life as smoke wafts up to my balcony. I can tell everyone's eager to unwind, relax in their routines.

But me personally?

I've never felt more jittery.

Alan told me no more personal business. But I'm putting his decision on hold for now.

I *have* to find Alistair Jensen, no matter the cost.

FOUR
Alistair

After Robertson, the Imar Family representative, has finished showing me around the hundredth floor of the Burj Khalifa, I find myself imbued with the desire to party.

And I mean *party.*

The sandstorm outside finally coming to a close, I step into the lobby of the Burj and head over to the front desk. A cheery young woman greets me, wearing a fancy floral-print suit and her hair tied up in a bun. She's cute enough, and I know she's the type that'll be eager to unwind after a long day of work. I smile at her as I approach the desk, and she greets me with the happiest voice I've heard in the entire United Arab Emirates since my arrival.

"How can I help you today, sir?"

I chuckle as I lean over the desk. "You look like a girl who's been to her fair share of nightclubs."

She pauses, grinning cheekily to herself as she puts on a customer service persona.

"Are you looking for something here in Dubai, sir?"

I nod, grinning. "What's your favorite?"

"The hotel recommends a few spots close to the Burj—"

"No, no, no," I say, waving a hand to cut her off. "Which one is *your* favorite?"

The girl smiles mysterious at me. I know she's interested, at the very least.

"I'll have to say...*The Spire,*" she grins.

"And what's your name, Miss?"

"Aaliyah," she says.

"Aaliyah, I'm Alistair," I say, extending a hand. She shakes it, and I see her eyes widen slightly. She knows who I am. Now comes the easy part. "Aaliyah, when's the last time you've visited The Spire?"

"Last week," she says.

I feign a swoon, pretending I've just heard the worst news of my entire life.

"I think we're going to have to do something about that, then," I reply.

Aaliyah shows me around The Spire after the bouncer lets us inside. It's packed here, with levels going up and up, ten stories tall. I can see the Burj Khalifa through the window here, and I know this has *got* to be the best nightclub in Dubai; Aaliyah wasn't lying to me before. She walks me around the length of the building, up to the tenth floor as we pass by levels upon levels of different clubs, each one a different theme. One has pink strobe lights flashing over a rave. Another is lit only by the glow of the attendee's glow-sticks. It's not the tallest building in Dubai, that's for sure, but it's the nightclub with the highest elevation, almost a thousand feet up off the ground. Luxury at its finest.

And that's all I need.

We walk up the massive spiral ramp as Aaliyah looks over to me and grins. She's changed out of her floral-pattern suit jacket into a skimpier dress, which I like.

"So, Mr. Jensen, you never told me what you were doing in the Burj today," she says, probing me. I smile. She's curious about my business, and I'm more than willing to

"I was buying your hundredth floor," I reply as we walk up past the eighth floor, a foam party surrounded by models in bikinis and speedos. "But that's in the past. You could say I was there to meet you. Call it luck, call it fate. I call it destiny."

She smiles. "You use that line all the time?"

"Only when I want to," I grin back.

Aaliyah and I reach the top of The Spire, a glass-domed club atop the building just a few blocks south of the Burj. I can see the tower from here, extending high above us into the night sky. A DJ cranks a record, spinning discs from their booth high above the crowded dance floor below. Pink and green lights flash up past the dome and into the sky, where you can see the stars beginning to shine. Aaliyah and I walk to the center of the dance floor, and she instantly wraps her arms around me as we begin to sway to the swanky music.

All I need is this moment.

It's impossible to feel alone. And that happens all too often nowadays.

But when I'm out, dancing free and solo with a girl? All else fades away. The money troubles. The stress of the computing industry, the real estate deals. The baggage of past relationships, the stress the ex-wife left me with. All gone in an instant.

I'm not alone when I'm with someone, and that's the only time I can make this god-awful emptiness goes away. Even when I'm in a crowd I can't help but feel alone. But not now, not in this moment. And it's all I could have asked for.

Aaliyah looks up and into my eyes, and I can tell she's already smitten with me. We haven't said more than a hundred words to each other, but I'm already ready to stop this feeling of isolation I've felt ever since I entered the UAE this week.

Around us, the beat sways the crowd to the rhythm of the music. The world slinks away, my troubles mere ghosts in the past. I don't know how long we spend dancing in The Spire. Hours go by, maybe more, maybe less. I don't really care how long it takes to feel whole again, all that matters to me is that it happens.

After a while, Aaliyah looks back up at me, her arms now wrapped tight around my shoulders. My hands are on her hips, guiding her closer to me with each passing moment. I can feel her body heat up against me, and I know she's feeling the same heat inside.

Now's my moment.

I wink at her. "Tired?"

She smiles. "A little," she replies. "Why?"

I nod at the tower behind me, the Burj Khalifa cutting up into the sky like a knife.

"Let's go take a load off. I've got a room back in the Burj, If you don't mind going to your work after-hours."

Aaliyah laughs, her fingers gripping my shirt tight. She nods. "I don't mind."

"You wanna get out of here?"

She nods. "Let's."

◆ ◆ ◆

After the deed, I throw on a bathrobe and step over to the plate-glass window as I inspect the city skyline. I'm staying in the hundred-and-twenty-fifth floor of the Burj Khalifa, an easy room to rent when you're as rich as I am. No shit.

Behind me, I can hear Aaliyah snoring softly as she rests in my bed. She's a good girl, eager to please. Fun to be around. It'll be a shame when I have to leave her like all the others. But in my heart, I know she'll be better off without me once I'm gone. They all are. It's a fact, an unchanging truth of the universe. When Alistair Jensen enters your life, you better count your blessings when he leaves you in one piece.

I sigh. It's not easy, knowing yourself. And I know I hurt people, whether I mean it or not. Aaliyah's a sweetheart, and I know she'll find true happiness once I'm gone and out of the picture. Just like the others before her did, and just like the ones who'll come after her.

Below me, I can see the still-crowded city streets below. The cars and people are even tinier than from the view from my office below, and the desert surrounding Dubai is calm and tranquil. No sandstorm in sight.

In the morning, I'll probably get breakfast with Aaliyah. Since she slept over here, it'd be rude not to. After we say good-bye I'll never see her again. No numbers exchanged, if she asks I'll give her my card. My secretary's used to routing calls from one night stands, telling them that I'm always busy—but she's always careful to tell the girls I'll call them later, if I find the time.

For now, sleep.

I head back to bed, pulling the covers up to my neck as Aaliyah sleeps soundly next to me.

I've never felt more alone.

FIVE
Samantha

The next morning, I wake up in a haze. I know I have that business card *somewhere,* I just have to find it. Alistair Jensen's office number'll be on there, and I can try to get in touch with him there.

As the speaker-boxes and megaphones around the city blare the morning prayers outside, I root through my purse as I dig past makeup, badges, credentials and passports to find the business card Alistair gave me all those nights ago back in Paris.

My fingers brush against pristine card-stock, and I grab the business card and pull it out from the bottom of my purse.

All-white laminate, with raised gold lettering and a symbol of a dove resting on a branch.

Alistair Jensen, Pemberton Computers, CEO.

And there's an office number just below that. I pull out my cell phone, cursing the international fees as I dial the number to Alistair's office. I have no idea what time zone I'm calling, so hopefully I don't get sent to voicemail—

"Alistair Jensen's office, this is Beatrice, how may I direct your call today?"

Gulp.

"I—I—Sorry. This is Samantha Jacobson, I'm a...personal friend of Alistair. We met back in Paris. He gave me this card a few weeks back and told me to call him. Is this a good time to speak to him?"

"I'm sorry, but Mr. Jensen isn't in his office today. He's out of the country on business purposes. I'll relay a message to him when he returns stateside, if you like."

"Where is he?"

"I cannot disclose that information, ma'am," Beatrice the secretary replies in a sweet tone. I can tell she's done this a thousand times before, deflecting other calls identical to mine. "But like I said, I'd be happy to take a message."

I sigh. "No, that's okay. I'll…find another way to get in touch with him. Thanks so much," I say as I hang up quickly.

Shit. Now Alistair's going to know I called his office. Maybe. Or maybe his secretary'll forget to tell him. Either way, I'm nowhere nearer to my goal of finding him than I was previously.

I guess I'll have to take matters into my own hands.

I go back to my phone's contact list, scroll down to my best friend's contact. Tracy Jennings has been my BFF since grade school, and now that we work for the CIA together, I've got someone stateside who's always got my back. Unlike Alan, my stoic of a supervisor. He's put a deadline on my overseas work, and I need every tool in my arsenal to make sure I use my time wisely before I'm chained to a desk in the Langley Office.

I dial Tracy's number, and she picks up on the first ring.

"Samantha! It's so good to hear from you. How's Morocco?"

"Marrakesh is good," I reply. "How's Langley?"

"Oh, you know. The old nine-to-five routine. I wish I had your job, Samantha. Field agent. More like *secret* agent."

I laugh. "Thanks, Tracy. Hey, what time is it there?"

"Four-fifty-six. Sorry, in the afternoon. Almost quitting time. What's up?"

"I need a favor. I promise I won't take up too much of your time. I need you to find someone for me. And Alan doesn't need to know about it, okay?"

"Who is it?"

I take a deep breath. "Alistair Jensen."

"Alistair Jensen? You mean, *the* Alistair Jensen? The one who basically owns the computing industry nowadays?"

"Yeah. That one."

"Why? Is it related to the Malstrom case?"

"Tracy, I'd rather not say. I just need you to find him for me, okay?"

"Okay," Tracy says. "Like you're asking me to find Bill Gates or something like that. Is everything okay, Samantha?"

"It's complicated, Tracy. But I promise I'll explain everything when I'm back stateside. I just have to figure something out first."

"Where Terrence Malstrom is?"

"Yes, and something else, too. Just help me with this one thing, okay? Then I'll owe you a favor, I promise."

"Sounds good," Tracy says. I can hear her typing away, plugging information into her computer to login to the CIA's security mainframe. I can hear her plugging Alistair's name into the search field, and there's a pause that hangs in the air while I hear Tracy working.

After a minute of silence, I hear her speak up. "Looks like we got a hit for Alistair Jensen, and…it's in the United Arab Emirates. Dubai."

"Anything else you can find?"

"Let me check…hang on just another minute, Samantha. I've got this."

Another pause, and I can hear Tracy plugging more information into her computer. Honestly, she's a lifesaver. I wouldn't be this far without her, and I know if I manage to find Alistair Jensen, it'll be because of Tracy's help.

I'll owe her when I get back home. Big-time.

"Here we go. I found a credit card, swiped…in the Burj Khalifa," Tracy reads. "God. And you're going after this guy?"

"Not exactly. He's not working for Malstrom. This is personal, Tracy. So I need the utmost discretion from you, okay?"

"You can count on me, Sam. Just tell me what this was all about when it's over, alright?"

I grin. "You got it."

"Hey, don't hang up yet. I've got something for you."

"Oh?"

"Yeah, hang on. Let me send the files."

Tracy types something into her computer, and I hear her clicking around. A moment later, she speaks up again. "Okay, check your email. I've sent you a few things."

I pull my phone back from my ear, scroll to my email after putting Tracy on speakerphone. "What did you send me?"

"Some tools. Apps to help you find Alistair. Smoothly and efficiently."

"Walk me through them."

"Okay, check out the first attachment. It's an app called *Locator,* which sounds simple enough. It's something our IT's been working on for the last year. A friend sent it to me last week, and I've played around with it. It's useful."

"*Oooh,*" I croon. "Your friend from IT sent it? Louis?"

"Shut up," Tracy giggles. "And that's none of your business, but yes. Louis hooked me up pretty good."

"I hope you guys hooked up, too—"

"Now stay focused, Samantha," Tracy says, interrupting me. "The next app's something I've coded myself. It's a secret recording application, activated by the sound of your voice alone when the password is spoken."

"Password?"

"You'll set it yourself when you first open the app. The app records everything it hears, activating without a sound or a beep or a flash. And the recording is sent to a secure dropbox, but you can set the destination where the recording'll go."

"What's this one called?"

"*Recorder.*"

"Not too good with naming, are we?"

"The CIA didn't hire me for my creativity, Samantha. Now, how are you planning on getting to Dubai?"

"I didn't think that far ahead—"

"Well, I've got an idea. I came up with it while we were talking. Do you want to hear it?"

"...Yeah?"

"Normally you have to request plane tickets from Alan, but I remembered you wanted to keep this secret from him. Well, how about *I* take a vacation?"

"Tracy, I don't know if it's safe for you to meet me—"

"Figuratively, not literally. I'll file the paperwork with Travel, put the request in with my name attached."

"Won't Alan find out?"

"Not if it's for earned vacation time. That's up to HR, where they'll approve or disapprove the vacation. Alan can't interfere. And I'll be 'taking' the vacation this week. You'll get my ticket in my place, I'll have it in your email box tomorrow. I'll put you in Dubai by the end of the week. Your name will be on the flight and everything, Alan none the wiser."

"Tracy I don't know what I'd do without you. Why are you helping me?"

"Because I want to," Tracy says. "And you're my friend. I owe it to you."

"You're a lifesaver, Tracy. I'll wait here for the plane ticket. And thanks again, really. I mean it."

"Good luck, Samantha."

I spend the rest of the day walking through the streets of Marrakesh, my work assignment now dropped in lieu of a personal assignment I'd given myself. The afternoon is bright and sunny, the hot desert air of Morocco causing me to sweat underneath my windbreaker and blouse. I shouldn't have work khakis to this country, but blending in means dressing modestly. And I'm thankful to avoid the gaze of onlookers here, who single out tourists constantly. Laying low is a priority, and I keep to myself as I wander the city streets and find my way to a market a few blocks from my hotel.

Terrence Malstrom and the CIA's manhunt can wait. It's Alistair Jensen I need to find now, before Alan yanks me back to Langley, Virginia to chain me to 9-5 office desk job. They're going to find Terrence with or without me, that's for certain. I've done enough for the cause. I'm dreading the day the desk job comes, but this baby's a ticking clock I can't escape. It's the most important assignment of my life, and it's thrown me completely off guard.

I'm still not planning on telling Alistair about the baby. In all honesty, I don't know what I'm going to do when I see him again. With Tracy's help, I'll be able to find him in Dubai if he hasn't left by the time I get there. If he's gone, I don't know what I'll do next. I just have to hope he's still there by the time my plane lands.

The market's crowded, bustling in the hot afternoon. Booths and stands are set up, tents with tired-looking merchants inside, peddling their wares to anybody who'll give them the time of day.

I'm just here to stop the feeling of loneliness. I know I'd go crazy alone in that hotel room, faced with the reality of my sudden and completely unexpected pregnancy. Here, I'm just a face in a crowd. A nameless tourist, one who's able to blend in well enough. And for that I'm ever grateful. Blondes like me usually stand out in a crowd here, but today I'm invisible.

I stop by a tent, buy myself a bottle of water to stay hydrated in the hot afternoon. The merchant, a man in white robes with a cocky smile, overcharges the shit out of me, but I couldn't care less right now. Everything's blurry, hazy. I can't stop thinking about this baby and the father a million miles away in Dubai.

I feel my phone buzzing in my pocket, another email from Tracy. She must've stayed late at Langley, met with HR for that 'vacation' she's taking. Sure enough, I see the plane ticket attached to the email. My flight's set to leave from Marrakesh International early tomorrow morning, landing in Dubai a few hours later. Where I'll be on the lookout for Alistair *fucking* Jensen, of all people. Like finding a needle in a haystack, if the needle is a world-famous CEO who's nearly impossible to get close to. And if that same needle in that haystack is the father of your baby, then you better be careful not to get pricked.

I spend another few hours wandering the marketplace, scoring a lamb gyro to eat as I walk back to my hotel. My bags are already packed, and I've been ready to get out of here for a while now. The Malstrom trail was already running cold, and Alan'll never notice my brief stint in Dubai if Tracy keeps our little secret to herself.

I'll owe her big time for this, that's for certain. Maybe she'll need help with that Louis fellow over in IT, but maybe not. Maybe they've already hooked up like Alistair and I did weeks ago.

When I make it back to my hotel room, I make sure my bags are all finished up with packing. I take my shirts and coats from the dresser, folding them into my suitcase as I get ready to leave the country. I collect my toiletries, grabbing an extra roll of toilet paper from the cabinet under the sink and pack that into my bag, too.

Then I see it in the trash can.

The pink stick, the test that announced the end of my life.

I reach down, grabbing the pregnancy test and inspect it. Sure enough, the two lines are still marked, and I have the evidence that I'm pregnant.

I wash the stick off, rubbing soap all over to clean it, and then I pack it in my bag, too. I don't know why I'm hanging on to it, but I am. Maybe it'll serve as a reminder. A keepsake, when all this is said and done. I don't know.

I inspect the hotel room one more time, finding it to be perfectly empty.

And just like that, I'm ready for my new mission to begin. The most important mission I'll ever have in my entire life.

And it all starts with finding Alistair Jensen.

The next morning, I board my plane to Dubai early as I collect myself emotionally. I stuff my carry-on in the overhead compartment, sitting down in my seat as I worry about this and that and what I'm going to do if I *actually* find Alistair. I'm off the radar now, working solo. Alone. With a personal mission, one that I'm not sure how it's going to end.

The plane takes off, and I hold my stomach gingerly as I stare out the window, the runway disappearing beneath us as we disappear into the clouds.

I don't know what I'm going to do. If I'm not going to tell him about the baby, why am I seeing this guy in the first place? Is it for security? Wishing that he'll sense my pregnancy and ask me to marry him? Hell. No.

I really have no idea what I'm doing here.

But I know I want to see the father of my child one last time before this all goes haywire. Before I'm forced back home, stateside, chained to a desk where I'll work a 9-5 until I hopefully retire.

This baby's going to be the end of my career, and I want to see the man responsible.

I put the eye mask on, leaning back in my seat as I try to get some rest. After all, I've got one hell of an assignment ahead of me.

I take a cab from the Dubai International Airport to the Burj Khalifa a dozen miles away. As the taxi rolls into the city, I can see a sandstorm brewing on the horizon, just beyond the city's border. I understand they're a regular occurrence here, storms strong enough to knock you off your feet. But I better be careful either way.

"Hey, should we be worried about that?" I ask the driver, hoping he speaks English.

"No, ma'am. They're common here," the driver replies. He's an older man, wrinkled, wearing robes and a golden belt that tinkles when the car moves. His smile is kind, and he peers back at me via the rear-view mirror often while he speaks. "Sandstorms are just a way of life to us here. Like tornadoes for you Americans."

"Not all Americans. What do you go when you get stuck in one?"

"Wherever you can. You run. Hide," the driver says. "Not much else you can do."

"I'll keep that in mind," I reply. "How much further to the Burj?"

"Why? You in a hurry?"

"I am."

"Fifteen minutes, tops. Got a hot date?"

"Something like that," I reply as I stare back out the window. The sandstorm's gaining traction, and I can tell it's going to hit us soon. Hopefully I'll be inside the Burj by the time that happens.

The taxi pulls up to the tallest building in the world a few minutes later, and I hop out as I tip the cabbie a little extra for his wisdom. I turn, facing the massive monument as I gaze upwards. The Burj Khalifa shoots upwards, extending into the sky, cutting into the clouds like a knife.

I step inside, through the glass doors as I enter a marble-covered lobby. Everything here is sharp, pristine, and I feel like I'm dirtying up the place just by being here.

I spot a receptionist behind a counter, and I walk over to her. I see a name-tag on her floral suit, Aaliyah.

"How can I help you today, ma'am?" Aaliyah asks me cheerily.

"Yes, hi. I need help finding someone," I reply. "Is that...possible? They might still be here."

"Maybe," Aaliyah shrugs. "Who did you have in mind?"

"Alistair Jensen."

Aaliyah flinches at the mention of his name. She looks at her computer screen, types something in and looks back at me flatly without emotion, her customer service persona dropped.

"I'm sorry, ma'am. It looks like that information's confidential. I do apologize."

I nod, defeated. "That's fine. Thanks anyways."

I step away from the desk, look around the lobby. There's a group of seats over by the door, a group of fine leather armchairs and couches. I head that way, plopping down in an armchair as I pull out my phone and fire up *Locator*.

The app is nothing more than a simple search box, and I type in Alistair's name and hit ENTER. The field populates, pulling up lines of data and codes I can't read at first. There's strings of numbers, three-letter codes in all caps that don't make any sense to me. I scroll down the list, and then I start to piece together the data. I can see dates, typed out like 1.3.2019 and so on. Then the strings of digits make sense, too—those are card numbers. Geez. And the three-letter codes must signify location. These are purchases, and I scroll back up to the top of *Locator's* list to inspect the most recent purchase.

The date's today, and I see a timestamp from ten minutes ago. There's a string of number, and a code: TXI. *Taxi?* That's got to be it. What else could it be?

So, Alistair Jensen's in a taxicab. Where, I have no idea. Maybe he's heading to an airport. Maybe he's about to get on a cruise ship, about to leave the UAE for good. Maybe I'm too late. But, hey, it's a start. Tracy said he's been in and out of the Burj Khalifa, and I know this is where he's spent most of his time while in Dubai. But for the life of me, I can't see him anywhere.

I sigh, closing my phone and leaning back in my seat. I watch as people pour in and out of the lobby. Businessmen, men in suits and ties. Men in robes, wearing headdresses and turbans. Money comes in, less money goes out. It's the way the world works, and I know Alistair's going to be spending money here in some fashion. Why else would a man as rich and powerful as him visit the Burj?

I rub my eyes. I'm already jet-lagged from the trip, and I've yet to find a hotel or a place to stay while I'm here. I don't know why I'm so eager to find Alistair, but I've taken it upon myself to start here.

And it looks like my search is coming up empty, at least for now.

I stand up, putting my phone back in my jacket pocket as I start to head to the doors.

And then I see him.

It's him, it's unmistakable. I've seen that face in magazine articles, on web journals and blogs. Financial reports, earnings reports. The cover of magazines, the face that's been hailed on the evening news as the savior of the modern computing industry.

And that same face is in my memory. From Paris, France.

I stand, shocked and dumbfounded as I watch Alistair Jensen enter the Burj Khalifa's lobby.

He's wearing a suit, casually unbuttoned at the top, his bare chest just barely peeking out. His tie is loose, and his jacket is swaying open with the breeze that comes inside. He's still the same man from Paris, and his rugged handsomeness hits me all at once when I see him again for the first time in weeks.

He's smoldering. He's walking next to a man in a robe and turban, and they're laughing about something one of them must've said. Alistair's smile is gorgeous, perfectly chiseled across his face.

Now I remember why I spent the night with him in Pairs.

Irresistible. In every definition of the word.

Behind him, I can see the sandstorm's finally caught up to us outside. The breeze buffets up against the Burj's countless windows, tinkling as it collides against the glass. Alistair's just barely made it inside by the time the storm reaches us.

The storm rages outside as Alistair Jensen passes me by, and I feel my voice caught in my throat as he passes without even a glance my way.

He reaches the elevator, and his friend presses the button to call it down.

I'm frozen in place, and I have no idea what I'm going to do if he disappears from me again.

It's now or never.

The elevator dings, the doors open. Just as Alistair and his friend step inside, I find my voice, calling out as loud as I can.

"Alistair! *Alistair Jensen!*"

He looks up, and our eyes lock as I see a look of recognition splash across his face.

So, he *does* remember me.

SIX
Alistair

"Alistair! *Alistair Jensen!*"

I hear the voice cry out from behind me as I step into the elevator, and I sigh quietly to myself. Another adoring fan, perhaps? Or an old colleague, ready to say hello again?

I look up, and then I see her.

The woman from Paris. I remember her—vaguely. American, works for the government. We spent the night together, of course. And I can't remember her name for the life of me. She's blonde, dressed in khakis and a blue windbreaker with a logo on the front of her jacket. I can't quite make it out, but I know she works for a government somewhere.

And she's walking right over to us.

I press the stop button on the elevator, excusing myself from Mr. Imar as I step out to meet the woman. We cross the lobby, meeting in the center just next to the front desk. Around us, businessmen and guests pass us by, stepping into the elevator. I turn around, Mr. Imar has vanished from view, riding the elevator up without me. Great. Just great.

"Hi," I say reluctantly. She's looking at me nervously, and I flash a quick glance over at Aaliyah, hoping things won't get ugly.

"Is everything okay, Mr. Jensen?" Aaliyah calls from the front desk. The woman from Paris flashes her an angry glance, and I'm confused even more so now.

"Everything's...fine, Aaliyah," I call back. I look at the woman from Paris, trying my best to remember her name. Rebecca? No, that's not it. Delaney? Something with a 'D', I believe.

"Hi," the woman from Paris says. Her tone is short, curt. She's thought this conversation over a million times in her head, I can tell. Her words sound rehearsed, and she cuts right to the chase: "Do you remember me at all?"

I blink. "I...do, of course." *No I fucking don't.*

"Really." She doesn't believe me. *Shocker.*

"Yes, really. We met in Paris," I reply. "What's this about?"

"I wanted to see you again," she says. "You told me some platitude about our story not being over in Pairs. And I wanted to see if that was true. To see if you remembered me at all, which you clearly don't. I guess that's the answer I needed."

Answer? Who is this? What is this woman talking about?

And then it hits me, everything coming back to me in an instant. The night in Paris comes back to me all at once, and I blurt out the details as they rise up in my mind.

"Your name is Samantha Jacobson. You work for the CIA; you've been an international field agent for the past two years. You're looking for that Terrence Malstrom fellow from the news, at least, that's what you told me when we met. And speaking of, we met in a hotel bar in Paris. You were drinking a tall glass of ice water. I remember everything, Samantha."

She cocks an eyebrow, letting a smile start to creep across her face. "I'm impressed. You really had me going for a minute there."

I nod. "I know. Sometimes it takes me a second. I'm sure you can understand, Samantha, with how many people you must meet in your line of work. But you're still not lucky enough to have met Malstrom, or should I say, caught him. You told me all about your manhunt back in Paris. I have to admit, I'm impressed. You're dedicated."

Her smile widens. "So. You do remember."

"What can I do for you, Samantha?"

Her smile's out in full force. "I wanted to ask you something."

"What's that?"

"Would you like to have dinner with me sometime? I'm in

Dubai for the better part of a week, and I was thinking—"

I wince. I just can't help it.

This just got awkward.

"I'm sorry, Samantha, I've got meetings to attend to this week. I'm incredibly busy, you see, I'm in the process of moving a new branch into the hundredth floor," I point upwards for emphasis. She doesn't look impressed one bit; Samantha looks at me blankly, as if her mind's shutting down and rebooting.

"R-right," she says. Her voice is quiet, and her words come out meekly. She looks down at the floor. I've hurt her, I can tell. But business is business, and right now I don't have time for old flames. If I did, she'd be the first one I'd call. "I get it," she says flatly, without emotion.

"I'm sorry, Samantha," I say again. "I'm just occupied with this deal, and the rest of my scheduled time in Dubai's packed to the gills. Really."

She nods, but keeps staring downwards, as if her life depended on it.

"I'm sorry for wasting your time," she says meekly.

And with that, she turns on her heels and walks out the doors of the lobby, heading into the street as she hails a cab. The storm's calmed down outside, just for a brief window as Samantha waves down a taxi and steps inside. I blink, stunned, but I quickly shake off the feeling. I turn back to the elevator, pressing the call button to take me upstairs.

What was that? Old flames don't reappear so suddenly, this wasn't a happenstance run-in. If she was in the Burj on business, why'd she leave after I shot her down? And she'd been practicing those words she said to me in the mirror, I could read it on her like a book.

Things aren't adding up here, I think to myself, confused as ever.

The elevator dings, and I step inside, completely alone. I press the button to the hundredth floor, and the elevator door closes a moment later.

SEVEN
Samantha

I hop in the cab as fast as I can, telling the cabbie to take me to Dubai International as quick as he can. The city disappears into a blur as the cab merges into the heavy traffic of the hot afternoon. I'm sick of this. I'm done, I'm going home. I've lost, and there's nothing more I can do about it.

Honestly, what did I expect to happen?

Alistair barely remembered me, and when I put myself out there, took a chance, asked *him* out—

He threw me away like yesterday's trash. *Meetings.* Sure, I don't doubt he's got meetings to attend to. But dinner with someone he's hooked up with before's too much to handle, I guess?

Well. That's that, I suppose.

I tried. I asked him out for dinner, and he said no. I can't do much more than that. That's all, folks.

I considered telling him about the baby, I really did. But I know he'd just shoot me down again right there in the lobby of the Burj Khalifa, and I'd look like an even bigger fool for having tried. It's not like the baby was going to change his mind in the first place. If he didn't want to spend time with me alone, then I know a baby wouldn't fix that. If anything, he'd feel a sense of obligation to the child, but I'd still be as worthless to him as I was back in the lobby. Maybe I would have felt worse that way. I can't know for certain.

The cab pulls up to Dubai International, and I hand the driver the rest of my Dirhams and US dollars from my wallet. Take it all, I don't give a shit. I just want to go home. I can see the sand-storm re-approaching on the horizon, a second wave, and I turn to face the airport hoping to God I'll be able to get out of here in time.

I head inside, not taking another glance at the storm behind me.

◆ ◆ ◆

When I make it back stateside, almost a full day's passed. It took a while to move my flight up (Tracy's flight, really). And when I finally managed to get a seat on a flight heading back to the US, the sandstorm had finally reached the airport, putting us on a two-hour delay. Then, layovers in Europe. Another layover in Philadelphia, and *then* my flight finally made it back to Langley, Virginia.

As I step through the double-doors to my office in Langley, I feel a terrifying sense of dread hanging over me. I've used up all my time as a field agent, only a few new leads to help us catch up to Malstrom. I've wasted the CIA's time, I've wasted my super-visor's time, I've wasted Tracy's time. I've wasted my time. What little I have left until the baby arrives, that is.

It's a ticking clock, and I'm dreading what comes next. Preg-nancy, my body host to new life. And don't even get me started on the birthing process. Seriously, I'm not looking forward to it, but I'd held hope that I wouldn't have had to face it alone.

But then Alistair Jensen, the baby's unmistakable father, shot me down from the heavens with his cold, calculated rejec-tion. I could tell he was following a script, going over lines he'd practiced before on other women. I'm just another brick in the pile, another drop in the bucket to him. I'm nothing. Worthless. He practically said so himself.

I walk through the old office, waving at familiar cohorts as

I pass them by. There's Jenkins, from accounting. He's mugging the water-cooler. And there's Tricia, trying to photocopy *another* file that could easily just be a PDF. I see my supervisor's office up ahead, and I'm dreading this conversation with Alan already. I know he's going to tear me a new one, ask why I wasn't able to find more leads on Terrence Malstrom. Why we haven't caught the guy just yet.

Of course, it's not entirely my fault. It's our department's job to catch the guy, but Alan's always seen me as a headstrong figure. And if I can't get a lead on him, then who else could?

I sigh, my hand clutching the doorknob to Alan's office. I pull the door open, stepping inside.

Alan's sitting back in his desk, staring at his computer screen. His office is tiny, with barely enough room for his corner desk and a bookshelf. His face is tired, eyes baggy. His usually well-groomed goatee is disheveled, his polo shirt wrinkled. He's exhausted, and I know I'm probably at least half to blame.

"Samantha, sit down," he says. Alan's always short with his words, so I know he's going to cut right to the chase.

"What's this about?" I ask. "I got your email, but I'm still confused—"

"We followed up on some of your leads on Malstrom," he says. "They're good. We've managed to find that informant you spoke to in Morocco, and he's revealed a safehouse we'd not known about previously."

"Where is it?"

Alan sighs. "It's in Spain, of all places. I know. I couldn't believe it either."

I cock an eyebrow. "You want someone to check it out."

My supervisor stares at me blankly, his eyes burrowing holes into my head. "Not you," he says sternly. "Not after the news you've bestowed upon me. We're sending someone else."

Right. He knows I'm pregnant. Hard to forget.

"Then who?" I ask. "You're planning on sending Ackerman? Richardson? Daniels?"

Alan shakes his head at all the names I offer.

"Then who?" I ask again.

"They're sending me," Alan says.

I want to laugh, cackle in utter disbelief. I know Alan used to be an agent working overseas, but he's been stuck behind a desk for over a decade. *"What?"*

"I'm going to check out the safehouse in Spain," Alan says. "You know I've got experience in the field. Hell, why else would the eggheads here put me in charge of the department? On top of that, I'm the only one here fluent in Spanish. So there's that."

I want to tell Alan that he's just going to put himself in danger. To hell with his fluency, make another agent get a translator. But I know he'll just ignore my protests, and he'll just chalk it up to misogynistic emotionality. Maybe he'll take a dig at me because I had the gall of getting pregnant during a work assignment. I know I'll just freak out if he says any of those things, so I elect to keep my mouth shut. Plain and simple.

"Well, I wish you the best of luck," is all I say.

Alan nods. "I'm just going to check it out, that's all. I've worked in Spain a few times before, many a year ago. I'll be fine, Samantha, don't worry about me. We want both of you to be safe, you and your—"

I nod. He's still careful with his words, but I get the hint.

The CIA won't put a pregnant woman in harm's way, even if she's a dedicated field agent of two-plus years. I get it. I *hate* it, but I get it.

"Look, this isn't all bad," Alan says. "You'll have stability. A routine, a schedule and a paycheck you can build a life around. You'll be taken care of. And it's not so bad here, really."

I nod, accepting my fate.

This is the best I can do, this is all I have to work with.

I might as well take what I can get. It's not like Alistair wanted me anyways, and even if he did, I'd still have to find a job one way or another. I'll *never* be a housewife to a billionaire. I'd feel like a trophy in a case, a feeling I'll never desire.

"Come on, let's show you to your desk. Tracy's going to excited to have a deskmate, finally," Alan says as he stands up slowly. He's tired, creaky with middle age. But I follow him out of the office, excited to see my friend again.

◆ ◆ ◆

My BFF squeals when she sees Alan and I approaching the two-seater desk.

Tracy's been a great friend of mine for ages, but it's always good to see her again. Her dark brown hair's tied up in a ponytail, her work blouse the *perfect* amount of wrinkled and pressed. Her skirt's cleanly pressed as well, and I can't help but notice how comfortable she looks in this environment. It's like she was *made* to work in the Langley office. She's the definition of professional desk-worker, someone I can really see myself taking after if I'm really going to be stuck here for good.

My friend jumps up, pulls me in for a gentle hug as Alan bids us *adieu.*

"Tracy, show Samantha what you've been working on," he says. "We'll get her trained within the week, and by this time next we'll have her cracking case files all on her own."

Tracy beams. "You got it, sir," she replies. Alan nods, approving of our setup, and starts to walk back to his office.

"So, where do we start?" I ask. Tracy sits down in her chair, rolling another office chair over to me. Our collective desk is set up for two people to work, two computers, two mice and keyboards, two chairs. One massive cubicle. She pats the chair next to her, and I sit down, grinning.

"You're going to love it here," Tracy says, brimming with happily positive energy. I can tell she's excited to have me back stateside, given the circumstances. And I know she's a friend I can always count on, no matter what. "Seriously. Give it a week or so, and then you'll be looking *forward* to coming to work. I swear."

I chuckle. "We'll see about that. I'll miss field work."

"But you'll be here. Helping agents just like you out in the field. And for that matter, do you know why they pulled you out of the field to begin with? I think it's crazy that they'd bring you back so soon."

I never told Tracy I was—*am* pregnant. She helped me find Alistair Jensen just because I asked her to. She's that good of a friend, and I know I owe her the truth. I look around the office, making sure we're in a private conversation. When I'm certain we're alone, I bow my head low and motion for Tracy to scoot closer to me.

"I'm...pregnant," I tell her cautiously. Tracy stifles a gasp, covering her mouth with her hand.

"*What?*" she breathes. I nod.

"Yeah. And you can probably guess who the father is."

"No," she says, unable to process my words. Her eyes dart back and forth as she puts two and two together. "You can't be serious—*Alistair?*"

I nod gravely. "We met in Paris, when I was following a lead on an informant for Terrence Malstrom. And I ran into Alistair in a bar, we hit it off before I even knew who he was...and then, you know. Things happened upstairs."

Tracy nods. "I get it, Samantha," she says. "Are you going to...?"

"I don't know what I'm going to do," I reply honestly. "All I know is that Alistair wants nothing to do with me. I found him in Dubai, by the way. Asked him to get dinner with me. He said no, that he was too busy, and that was that."

"Did you tell him about the baby?"

"I didn't. He has no idea. Tracy, I'm done talking about this now, okay?"

She nods, sitting back up in her chair. "Okay," she says. And that's that.

I wheel over to my desk, flicking on my computer. I login to the CIA mainframe with my credentials, and Tracy watches me as I pull up my home computer screen.

"Okay," she says. "Let's get you started on system training. You ready?" she asks, overeager.

I nod slowly. "Let's just get this over with," I sigh.

◆ ◆ ◆

It's a long day of training with Tracy, and by the time five o'clock rolls around I'm positively brain-dead. My brain feels like a sponge, soaking up all the information that Tracy throws my way. Now I just need to wring it all out, preferably into a bucket somewhere. It's getting dark outside, the sun's already setting through the windows. Golden light seeps inside as Tracy and I get ready to leave.

"So, what did you think of your first day as my deskmate?" Tracy beams as we gather our things. I throw on my windbreaker, grab my purse as I shut my computer down and push in my chair. I'm exhausted, to put it mildly.

I shrug. "It's okay, I guess. Not to knock your training abilities, I mean. I just miss the field already, that's all."

Tracy nods sympathetically. "I understand," she says. "You'll get used to it here, I promise."

"Thanks, Tracy. That means a lot."

"Hey, want to get a drink? I'm buying—" she suddenly trails off, remembering the baby. "Well, we can skip out on the bar scene. How about a soda? I'm still buying."

I nod, grinning. "That'd be nice. Sure, why not?"

Fifteen minutes later, our cars are parked outside a local tavern, Derby Rollers. Tracy and I head inside, ordering two sodas at the counter. The bar's a quiet enough scene, with only a few patrons scattered around the old musky room. Framed pictures hang on the wall, and a few TV's play local and national sports games. Tracy and I find a seat alongside the back wall, sitting across from one another as we slide into the booth with our drinks.

"So," Tracy starts. "You found Alistair in Dubai?"

I nod, staring down into my glass. "Yeah. I used that *Locator* app you sent me."

She beams. "How did it work for you?"

"It worked. I found out he'd taken a cab to the city—never-mind. It's in the past now, I don't need to think about it."

Tracy looks down into her glass, too. A moment later she looks back up at me, a look of determination splashed across her face. "I don't think it's over, though," she says. "It can't be. Not like this."

I sigh, defeated. "Tracy, I wish I shared your optimism. Really."

She nods. "Hey, the glass is always half-full. Think about it that way."

"Yeah, whatever," I reply, taking a sip of my soda. "Hey, what about you?" I ask, changing the subject. "You and that guy from IT. Louis. What's up with that?"

Tracy's face flushes red. "Stop it. You don't care," she laughs.

"I do!" I play along, laughing as I shift the focus over to my friend. "Look. You helped me chase down the father of this child. No matter the outcome, I owe you for that."

My friend grins. "You certainly do. Don't think I'd forget so suddenly."

"How about I help you out with this Louis guy, then?" I ask.

Tracy shrugs, smiling as she looks down into her drink. "Not sure how much help I need with that at the moment," she says mysteriously.

"You didn't," I grin.

She looks back up at me, beaming. "We did."

"No!"

"We hung out last week, and then…"

"No!" I shout again playfully, lightly punching my friend's arm for emphasis. "You can't be serious."

"We spent the night at my place," Tracy says, her face redder than a ripe tomato. "We exchanged numbers, and we've made plans for this upcoming weekend already. He wants to take me to a concert here in town."

Hey, I'm happy for her. But now that means I'll be practically alone this entire weekend. It's already Monday, but I'm dreading this week coming to a close. Alone at work, alone at home.

"I'm glad you two finally did it," I smile. "It's been long overdue."

"Really?"

"Really," I reply. "You two deserve each other. I can't wait to see the look on Louis's face when I run into him at work."

Tracy grins. "You'll see him eventually, I promise. We'll all have to go out sometime, I swear."

I take a sip of my drink. "It'll happen soon," I say.

We look around the bar, checking out the other patrons around us. There's a man in a suit, leaning over the bar as he sips out of a shot glass. A group of guys and girls crowd around one of the TVs blaring a basketball game. The bartender leans up on the counter, playing a game on his phone. I'm surrounded by people, my best friend across from me with the best news I've heard about her in weeks. But I still feel alone, I feel that same hole in my heart from before.

Alistair's rejection still stings, I'll admit it.

But I wish things had gone differently between us. I don't regret Paris, that's for certain. But if I could do it all over again, I might have changed my approach in Dubai. Handled things a little more carefully over there.

But the past is in the past. And Alistair doesn't want anything further to do with me, that much was made abundantly clear.

Tracy and I finish our drinks, and she clears her tab with the bartender after he finishes his cell phone game. We step outside into the cold foresty air of Langley, Virginia, and for the first time since returning stateside I finally feel like I'm back home. And I guess it's for good now.

"Hey, thanks for tonight," I say. "I'd probably go insane if it wasn't for you."

Tracy smiles. "Hey, don't give me all the credit. I'd be going stir-crazy at work if I didn't have you as a deskmate."

"Oh, shut up," I say playfully as we stand next to one another in the parking lot. "You love that desk job. You'd flourish without me tying you down with training."

Tracy shakes her head. "Not true. I wouldn't be there without you, and that's a fact."

"Really?"

She nods. "Yeah, really. You being out in the field gave my day excitement, and having you as a deskmate gives me something to look forward to every day. Don't count yourself out, Samantha. You're a lot more than you give yourself credit for."

I smile. "Thanks, Tracy. You're a true friend."

We say goodbye, a brief hug between friends as we get into our cars and pull out into the road.

As I drive the long route home, forty-five minutes until I've finished my commute, I can't help but reflect on the rollercoaster of a week I'd just been through.

Finding out about the pregnancy.

Remembering the father, tracking him down with Tracy's help.

Finding him in Dubai, asking him out. The rejection that stung.

It's all so much, I can't believe it's been less than a week since I first took that pregnancy test. But life comes at you fast when it wants to, and Father Time couldn't give two shits if you think you're ready or not.

I've accepted my fate.

I'll keep the desk job here in Langley. It's not my passion, but it'll be enough to get by. And this baby's going to need all the care it can get when he—or she—enters the world.

I'm going to be a mother.

It finally hits me on the drive home.

Another human being is going to entrust their entire life, their entire world to me. And they didn't even ask to be born.

With or without Alistair, I know I can do this.

The drive home is long, dark, and I'm nervous about going it alone. But in the end, I make it home safe and sound. No help required.

EIGHT
Alistair

After Dubai, I finally have enough free time for a trip back home. Once I've got the hundredth floor of the Burj Khalifa in my possession, I've finished my task set out for myself. I take a private jet from Dubai International to Italy, where I take another flight back home to Washington, D.C., a fifteen-hour trip in total. No matter, I'm able to get plenty of sleep in my seat; I'm the only passenger on board. The flight attendants wait on me hand and foot, bringing me hot towels and a fresh eye mask every time I need to get some shut-eye. Before I know it, we're touching down in D.C., and I've got an entire week ahead of me with nothing on the docket.

After getting off the plane, I hop into the limo that's waiting for me on the tarmac. My regular driver, Kennedy, a young man in his prime with a killer beard and a nice smile, tells me he'll take me anywhere I want to go. I rub my five o'clock shadow, wondering if I should grow mine out, too.

"I want to stop by the office first," I tell him through the partition window, scratching my chin. "I've got some business to attend to after Dubai."

"Right away sir," Kennedy says cheerfully. He rolls up the window separating us, and the drive to the office is smooth and fast. I take a moment, collecting myself in the backseat as I crack open a bottle of ice-cold spring water, sipping it as I stare out the window.

It's been a long time since I've been back here. A long, long time. I'm staring to remember landmarks as we pass them on the way to the office, and I remember cheerily that Pemberton's main office is only half a mile from Pennsylvania Avenue. I'm a stone's throw away from the President himself, if that's any consultation. But I've never had the pleasure of meeting him in person. Only phone calls.

Kennedy whisks me to the office, dropping me in front of my building as I hop out the backseat.

Pemberton's Corporate Office is huge, a sprawling campus five stories high. The parking lot here is almost as big as Disney World. My office is just up ahead, the fifth floor in the center of the campus. The office isn't nearly as big as the Burj Khalifa, of course, but it'll do for my purposes. And I'm more than happy to be back home.

I step inside, pushing through the revolving door as I step into the lobby. I can see the company masthead, a dove resting on an olive branch, and my faithful employees walk to and from as they cross the marble floor. The front desk is busy today, secretaries and receptionists answering constantly ringing phones, routing calls, putting clients on hold as they transfer them to the correct department.

I wave hello at the front desk workers, passing them by as I step over to the elevator, pressing the fifth floor button. The elevator dings and I step out, walking into my personal office on the top floor.

The best of the best are working here upstairs; I've chosen to surround myself with the most dedicated thinkers that Pemberton has to offer. Engineers program code into surgically-opened computers, interns rush to and fro as they deliver coffee to the other executives on my floor. I'm home, no doubt about it. The busy energy keeps me awake, keeps me focused on my mission at hand.

I unlock the door to my office with my personal key. My office is cold and dark when I step inside, and I flick on the light as I close the door behind me. The room's dusty, clearly having not been used in months. For a moment I want to curse the cleaning crew we've hired, but then I remember the locked door outside, the key that only I have to the CEO's office. No wonder they haven't been able to clean up in here, nobody can let them in.

I sit down, brushing aside a thin layer of dust from the blotter atop my desk. I boot up my computer, logging into the corporate mainframe as I send an email to the higher-ups in the company. I tell them we've secured the hundredth floor of the Burj Khalifa, and the branch managers in Dubai can begin to move in whenever they please.

After that, I shut my computer down, finished with my work for the week.

Nobody said it was hard work being a CEO, and I'd be inclined to argue with anyone who says otherwise. It's not hard work. But my brain powers the entire company, and without me, the whole ship would go down.

I step out of my office, flagging down one of the many secretaries we have working on this floor. She scurries over to me eagerly, a young woman no older than twenty-five, dressed in a neatly-pressed blouse and skirt. For all I know she could be my personal secretary.

"Ma'am, what's your name?"

"Beatrice," she smiles. "Beatrice Langley."

"Miss Langley, have somebody attend to my office. I'll leave the door open. Have it cleaned up in there. I'll keep the door locked, you can just pull it shut when they're finished inside."

"Yes, Mr. Jensen. Anything else?"

"That'll be all, Miss Langley."

As I lock the door to my office, keeping the door cracked open, I can't help but feel a twinge of a forgotten memory tugging at my brain. I walk to the elevator, pressing the call button as I head down to the lobby.

Langley.

Langley, Virginia.

The woman I met in Paris, Samantha Jacobson, works in Langley, Virginia for the CIA.

I've been thinking about her non-stop ever since she found

me in the Burj's lobby. Sure, I've been busy, but that doesn't mean I haven't been able to think about her ever since we parted ways in the lobby of the tallest building in the world.

Samantha wanted something from me. She asked me out for dinner, something a lot of girls do on a daily basis. But I can read those women like a book, every time: they want my money, my status, my fame. In some form, I'm a mind-reader. But I can't get a read on Samantha, not for the life of me.

And it's killing me inside.

I step outside my office, into the golden afternoon. The sun's shining overhead, and I feel like I've got the weight of the world stacked on my shoulders.

Samantha Jacobson. I need to know more about her before I make my next move, and there's nowhere better to start than her place of work.

I hop into the limo that's waiting for me outside. I tell Kennedy to take me back home, and to give me some privacy while I make a few phone calls.

"Got it, boss," he says as the partition window rolls up. When I'm sure I'm alone, I pull out my phone and start my research.

I search for the number to the Langley, Virginia office that I know the CIA's housed in. The call goes through, and a receptionist picks up on the first ring.

"Langley Office, this is Marta, how can I help you?"

"Marta, I need help finding one of your employees. Can you see if they're available, please?"

"Absolutely, sir. May I ask who's calling?"

"Alistair Jensen."

"And to who may I direct your call?"

"Samantha Jacobson. I'm sorry, I don't know which department she's in, but I know she used to be a field agent. I bumped into her last week overseas. I'd like to relay a message to her if that's possible."

"One moment, sir, I'll connect you."

The line goes quiet, and a moment later I hear a click. Then the phone starts to ring again.

I'm nervous when the ringing starts, and when somebody finally picks up I can feel my heart racing in my chest.

"Hello?" it's a woman's voice, but it's not Samantha's.

"Hi, this is Alistair Jensen. I'm looking for a Samantha Jacobson?"

The woman on the other line gasps, and I hear her mute the phone line for a brief moment. "Alistair? Alistair *Jensen?*" she says a moment later.

"Yeah?"

"Sorry, this is just—I'm starstruck. Sorry. My name's Tracy, I'm Sam's deskmate."

"Oh. Okay, well, is she available?"

"She's busy right now. On a conference call. Is there something I can help you with?"

"She found me in Dubai, asked me out to dinner. I was hoping to speak to her about that, if possible—"

I hear Tracy mute the phone again. She must be covering the receiver with her palm, because I hear a few words muffled through the phone. I can hardly make them out, but I manage to make out a few choice words.

"…Alistair…calling…father, isn't he?"

Father?

What's going on?

"Hello?" I ask, equal parts confused and concerned. Tracy picks the phone back up.

"Hey, hang on just a minute. I think Sam's coming this way."

She palms the receiver again, and this time I hear the entire conversation.

"*It's Alistair,*" Tracy says. I can her her voice, faint. I have to strain to hear her words. "*I think he wants to talk to you.*"

"*I'm not in the mood right now, Tracy.*"

"*But he's the father! Didn't you want to see him in the first place?*"

Holy. Shit.

Samantha's pregnant.

And it sounds like I'm the father.

My entire life flashes before my eyes as I feel a responsibility lowering itself onto my shoulders. The weight's heavy, that's for certain. I feel my world start to spin, my entire life yanked out from under me like a loose rug on tile. I'm at a loss, completely and utterly bewildered.

I know some women try this stunt on me, try to collect alimony payments and maternity entitlements. It's just part of the game, really.

But *nobody's* done it this way. Secretive, trying to dodge the question at hand.

Which leads me to believe one thing: that this is real. That Sam's *really* pregnant, and that I'm really the father.

How did this happen?

My ears are ringing, and I feel like I'm going numb.

I suddenly notice I've dropped my phone, and I pick it back up, holding it to my ear. A familiar voice crackles through the line, and I feel my voice catch in my throat.

"Hello? *Hellooooo?*" I hear Samantha calling as I come back to reality.

"Hello? Samantha?"

"Alistair? Is that really you?"

I gulp, more nervous than I have any right to be. I don't know for *certain* that Samantha's pregnant with my child. It could be a fluke. A test to get closer to me after a failed attempt back in Dubai.

I have to play my cards right. I only have one shot at this. I try to stretch my voice, sounding as casual as I can given the circumstances.

"Samantha, hey. I wanted to get in touch with you. I think we got off on the wrong foot back in Dubai."

She sighs. I can hear her exasperation from here. "You think so?"

"I know so. Look, I'm sorry. I feel terrible after last week. I want to make it up to you, Samantha."

"No, you don't." Her voice is sharp, curt. I've hurt her, I can tell, and I feel the need to make things right.

"Yes, I do. I feel awful for rejecting you. Honestly. I want to take you out to dinner, just like you offered me back at the Burj."

"Well, my offer's off the table. Sorry."

"And I'm putting a new one in its place," I reply. "Samantha, I can't get you out of my head. Ever since Dubai I've been racking my brain, trying to figure out why things happened the way they did between us."

"Well, let me solve the puzzle for you: I'm done, Alistair. I put myself out there, and you shot me down. Threw me in the garbage, just like that. I'm out. Have a good life."

"Don't hang up, please. Samantha, let me do this. Just one meal, and then it's over."

"Why?"

"Because I want to."

"Okay," is all she says.

I sigh.

Paris was something else. Something new, something I'd never experienced before. The night we shared was unlike any other, secrets bared that I'd never dared to tell anyone else before in my life. She asked me about my past marriage, and I remember blubbering on and on about my ex-wife to her. Samantha *gets* people. A field agent for the CIA knows when you're full of shit and when you're not.

And she came back to me. After our night together in Paris.

If she knew I was full of shit, she'd never consider giving me the time of day. I know that for a fact.

But *something* drew her back to me.

And I intend to find out what that is.

What the truth is.

"There's one more reason I want to take you out for dinner."

"What's that?" she asks.

"I know about the baby."

NINE
Samantha

"I know about the baby."

His words cut deeper than any knife, cutting me through to my core. My world starts to spin, and I feel myself growing faint. Tracy's sitting on the edge of her seat, keeping a lookout for any supervisors that might come out way. I hang onto my desk for balance, staying seated in my chair. I don't know if it's nerves or nausea keeping me down, but I don't intend on finding out anytime soon. I clutch the phone tight, hanging onto it for dear life. It's the only lifeline I've got.

"What?"

"The baby, Samantha. I know about the baby. I heard you and Tracy talking about it. That's why you came to Dubai, right? Because you're pregnant?"

No use beating around the bush any longer.

"Yeah, I'm pregnant," I reply. "I should have said something in Dubai, but…"

"But?"

I sigh. "I didn't think you'd believe me. I was certain you'd get hundreds of women claiming the same thing every day, and that I'd be just another drop in the bucket to you."

"You're not just another drop in the bucket," he says. "And you're right—I do get plenty of solicitations from women claiming I'd gotten them pregnant. But you're not them. I can tell you're different. Unique. I meant what I said to you back in Paris in the morning, just before we went our separate ways."

Well, go figure. Alistair Jensen thinks I'm unique. If he's trying to flatter me, butter me up, it's working. I grin, a hint of a smile cracks across my face.

"You really think I'm different?"

"In a good way," Alistair stutters, tripping over his words. "I think it'd be easier to explain in person. Trust me."

I lean over my desk as I shoot Tracy a look of excitement.

"Okay, Alistair Jensen. You win. I'll go out with you. Dinner, right?"

"Right. I'll have my secretary call you later this week, arrange the details. I'll come pick you up, Friday night if that's good for you."

I shrug. "Friday's fine with me. Are you…in Langley?"

"No," Alistair says. "I'm in Washington, D.C., but it's only a quick flight there. I can be on my plane and take off in fifteen minutes flat."

Right. Billionaires tend to own private planes. I might've forgotten about that, given the heaviness of the moment at hand.

"So, what do you have in mind?"

Alistair chuckles through the phone. "Dinner. I'll say nothing more than that."

"Really?" I chuckle lightly, playing along.

"Yes, really. It's for me to know, and for you to find out."

I give Alistair my contact information for his secretary, and just like that, the call's over.

I've got a date this Friday. With *Alistair Jensen,* no less. Is this really happening to me?

I look over at Tracy and grin.

"I guess that went well?" Tracy asks, already knowing the answer before I have a chance to respond.

I nod eagerly. "We've got one hell of a week ahead of us," I reply. "Better get to it."

The rest of the week goes by in a blur. Day in, day out, I'm only spending time in the office with Tracy while she shows me the CIA's inner workings. By the time Friday rolls around, I'm practically an expert on spreadsheet functions, server maintenance, and filing applications for field agent requests.

I miss my work in the field, but I'll make do with what I've got. And besides, I've got bigger things to worry about.

Alistair's secretary calls me on Thursday, giving me the schedule for Friday: Alistair'll pick me up at eight on the dot, and we'll go out to eat after that. Simple enough, I guess.

Tracy comes over to my house after work on Friday, helping me get ready for my dinner with Alistair. My place isn't the greatest, just a small house outside Richmond. Something I can come back to after a long trip overseas. One bed, two bath, a living room that's no bigger than my dorm room back in college. Nothing too fancy. Tracy and I run upstairs to my bedroom, flinging open my closet as we search for the perfect dress. We rifle through dress after dress, weighing our every option as I stand back and drape each dress over my midsection, trying to find the perfect fit.

We settle on the perfect one for the occasion: a skimpy black cocktail dress, with a hidden zipper in the back. It's sexy, mysterious, enough to keep Alistair guessing all night.

"How about this one?" Tracy asks, holding the dress up.

I stare, amazed. "It's perfect. How did you know?"

Tracy giggles. "I've got an eye for perfection," she says. "Come on. Put it on, let me see how you look."

I duck into the bathroom, closing the door behind me as I start to undress. I shimmy into the dress, careful to zip it up slowly in the back. I step outside, Tracy finishes zipping me up and I step over to my mirror, admiring myself.

I look fine as *fuck*. I do a twirl, inspecting myself just like Alistair's going to do a little while later. And when I like what I see, Tracy and I head to my shoe rack, picking out a black pair of high heels that compliment my dress perfectly.

I sit down in front of my dresser, my makeup spread out in front of me as I check myself out in the mirror again. Tracy plops down on my bed, playing on her phone as I apply my foundation, mascara, straighten my eyelashes. It's all so much effort, but I'd like to put my best foot forward tonight. After all Alistair and I have already been through.

And we've got one hell of a surprise waiting for us. In a few months, I'll be showing. And rude-ass coworkers and family members are going to pry, asking who the lucky father is. I need to know what I'm going to tell them; I need to know if Alistair wants to be a part of our baby's life or not. He knows about it, the cards are all on the table. Now it's time to see if his bark matches his bite.

It's all going to be settled tonight, I tell myself. I'm not going to wait on this man hand and foot for an answer, no ma'am. I can do this all on my own, I've decided. It's just going to be up to Alistair to let me know just how big of a role he wants to play in our child's life.

When I've finished with my makeup, I turn and face Tracy, my arms extended like a sacrificial lamb. "How do I look?"

She grins. "You look like you're about to go out to dinner with a billionaire," she replies. "You look amazing, Sam. Really. Now, if we can do the same to me before my night out with Louis —"

I laugh, waving a hand. "Of course, Trace. We'll take turns, you and me."

She beams. "Well, hey, best of luck tonight, right?"

I nod, sighing heavily. "Yeah, I'm going to need it."

Tracy and I exit my bedroom, and I walk her outside. She stands by her car, waving goodbye as I return the favor from my front porch.

"You got this!" she calls out.

I nod sweetly, and she hops in her car, firing up the engine. A moment later, she's backing out of my driveway, onto my crowded suburban street, and she pulls away a second later.

I'm alone. Left to my own devices. I check my phone, it's six-fifty-seven. Still an hour before Alistair's here to come pick me up.

I head back to my room, crashing on my bed.

I hold my stomach gingerly.

This'll all be worth it, I tell myself. *One date with Alistair, and I'll have all the answers I need. I'll know if I have to do this alone, parenthood. I'll know if Alistair meant what he said about me being unique. And, most importantly, I'll know how I feel about* him. *And that's what matters at the end of the day, right?*

I sigh, blowing hot air from my nose as I play on my phone. Some game that was free on the app store, don't ask me.

Whatever tonight brings, I just hope it's all for the best.

I put my phone down, close my eyes for just a moment as I steady myself.

And then, before I know it, I hear my doorbell ring. I check my phone.

Eight o'clock.

It's showtime.

I run downstairs, my high heels in hand as I fling the door open to see Alistair Jensen, dressed sharply in a three-piece suit and tie, waiting for me on my front porch.

TEN
Alistair

"So, do you prefer Alistair? Or do I have to call your Mr. Jensen while we're out?"

I laugh. "Alistair works just fine," I tell the woman seated across from me. "That'd be a strange imbalance, wouldn't it?"

Samantha blushes, a hint of red blotting her cheeks. "I guess. I just wanted to play it safe, you know?"

"Of course. Now, my turn: do you prefer Samantha, or should I call you Miss Jacobson?"

Samantha laughs. "Okay, now I see my question was a bit silly. You'll have to excuse me. I've never been to a place as fancy as this."

I nod, looking around. This place is fancy as *shit,* I'll give her that. Probably the most expensive place that's within an hour's drive from Langley. Tonight, I've taken Samantha to the highest rated place in the tri-state area, a four-star Michelin restaurant that's as costly as it is in-demand. *Retrait,* this place's called. I'd been able to get a reservation here tonight, no problem, but I don't want to think about how much it cost me. Around us, patrons eat their fancy French meals. I see calamari, escargot, fancy sparkling water poured from bottles. Waiters check in on tables, and I can see a line forming outside the restaurant.

But that's not what matters.

What matters is the woman across from me. She's here, she's happy. And now we can finally hash things out as adults. We can figure out this baby situation, get it under wraps. Literally *and* figuratively.

"So, want to get down to brass tacks?" I ask, unfurling my napkin and setting it on my lap.

Samantha shrugs. "What did you have in mind?"

"The baby. What should we do about...it?"

Samantha opens her mouth to speak, but she's interrupted when our waiter appears, a slender young man with a wisp of hair under his chin.

"Can I take your orders?" he asks.

I nod. "We'll take that calamari, side of escargot," I reply. I look over at Samantha. "That work for you?"

She nods. "Sure, I guess."

"Excellent," the waiter says, scribbling down our order. "I'll have that sent out as soon as possible, Mr. Jensen."

As the waiter leaves, Samantha cocks an eyebrow. "How did he know your name?"

I shrug. "Takes a lot of money to get in here without a reservation. I guess they'd want to learn my name after I spent a few thousand—*nevermind*," I wave my hand, dismissing her question. "None of that matters. Now, where were we?"

"About the baby?"

"Yes. What should we do about it?"

My date crosses her arms, putting a metaphorical wall between us as she spares me a stern look. "It's not an it," she says matter-of-factly.

"You know the gender?"

She shakes her head. "No. But that doesn't make them an *it*," she replies.

"Okay, what should we do about them?" The word sounds funny, but I'm not going to question her.

"I don't know," Samantha says. "I was hoping to hear your thoughts on the matter first. If that's alright."

I shrug again. "I thought we'd be able to start a family," I say. "This was the sign I needed. And you're here, with me. What else would we possibly need?"

But Samantha's not buying it. "Last week you tossed me aside. Back in Dubai. And now you've had a sudden change of heart?"

I nod. "After I found out about the baby, yes."

"And you want to start a family with *me.*"

"I've never wanted anything more."

In reality, I'm petrified. I've never followed through with a woman like this before, pregnancy or no. Second dates are never my strong suit, and I'd consider our night in Paris the first date between us. I'm in uncharted water, up to my neck in self-doubt and guilt. In reality, I don't know what I want. As I tell Samantha I want to start a family, I can't help but feel I'm lying. Not that I'd purposely mislead her. I just don't know if my words ring true.

And Samantha can see right through me. Her arms still crossed, she stares me down from across the table.

"I do this for a living, Alistair. Interrogating witnesses and informants is my speciality."

"Oh? And I'm…a witness?"

"In some sense of the word, yeah. And I'm going to cut to the chase. You're lying to me, in one way or another. Either you're completely uninterested in starting a family, or worse: you have no idea what you're doing here. Both options scare me."

I blink. She's good at this, I'll give her that. "Why's that?"

"Because I see that you're a man who's never been told no. Hell, this date is an example of that. Imagine what the hostess would say if I called here, asked for a table tonight without a reservation. They'd laugh me out into the street. But not you. Your money can buy you anything, Alistair. But you can't buy me. You can't buy affection. And you can't buy family, not as easily as you'd think."

I'm shocked. Dumbfounded. I offered Samantha an olive branch, and in return, she spat in my face. I've got half a mind to end the date here, pay for her ride home and end everything between us. But I tough it out, telling myself it'll all be worth it in the end. For the baby. For us, if that's even a remote possibility anymore.

"So what do *you* want to do, then?" I ask, letting Samantha speak for herself.

"I want to raise the baby alone," she says. "That's it. All there is to it. I don't even know why I'm here anymore, to be perfectly honest. I came here on a chance that you'd be reasonable, that you'd be understanding. But now you're telling me you want to start a family with me? Do you really have any idea how much work that is? How busy your life gets when there's a baby involved? Because I don't think you have the slightest inkling of what we're facing here. Parenthood is real, Alistair. More real than I think you've ever known."

Her words cut deep, like a knife to my back.

Hang me out to dry, why don't you?

"Your attitude. Is this about me rejecting you in Dubai?" I ask, point-blank.

Samantha's mouth hangs open, a look of disgust chiseled on her face like a statue.

"You did *not* just say that," she says.

"What?"

"That I'm not going to drop my life and start a family with a man I hardly know because he *rejected my invitation to dinner*. You know this is bigger than that. Don't pretend otherwise."

I've almost hit my limit here. I'm pissed, annoyed at her playing the *holier-than-thou* card so early into the date. Like she knows the half of what parenting means. "Okay, that's not what it's about, then, I'll concede. Tell me, please. I beg you. Enlighten me."

Samantha scoffs. "If you have to ask, then it's already hopeless."

"No, it's not. You're just as full of it as I am, admit it. You're as nervous as I am. Why can't you just meet me in the middle, Samantha?"

"Because *you couldn't do the same if your life depended on it!*" Samantha barks, and I hear the restaurant go silent as everyone turns to face us.

The awkward pause hangs in the air, a moment I can't escape from. A moment later, the other patrons go back to their meal as the skinny waiter from before brings us our food.

"Escargot, and an order of calamari," the waiter says, setting the plates down between us. His face is grim, he's definitely heard Samantha's outburst. He scurries off back to the kitchen as quick as possible, leaving us alone to our own devices.

"So, you were saying?" I chide Samantha, daring her to burst out at me again. Instead of that, she shakes her head, staring down at her plate of snails.

"You heard me well enough," she says. "I'm done here, Alistair. I want out. Take me home, I don't care anymore."

"Given up already? I thought it was *me* who wasn't accommodating? What was that you were saying, about meeting each other in the middle?"

"Shut up," Samantha says flatly. She's done. Her arms are crossed, she's staring down at the floor in contempt.

I scoff. "Only if you'll admit you were wrong."

"I wasn't wrong. You're being a jerk," she says. "I can't believe I thought you'd changed. You're nothing more than an asshole in an expensive suit. Only difference between you and a shitty used car salesman are the zeroes in your bank account. You're a charlatan, someone who thinks charity is below him."

"You're wrong about that."

"Which part? The bank account, or the charlatan part?"

"The charity part. I'll have you know my company donates *millions* each year to charity, providing clean water for villages in need—"

"Your company does charity. Not you."

"I'm the CEO, so I fail to see why that doesn't apply to me."

"Because if you cared even remotely about charity, you wouldn't hoard cash like a fucking *dragon*. You'll *never* be a good father with that kind of attitude," Samantha hisses.

I nod, accepting the fact that Samatha doesn't know jack shit about capitalism or fatherhood. Good thing you don't have to be good with money to be a parent, otherwise I'd be the only one here who qualifies.

"Sounds like you've made up your mind," I reply.

She nods. "I have."

We sit in silence for a moment, picking at the plates in front of us. I've completely lost my appetite, and I'm sure Samantha's feeling the same as well. I flag down the waiter, who watches us nervously from the window in the kitchen. He scurries over to our table in an instant, looking between us frantically.

"Check, please," I say, and the waiter nods, disappearing back to the kitchen in an instant. Samantha and I sit in silence while we wait, a god-awful awkwardness hanging in the air between us.

I hate how things went down tonight, but I can only blame myself so much. She's made half of this mess, too, and I know Samantha's going to tell herself she's been completely in the right the whole time.

It's hopeless, salvaging this.

I just want this night to be over.

The waiter reappears, handing us the bill. As he scurries off, I flag him down again. "Wait," I say, holding out my card for him to take. "Let us get out of here already."

"Right away, sir," the waiter says meekly, disappearing back into the kitchen.

A moment later, he's back with the receipt. I sign a zero tip, scratching out a half-baked signature.

Samantha and I stand up, grabbing our coats as we leave the restaurant *Retrait.*

The night's air is cold and a sudden gust of wind stings my back as we step outside. *Retrait* is on a main street, surrounded by restaurants and pubs as cars zoom past us on the road. Samantha and I can't even stand to look at one another after that trainwreck of a date back there. I don't even give a shit about leaving the leftover food behind; I just want out of here. If she's dead set on raising this child without me—a child she *had* to confront me over—then so be it. There's only so much I can do, only so much money can buy. And Samantha's respect isn't going to be bought anytime soon.

I pull my phone from out of my jacket pocket as I dial Kennedy's number. I need to get out of here, and I'll be more than happy to pay for Samantha's ride back home alone. I just don't think I'll survive another minute next to her, and I'm positive she feels exactly the same.

"Yes, boss?" Kennedy picks up on the first ring.

"I need a lift. Date's over," I tell him flatly.

"That quick?"

"Yes. And I'm going to need you to find Miss Jacobson a driver of her own for tonight. She'll be taking a separate car back to Langley."

When I say that, Samantha's gaze darts up at me, and she shoots me a look of pure disdain. *What? You wanted to stretch this out more?* I want to bark at her, but I know it's no use. She scoffs, sighing as she crosses her arms and rolls her eyes.

"Boss?" I hear Kennedy's voice through the phone as I press it up against my chest and look down at Samantha.

"Was there something you needed?" I ask her sarcastically.

Samantha scoffs again, tapping her foot impatiently. "I don't need a ride home," she says. "You can shove your charity up your ass. I can get back to Langley just fine on my own."

I shrug. "Suit yourself," I tell her. I lift the phone back up to my ear to speak to Kennedy. "You heard that? She doesn't need our charity. Nix the ride for her, I'll see you as soon as you can get over here."

"Yes, boss." I can tell Kennedy doesn't give a shit about her, doesn't give a shit about any of this, but I need to use him to make a point. Which has been made elegantly.

Samantha starts taking matters into her own hands, stepping off the curb to try and wave down a cab. Out here in Richmond, taxis are few and far in between—we're not in New York City or anything, so I don't really know what she expects.

I watch as Samantha stretches her arm out as far as she can muster, doing her best to flag a ride down before me.

I see Kennedy's limo pulling up from down the street, and I shoot one final look back at Samantha as the limo parks in front of me.

"You sure about the ride?" I ask, giving her one more chance at an out.

"I've never been more sure about anything in my entire life," she groans, not even bothering to shoot me a second glance.

I shrug again. "Fine," is all I say.

And I start to get into my car.

With my hand gripping the door handle as I pull it open, I watch Samantha as she overextends herself, stepping further out into the street as she tries to flag down a ride.

And then it happens.

Everything goes slow-motion as I watch in horror as Samantha slips, her ankle buckling under the pressure of the high heels she's wearing. She yelps, leaning back to balance herself, but it's no use.

Samantha slips and falls into the road with a *thud*. The cars passing her just narrowly avoid running her, over and an occupied taxi honks and swerves mere inches away before it's set to run over her head.

I don't waste a single second.

I slam my limousine door, rushing past the car to dash over to Samantha.

She's still collapsed in the street, clutching her arms over her head as she tries to roll away from the traffic. Another car honks, swerving past her head as the driver merges into the opposite lane of traffic. I lean over Samantha, grabbing her by her shoulders and waist as I pick her up.

She's light as a feather, and I find it easy to pick her up entirely, carrying her back to the sidewalk. I can hear sobs faintly escaping her, and I feel her head press into my shoulder instinctively.

I shift my weight, holding Samatha by her waist alone. I

reach the sidewalk, setting my date down slowly and carefully. When her feet touch the ground, light as a feather, I start to pull away. Her arms are locked tight around my shoulders, and I feel it hard to pull away from her grip.

But she just won't let go of me.

My hands still around her waist, I look down at my date for the evening.

And she looks up at me.

The look of disdain and frustration from before have melted away entirely; I'm left facing a woman who'd just stared death in the face only a moment ago. And she's already different, her demeanor shifting from anger to unyielding want. The look in her eyes say as much.

I can see their color now, they're blue. Bright blue eyes. I'm enamored, and I'm somehow able to forget the entire train wreck of a date we'd just shared only minutes ago.

"Are you okay?" I ask.

Samantha nods, still shaking from the experience. "I'm fine, just…Just a little scratched up, is all."

"That's good. I mean, not the scratched up part. But the you being fine part."

Samantha giggles just a little bit. "I know what you meant."

"Good," I say.

There's an awkward silence that hangs in the air between us, and I can feel the weight of the moment pressing down on me like an anvil falling from the sky.

"Hey, I'm sorry about earlier," Samantha says. "Really. I think I was a bit of a jerk, and—"

"You were *so* not the jerk. I was."

She smiles up at me, and I get another good look at those piercing blue eyes. I'd jump into them and swim if she'd let me. Hell, I'd *drown* in those eyes if I could.

"Well, agree to disagree, then?"

I nod, a hint of a grin creeping across my face.

"So, now what?" I ask.

Samantha shrugs. "I'm still going to call that ride home, I

think. But thanks for everything, really. I'm glad you came back to put me on my feet."

"No problem."

"Alright, Alistair. I guess I'll…see you around?" she says hesitantly.

I smile. "Sure. See you around."

Samantha ducks back into the restaurant, flagging down a hostess to call her a ride back to Richmond. I'd offer her another lift home, but if she's adamant on getting home alone, then what's the harm in doing so?

Samantha steps back outside a moment later, smiling at me as her high heels clack on the sidewalk.

"They're calling me a ride. A cab back to Richmond's a little costly, but I think I should be okay paying the fare," she says.

I put a hand on her arm, gently, careful not to overextend my welcome.

"You can ride back with me," I tell her. "Really. I can even turn away from you if you don't want to look at me on the way back."

She giggles. "I don't think that'll be necessary," she says.

"Oh. Okay, then," I say flatly, and I turn back to my limo, ready to head home.

"Wait."

I turn around, and Samantha's right behind me, only inches away from my face.

"I think I'll take that ride back," she smiles.

"I think we can make that work," I say, returning the smile.

I open the limo door for Samantha and she steps inside, grinning from ear to ear.

ELEVEN
Samantha

I'll admit, that date was a little bit of a train wreck. Just a hair, really. The argument over dinner, the awkwardness in the restaurant. And then, of course, I have to go and do something stupid like fall over in the street. Luckily Alistair wasn't okay with watching me die in front of his limo, and he plucked me out of danger, putting me back on the right path.

I think things are a little different between us after that.

After his limo finally made it back to my house outside Richmond, Alistair and I shared a quiet goodbye as we hugged in the back seat of the limo. I stepped out of the car, waved him goodbye as the limo pulled back out into the suburban street.

And that's it. Show's over, folks.

Back to reality.

As I sit on my couch, mindlessly scrolling through endless TV channels, I can't hep but feel utterly conflicted about the date tonight.

Sure, it was a train wreck, I've said it once and I'll say it again as many times as I need to. Alistair and I don't have compatible personalities, that much is painfully obvious after the dinner we'd 'shared.' But afterwards, out on the street, things changed.

Alistair Jensen saved my life tonight, and that's a fact I cannot deny. I could have died right there in the street. I could have been run over, my head crushed like a water balloon under a taxi's tires, ending my life and the baby's life before it even had a chance to begin.

But Alistair didn't let that happen.

I can't stop thinking about that moment. The moment after he set me down, when our arms were still wrapped tight around each other. I couldn't stop shaking, I couldn't let go of him. And he couldn't let go of me.

I swear, we could've kissed, right then and there. And I would've been more than okay with it. Really. I know how crazy that sounds, but I know it's the truth.

I know in my heart, deep down that *I* was the jerk to him. Alistair extended an olive branch, offering to start a family with the baby and I. And I practically spat in his face when he made the offer, telling him he's insecure and childish for even dreaming of something like that.

And I can't stand by those words anymore.

A man who risks his life, jumps into traffic to pluck his date out of danger isn't a coward. Not by a long shot.

Hey, at least I let him give me a ride home, right? On the way back, we made small-talk, nothing fancy. He told me about this horrible flight he took from Paris to Dubai only a few weeks ago after our chance encounter in the hotel bar. He'd left the hotel we met in, took the flight to Dubai, but the whole thing got delayed by ten hours. The wing broke, and the only tool they could repair it with was in another airport. Yikes. I'm sure Alistair's full of those kinds of stories, and the ride back home was pleasant enough with his company and tales of foreign travel. It's nice to hear more about his life, and I'm curious to know more of his experiences.

Along the ride back home, I saw a different side of Alistair. The billionaire CEO died somewhere in the street outside *Retrait,* and what I was left with was a man who wanted nothing more than to make me happy.

He wanted to be a father, start a family. He told me as much over dinner.

And I told him he'd never be a father. He'd never be a *good* father, I remember saying.

But that isn't true, is it?

Alistair's already a father, technically speaking. Hell, he

might've been one before we even met in Paris. I wouldn't know.

And he saved my life. And our baby's life, too.

That's one hell of a father, if I'd ever seen one before. My own father never plucked me out of danger like that, not from what I can remember of my childhood. Alistair's already overqualified in the life-saving department, and I know in my heart I'd be lucky to be paired off with a guy like him.

The TV channels blur together, an endless feedback loop of talking heads arguing over politics, science. It's obnoxious, to say the least, and I feel a deep sympathy for everyone else in the restaurant that had to overhear our argument over parenthood.

After all, we *both* want to be good parents. So what's the hangup?

I suppose it's me. I told Alistair I was done with him at dinner, even though I'd accepted his ride back home after he saved my life. I'm the inconsistent one. I'm the jerk, and I'm the one who should be so lucky to have a partner like Alistair.

I need to make things right.

I'd never be able to live with myself if I didn't.

I get off the couch, step over to my purse that's sitting on the kitchen table. I know I've still got that card from Alistair, the one with his secretary's number on it. I fish around, digging through my purse until I finally find the card-stock, and I resolve to put the card in a safer location for next time.

I know it'll be a long-shot, getting ahold of Alistair this quickly after our date. His secretary probably isn't going to give out her CEO's personal cell phone number, even if I tell her I just got back from dinner with Alistair.

Still, I have to try, don't I?

I dial the number on the card, holding the phone to my ear as it rings.

It rings once. Twice. Three times.

By the twelfth ring, I know it's useless. I hang up the phone, sighing as I place Alistair's business card on the fridge and tucking it under a magnet. I'll just have to try again later, no shame in that. I've got an entire weekend, alone, and with nothing on my schedule to give me something else to think about besides Alistair.

I guess it's back to reality.

◆ ◆ ◆

The next week goes by in a haze. I'm completely unable to focus on my work, and every word that Tracy says to me in training slides off me like water on a duck's back. I can't even see straight, unable to focus on the screens before me. Tracy shows me calculations, programs to assist the CIA in finding the FBI's most wanted criminals. Fingerprint scans, algorithms to predict crime in certain areas or countries, it's all fascinating, really. But I couldn't give two shits about any of it, not right now. Not when I've got Alistair Jensen on my mind. Our future's foggy, the path ahead of us uncertain. Hell, I don't even know if he *wants* to see me again, after our train-wreck of a date.

On Monday, Tracy tells me about her weekend with Louis. They'd spent the weekend at her place, unable to leave each other's side. They made breakfast together, had lunch out at a café in town. Dinner was takeout, and Tracy tells me all about the movies they *started* watching before getting physical with one another. And she spared me no details in that department, either. I get to hear *all* about Louis's shirtless bod, how Tracy likes it when he pins her—

"Look, Tracy, I'm happy for you guys. Really," I say, exasperated. I've spent the last hour trying to login to the CIA's fingerprint database, but nothing seems to work. Tracy's got a phone resign in the crook of her arm, on hold with the CIA's IT department as we try to get things figured out. "I just need you to let up on the details, okay? It's not like I told you the intricacies of how Alistair got me pregnant back in Paris."

"Well, you *could*—"

I shoot Tracy a look of disdain, and she reels back defensively. Her eyes light up, and I can hear a voice on the back of her line as she lifts the phone up to her ear. "Hello?" I guess IT must've finally bothered answering the phone. She nods a few times, smiling as she scribbles out a few notes on a pad of paper in front of her. "Okay. Yeah. No, that's fine, we can manage that—Oh. Okay, thanks. Yeah, that works. Okay. Thanks again, Louis."

She hangs up the phone, grinning from ear to ear.

"So, I guess your *boyfriend* had the answers?" I say mockingly, poking fun at my deskmate.

Tracy looks at me blankly. "What answers?"

"You were just on the phone with Louis? In IT?" I ask. Tracy nods.

"Yeah," she sighs dreamily. "We just made some plans for this weekend," she says. "And Louis wanted to know if you'd be interested in joining us at the farmer's market this weekend, and I told him I'd ask you first—"

I groan, putting my head in my hands. "So, nothing about my login credentials, then?"

Tracy gasps. "Oh my *God!* I completely forgot, Samantha, I'm so sorry. I'm just...you know. Let me call him back real quick. We'll get this figured out, I swear."

I groan to myself again as Tracy re-dials the line for IT, grinning like an idiot for another chance to talk to her boyfriend.

By the time Friday rolls around, I'm positively exhausted. I feel used, washed-up. All week I've had to listen to Tracy recanting her time with Louis from IT, and I feel like I'll never be wanted in the same way. At least not anytime soon.

Sure, Alistair wants to start a family with me. But we've already done that, haven't we? I mean, there's a baby in me. That's a start. But I still feel unloved, unwanted. I want what Tracy has, I'll admit my jealousy.

As we leave the office, Tracy asks me again if I'm interested in going with her and Louis to the farmer's market here in town sometime this weekend. I can't help but brush her aside, telling her I'll let them know before Sunday morning rolls around. I dash to my car, saying a quick goodbye to Tracy as I cower from the world behind my steering wheel. I'm hopeless. Worthless. I feel like shit, and there's nothing I can do to remedy it.

The drive home is long and tiring, and I start to let the tears flow when I'm halfway home. I have a hard time seeing through the tears, but I let my headlights guide me home, illuminating two hundred feet of road ahead of me at a time. Step by step, mile by mile, I finally find my way home as I continue sobbing behind the steering wheel.

I park my car in my driveway, rushing inside as I fumble with my keys and throw my door open. I'm finally home again, 'free' for the weekend, but I've never felt more alone.

I slump on my couch, not bothering to flick on my TV as I hold my head in my hands, sobbing quietly to myself in my empty home.

God, how pathetic.

Maybe it's the baby causing the emotionality, but I'd never know the difference. I'm happy for Tracy and Louis, I really am, but this has all been too much this week. I'm a wreck, and I've got nothing else to lose. I haven't heard from Alistair since our date last weekend, and I'm more than certain that he's done with me.

If he's done with me, I think to myself, *then what else do I have to lose?*

I get up, trudge over to my fridge as I grab Alistair's business card from under the magnet. I grab my phone, dialing his secretary's number as I hold the phone to my ear.

Here we go again, I guess.

It rings once.

Twice.

Three times.

And then someone picks up.

"Pemberton Computers, Alistair Jensen's office. This is Beatrice, how may I direct your call today?"

Oh my God. Somebody actually picked up for once. Now the ball's in my court. I have to say something, I guess.

"H-hello?" I say, chocking back a sob.

"Yes, how can I help you?" Beatrice says in her chipper tone. I can tell it's getting close to the end of their work day at Pemberton's. I shouldn't keep her long, I don't have much to say anyways.

"I need to leave a message."

"You'd like to leave a message for...?"

"Alistair," I reply, holding back the tears for just a minute longer. "Jensen. He'll know who it is."

"Sure, I can relay a message. What should I give him?"

"Just tell him Samantha called. Samantha Jacobson. I...I just wanted to tell him I had a good time last weekend, as crazy as that sounds. That's it."

"Oh. Well, I can certainly get that message to Mr. Jensen, if that's all you need."

I sigh. "Yeah, thanks. That's all I need. Thanks a ton, Beatrice."

"You're welcome, Ms. Jacobson."

And just like that, she hangs up.

I guess that's that. I've said my piece.

I don't have any choice but to face the real world, having done all I can to change my world for the better. And it's starting to feel like nothing's going to work.

When Sunday rolls around, I end up calling Tracy early in the morning as I make myself a fresh pot of coffee. My BFF picks up on the first ring, chipper and brighter than even Beatrice the secretary.

"Samantha! What's up?" she croons when she picks up the phone. I can't help but smile when I hear her voice, I'm excited to not feel the crippling loneliness this weekend's brought. I've spent the last day and a half cooped up inside, watching endless reruns on television as I wait for time to pass me by. But I'm not going to tell Tracy that, it'll just bum her out unnecessarily.

"Hey, I thought I'd check in on you guys. How're you and Louis doing this weekend?"

"We're great, Sam. We were worried we weren't going to hear from you. We didn't want to go to the farmer's market without hearing from you first."

"Well, I'm free as a bird today. I've just been sitting around all weekend. Care if I swing by, pick you guys up? I'll drive us to the market, no problem."

"Sure! Oh, hang on—Louis is calling me—*what, honey?*" I hear her voice trail off as she sets the phone down. I can hear them talking, my name's mentioned at least once. I can't make out their words, but I know I'm the subject of conversation between the two of them.

Tracy picks the phone back up a moment later. "You still there, Sam?"

"Yeah, what's up?"

"Louis just reminded me. We actually made other plans for this weekend, I'm really sorry, Sam. I totally spaced on them. We're supposed to meet his parents today for lunch, and then afterwards we're going to a—"

"That's okay Tracy, really. I'll find something else to do. You don't have to give me the details."

"You sure? I feel terrible, Sam, really, I just wanted to do something nice..." she trails off, and I can tell Louis is waiting for her to hang up the phone.

"I'll be fine, Tracy, really. Have fun with Louis, okay?"

I can hear Tracy sigh on the other end of the line. "Okay, Sam.

I'm really sorry about that. For real."

"It's fine, Trace. I'll see you at work tomorrow, alright?"

"Sure thing, Sam. See you then."

I hang up, sighing as I put my head in my hands.

Can *anything* good happen to me anymore? I feel cursed, like I'd broken a mirror seven years ago and I'm just now suffering the consequences. Maybe I walked under a ladder this week, or a black cat must've crossed my path somewhere. Because I can't find any rational law of nature that says I deserve this much bad luck. It's uncanny.

I throw my phone down in disdain, curling up into a ball on the couch.

Is this really all there is to adulthood? Work all week, wait for the weekend to come. Then you feel horribly alone; you can't wait for Monday to roll back around, and the cycle repeats itself again and again. I'm trapped. I can't work in the field, I can't even make solid plans for a weekend with friends. What else do I have? This baby, I guess. That's a start, I suppose, but I know it's not going to cure my loneliness. In fact, I really don't know what *would,* at this point.

I flick on the TV, start scrolling through endless channels of news reports, old sitcoms, game shows. It's all bullshit, is what it is.

I lean back into the couch, closing my eyes as I relinquish my weekend to another bout of depression and loneliness. I feel myself start to drift off, sleep welcoming me after a stressful phone call with my friend.

I don't know how long I'm stuck in that position, but something yanks me out of my temporary slumber.

It's my cell phone, still sitting next to me on the couch.

And it's vibrating.

There's an incoming call from an unknown number. CALLER BLOCKED, the ID says.

I gingerly reach for my phone, picking it up gingerly like it's a diseased rat.

Who'd be calling me from a blocked number, I wonder?

I take a moment, collecting myself as I mute my TV and take a deep breath.

And then I answer the phone.

"Hello?"

"Samantha?" It's a familiar voice, strong and deep. I'd recognize those oaky undertones anywhere.

"Alistair?"

"I heard you called my office on Friday. You left a message with my secretary?"

"Yeah, Beatrice, right?"

"That's right. She just got back to me about that call, I thought I'd check in with you. See how you and the baby are doing this weekend."

I feel my face flush, and I feel my heart skipping a beat.

"Yeah, we're doing okay," I reply honestly. "Pretty lonely outside of town, but we're still hanging in there. Just a little bored, that's it."

"Well, I wanted to call you. Hear your voice again, after the craziness last weekend. How's work?" Alistair asks, and for a brief moment it feels like we're able to hold an actual conversation between the two of us without breaking out into a fight. I feel like somebody actually gives a shit about me for once, and I'm not eager for that feeling to end anytime soon. I find myself tripping over my words, eager to indulge the billionaire in casual conversation.

"Work's work, I guess. I'm not a field agent anymore. After my supervisors found out about the baby, they pulled me back to Langley. It's been rough, adjusting to the new routine. But I'm still in training, so I guess it'll all get easier over time. What about you?"

Alistair chuckles. "Work's work. I couldn't have put it better myself. Same for me, too."

"They got you busy at Pemberton?" I ask playfully.

"You'd freak out if you found out how much work I *actually* did every week," he replies. "You don't even want to know."

"Sure I do," I say, grinning. I hope he can hear my smile

through the phone, because his call's already brightened my entire week more than it deserves to. And I *do* want to know how much work he puts in as CEO. I'm genuinely curious. "Tell me, I won't judge."

"Okay. I worked ten hours this week, nothing more. I had to take a conference call with the regional managers, get the Dubai team set up in their office."

"They've moved into the Burj Khalifa, then?"

"Oh yeah, and it's a real bitch getting all the office workers in order."

I laugh at that. Alistair's funny when he wants to be, and it's nice to have someone who cares to make me laugh for once. The god-awful date from last week melts away as I feel myself warming up to Alistair Jensen again, ready for him to catch me when I fall again.

"Hey, how're you feeling after last weekend?" he asks, and I instinctively play coy.

"What do you mean?"

"Well, to start: how're you feeling after that nasty fall into the street? You okay? Baby's...baby's safe?"

"Yeah, we're all good here," I reply. "Just a few scrapes from the asphalt. My field diagnosis? Nothing major, no stitches or surgery required."

Alistair chuckles. "Well, that's good to hear. I think I can finally get a good night's sleep after hearing that."

"How do *you* feel...after last weekend?" I ask, reluctantly. I don't want to overstay my welcome on the phone, and I feel like I'm walking on thin ice, touching on a tender subject. Our date last weekend was a train wreck, and I'm nervous to know what Alistair thinks about everything after the fact.

"I...I wanted to ask you about that, actually," he says, his voice as reluctant as I feel.

"Yeah? What's up?"

"I think you and I got things off on the wrong foot," Alistair says. "I came on too strong, and you got defensive. Naturally. I don't blame you for that at all. Guy shows back up, says he wants to start a family with you after radio silence for weeks? You had every right to say the things you did. I'm not holding anything against you, Samantha."

"You can call me Sam, if you like. And I'm sorry for that, Alistair, don't take things the wrong way—"

"You don't have to apologize," he says. "I mean it. I was wrong, and I hope you can find it in your heart to forgive me."

"Apology accepted," I say, beaming. "Only if you let me apologize, too."

"Okay, then. We're even."

There's a pause that hangs in the air, the line between us crackling and staticky.

"So, now what?" I ask, unsure of the future ahead.

"Well, I guess that's the billion dollar question, isn't it?"

Another awkward silence. I can't take this anymore.

"Hey, can I ask you out again?" I ask, blurting my words out suddenly. They escape me before I've a chance to think them over, weigh my choices. Now it's out there, and I wait with bated breath while Alistair mulls things over.

"Even after that trash can fire of a date last week?"

I smile. "Even after that train wreck. As long as we stay away from *Retrait,* I think we'll be okay. Maybe that place has bad energy. Threw us off our game."

Alistair chuckles. "I'd believe it," he says.

He pauses, and I hear him take a deep breath.

"Yes," he says. "I'd absolutely love to see you again, Sam."

TWELVE
Samantha

Alistair tells me over the phone that he'll be able to pick me up from my place in just a few hours. He's got a private plane, an airstrip just a few blocks away from his office. It won't take him long to get here at all. He'll be here in less than an hour, Alistair tells me, and when we hang up I rush upstairs to pick out an outfit to wear. Anything'll be better than the tank top and sweatpants I've got on, and I can't wait to see what Alistair has in store for us today.

I throw on a floral blouse with some torn-up and washed-out jeans. I step into some flats and I plop back down on the couch, waiting for Alistair to show up as I flick through the endless channels on television.

Before I know it, I hear a knock at the door. I scurry over, flinging my front door open excitedly.

It's Alistair, dressed in a button-down shirt and khakis, a perfectly casual Sunday getup. The top buttons on his shirt are undone, exposing a hint of bare chest. I can see his muscles peeking through the folds in the fabric, and I long for the night we spent together in Paris for the briefest of moments. I know it's a bit much, but I know one truth:

I *want* Alistair Jensen. I wanted him in Paris, I wanted him in Dubai, and I wanted him even during the most God-awful date I've ever been on.

And I still want him now. It's unwavering.

I shoved those feelings aside to protect myself, but now I don't see much of a point in hiding those desires anymore.

He leans forward, and I instinctively meet him in the middle as we embrace on my front porch. His body is big, strong. I can feel those muscles pressing up against my body, and I feel that same aching desire wash over me once again.

"So, you ready?" Alistair says as he pulls back, a cheeky grin spread across his face.

I return the smile, closing my front door behind me. "Never been readier," I grin.

Alistair shows me to his limo, opening the backseat for me as I plop inside. His driver waves at me through the partition window separating the cabin from the driver's seat.

"I guess you've already met Kennedy, my driver?" Alistair says as he hops in behind me, closing the limo door as we both get settled in. We're sitting across from one another, the backseat of the limo more spacious than I'd imagined.

I nod. "I guess we met last week, didn't we?" I call up to the driver.

Kennedy shoots me a bearded smile through the rearview window, his eyes inviting and kind. "Yes, ma'am," is all he says. He must not be a wordsmith.

Alistair leans forward, addressing Kennedy. "Hey. GPS show anything good in town?"

I want to mention the farmer's market, but I'm more interested in hearing what Kennedy finds for us. There's a moment of silence while the driver scrolls through the GPS, looking for a hotspot for our Sunday afternoon date.

"Here we go," I hear him say from up front. "I think I found something cute."

"What is it?" I ask, eagerly grinning.

"Metropolitan Art Museum, only a handful of miles away." Kennedy peers at us through the rearview window. "Up to you guys."

Alistair looks at me expectantly, a cheeky smile spread across his face. *God,* he's fucking handsome. I mean, seriously. That chiseled jawline, the perfect amount of stubble. And those dark hazelnut eyes of his. I could get lost in those for hours, only if Alistair would let me.

"I think that sounds just fine," he says.

I nod in agreement. "I've never been. Kennedy, how far is it?"

"Fifteen minutes, tops," the driver calls back from the front seat.

"I think it's settled, then," Alistair replies. "Take us there, Kennedy."

"Right away, sir."

The partition window rolls up, and a moment later the limo's pulling out onto the road. I smile over at Alistair, who's already returning the favor.

I guess we've got another shot at making this work after all.

Kennedy wheels us to the Metropolitan Art Museum in a flash, and Alistair and I step outside into the gentle breeze of the afternoon. I don't know if we're closer to Langley or Richmond, but at this point I honestly couldn't give two shits. I'm more interested in my date, the man who'd taken yet *another* chance with me to make things right. I'm forever indebted to him for that, and the baby I'm carrying spells out a future that Alistair might very well be a part of someday. If he'll have me, that is.

That part's still a little uncertain.

The Museum's tall, elegant, the whole thing made of light-brown sandstone. Columns extend to the ground, giving the whole place a mausoleum look to it. Banners hang from the rooftop, highlighting new exhibits and attractions for patrons inside. One banner advertises the Human Body, an exhibit made up of muscular skeletons, posed in a variety of differing fashions. Another advertises the restoration of old books. Honestly, neither of those sound all that enticing, and Alistair and I walk to the entrance together as we plan out what we'd like to see inside the museum.

"I'm thinking paintings," Alistair says. "I've always had an eye for a good self-portrait."

"Yeah? And why's that?"

"Because landscapes bore the shit out of me," he says quickly. I laugh at that, Alistair's sense of humor throwing me for another loop before our date's even begun. "What about you?"

I shrug. "I'll follow you anywhere you lead me," I smile up at my date.

Alistair returns the grin. "I'll take you up on it, then," he says mysteriously.

Before I have a chance to ask him what he means, Alistair takes off in a mad dash to the museum entrance.

I laugh, giggling at his antics as I chase after him.

◆ ◆ ◆

Inside, the security guards take our phones, belts, wallets, keys as we slide through the metal detector inside the front gates. We pass through, neither of us tripping any alarms as Alistair leads me into the Metropolitan Art Museum's front entrance.

It's so beautiful here, honestly. It's spacious, and I can see hundreds of patrons walking the concrete hallways to and from whichever exhibits they please. In the center of the entrance, a dinosaur skeleton with a massive sail on its back hangs over us menacingly.

"You know which one that is?" I ask Alistair, pointing up at the fossil with curiosity. I've never seen that one before, in all honesty. I could probably recognize a *Triceratops*, but that's about it.

"*Spinosaurus*," he replies. "Cretaceous period, the deadliest predator that's ever walked the earth. He could take down a T-Rex in thirty seconds flat. The most cutthroat hunter the world's ever seen."

"Sorta like you?" I ask playfully as I nudge my date's shoulder.

"*Exactly* like me," Alistair grins. "Well, maybe not so much anymore."

"And why's that?"

"Because now I have you," he says, looking down at me and smiling.

"What, so I'm your prey?"

He chuckles at that. "Only if you want to be. Come on, let's explore."

Alistair reaches out, offering a hand for me to take.

I feel my palms growing clammy, but I shove the insecurities aside as I take my date's hand, following close behind him as we make our way into the heart of the art museum.

There's so much here, I couldn't imagine seeing all of it in one visit. There's hallways upon hallways of old oil paintings, galleries of statues, and even a gift shop just beyond the front entrance. Alistair and I stick closely together, holding hands as we walk through each of the exhibits offered to us. We skip out on the old book restoration exhibit, something that sounds utterly boring without consequence. And the human body exhibit's going to make me sick to my stomach, I tell Alistair.

"Well, let's not let that happen," he smiles. "Come on, we'll walk through the halls of paintings, then."

As we walk across the length of the exhibits, passing countless guides and patrons along the way, Alistair starts to open up to me about his work.

"It's hard work, computers. You know, I never would've gotten into the industry without my father's guidance," he says. "Motherboards are too complicated. What about you? Who inspired you to join the CIA?"

"You really wanna know?"

He nods. "I'm dying to know."

I can tell he's genuine, so I don't skimp out on the truth. I sigh, taking a deep breath as I recant my admission to Alistair.

"I got plucked right out of college," I explain. "My school had a killer internship program. You could work just about anywhere you wanted as a senior in college, and I wanted to travel for work. So I chose the only option that'd let an intern travel in their first year on the job."

"So, the CIA?"

I laugh. "No, actually. I joined up with Mappignton's Cruise Line. I worked on a cruise ship for a year, got my dual-credits in from online classes. I almost minored in hospitality."

Alistair cocks an eyebrow as we pass by a row of abstract impressionist paintings from the mid nineteenth century. "Really?"

I nod. "Yeah, really. As crazy as it sounds. I was a hostess on a cruise line before I joined up with the government."

"What made you…?" he smiles cheekily, and I already know the joke before he's said it.

"Don't say it," I grin.

"I'm going to," Alistair says.

I sigh playfully, teasing Alistair. "Fine. Go ahead."

Alistair smiles, taking a deep breath as he takes pride in his upcoming joke.

"So, what made you jump ship?"

I can't help it. I burst out in laughter. I've heard that joke a thousand times before, but Alistair manages to stick the landing.

"I met an agent on one of my cruises," I explain. "He was an older man, looked a hell of a lot like Al Pacino."

"Was he?"

"What?"

"Was the man on the cruise ship Al Pacino?"

"No," I giggle. "He just looked like him. Anyways, he told me all about the CIA's internship program when I asked him what he did for work. He was a recruiter. Taking a bit of a vacation from work when he bumped into me in the cruise line's restaurant. After that, he gave me his card, told me to call his office sometime if I was interested. I called them the very next day, packed my bags, and left Mappington's on the nearest stop."

Alistair breathes a heavy sigh. "Wow. That's intense," he says. "I'd never expected you to be so…"

"Impulsive?"

"You said it, not me."

We pass by a hallway full of old Roman statues, painted and colored to resemble their original color schemes. Around us, patrons and tour guides crowd halls and pack themselves into tight groups. Alistair and I keep holding hands as we pass through another hallway, into the larger gallery of oil paintings.

"So, what about you?" I ask. "What made you want to become a CEO in the first place?"

"The money," Alistair says flatly as he stares straight ahead.

"That's it? Just cold hard cash?"

He nods. "That'd be it. I started Pemberton from nothing, hired more employees as the workload got greater. I started out with an office in my dad's garage. Now I work in the biggest corporate campus in all of Washington, D.C.. Not much more to say about that."

I nod. "No, I guess not."

We walk by a gallery of paintings, self-portraits from the fifteenth century onwards. There's a few of old artists, composers who'd commissioned artwork of themselves before they passed.

Alistair stops in front of one painting, the first exhibit we'd stopped to take in today so far. It's an old oil painting of a man and a woman, dressed elegantly in old-timey clothing. The metal plaque next to the painting explains it's from mid-century Spain, made up in the style purveyed by Queen Isabelle only a few decades earlier.

"What do you think of this one?" Alistair asks me as he stares up at the artwork. He's deep in thought, I can tell my date's enamored with the painting even before I spare a single glance at it.

To me, the whole thing reeks of rich people stroking their own ego. I figure I might as well be honest with Alistair—after all, what else do I have to lose?

"I think it's dumb," I reply. "Seriously, look at them. They look *bored as shit.* They can't even smile when they're getting someone to paint their picture?"

Alistair just shrugs. "That was just how you posed back then," he says. "Like the old photographs of the eighteen-hundreds. You weren't supposed to smile, it was harder for the artist to capture. Plus, if you had to stand motionless for hours on end, wouldn't your face start to hurt with all that smiling?"

I shrug, too. "I suppose. But why do *you* like this one, over all the others?"

Alistair smiles. "You're going to think it's weird."

"No, I won't."

"You sure? Okay, here goes: I like this painting because I see *us,*" he says.

I take another look at the painting, keeping my date's words in mind.

The couple's old, tired. They're wearing elegant garb, the man dressed up in the ruffly-looking suit of the times. The woman's in an old-timey dress, with buttons and sashes flowing freely every which way.

Then I see it. I see what Alistair means.

The painting isn't *us,* per se, but I see his point.

The couple's rich, that much is obvious. But you can see cracks in the frowns, a hint of feeling underneath. The woman's winkles curve up in such a way that admits a flirtatious smile hides underneath. And I see that same curled-lip look on the man, too.

They're abiding by the rules of their time, bound to conventions in society and art. The pose they strike isn't original, and the style of the artwork isn't the first of its kind, either. But the couple in the portrait still manages to find a way to let their personalities shine through. The more I look, the more I can see it clearly. They *want* to smile, but something's holding them back.

I get it now.

Don't hold back, Alistair is saying. That's what the painting means to him.

I nod. "Okay, you're right. I see it now."

Alistair smiles down at me. "Come on, we're burning day-light. Let's see if there's any others here we like."

Alistair takes my hand again. I feel his gentle, yet firm grip, and I feel a sense of belonging I'd never felt before as he leads me through the gallery.

◆ ◆ ◆

We spend the rest of the day mulling about the museum, never spending more than a few minutes on each painting we check out. Alistair checks his watch, noting the lateness of the hour as I peer out the front windows to see the sun setting over the horizon.

"Think we should be getting back soon?" I ask.

Alistair nods gravely. "Unfortunately."

We start to leave the museum, making our way past security and stepping out into the cool of the late afternoon. The sun's just about to set over the tree line just past the parking lot, and Alistair calls Kennedy to tell him to come pick us up.

"I still had a really good time with you today," I tell him as we stand out on the curb, just outside the museum. "Really. I wish we could've had more time to spend."

"If I could buy another hour with you, I would. No matter how much it would cost."

I feel my heart skip a beat.

That's the sweetest thing anyone's *ever* said to me, bar none.

I look up at my date and smile, hoping he'll take the hint al-ready. "I'd spend another day with you if I could."

God, I just want him to kiss me already.

There's a pause that hangs in the air between us, and I see Alistair shifting his weight slightly forward as he begins to lean closer to me.

I start to close my eyes, ready for the kiss of a lifetime.

Just when I can feel the heat of his body, the warmth of his skin about to press up against me, a car pulls up next to us as brakes squeak.

Alistair turns, leaving me halfway between kissing him and falling flat on my face again. "Looks like our ride's here," he says.

I nod. "Might as well start heading home."

Alistair motions to step off the curb, careful not to let me slip and fall this time around. He grips the handle of the back door, about to pull it open. He stops, turning to face me as his hands remains frozen in place.

"Wait."

I'm confused, and just when I start to ask what's going on—

Alistair Jensen leans down, kissing me squarely on the lips.

It's soft, sweet. I can feel his stubble tickle my chin, his arms carefully reaching around my shoulders to pull me in for an embrace.

I feel my knees buckling, my legs turning to jelly underneath me. I feel like I'm about to swoon, on the verge of collapse. But I hang on for dear life as I put my hands up to Alistair's chest, grabbing handfuls of his button-down shirt to keep myself steady.

The kiss is amazing, to say the least.

It's the best I've ever had in my entire life. Even our kiss back in Paris wasn't this good, I recall. Strangers meeting in the night is one thing, but a date with someone you're honestly making an effort with is all the sweeter.

Alistair pulls back, grinning down at me from where he stands.

"How was that?" he asks.

I have to take a moment to collect myself. I feel my brain short-circuit, and I feel my entire being reboot like a computer on the fritz.

"G-good," I manage to eke out. His smile is contagious, and I catch myself grinning back up at him. I miss him already, and the date's not even over yet. *How is that possible?* I wonder to myself, but I brush the notion aside. If it all made sense, none of this would be any fun.

"Great," he says. "Let's get you home then, yeah?"

"Yeah," I beam.

Alistair opens the limo door for me, and I hop inside as he follows closely behind. The bearded driver greets us, and Kennedy punches my address into the GPS. A minute later we're on the road, heading home.

THIRTEEN
Alistair

The week after our museum date, I feel like the days are dragging on endlessly. I don't even feel like putting in the ten hours or so I usually put in at Pemberton, so I don't bother going in to work at all. I'm not upset, I'm not in dismay.

I just can't get Samantha out of my head.

The date at the museum was perfection in a nutshell, and I can't get over the thought of the kiss we shared on the curb. It's probably the best ending to date I've ever had, to be perfectly honest. At the very least, it's a billion times better than watching her fall into the street. That's for certain.

For the first time in half a decade, a woman's got me completely distracted from my work at hand.

And I'm okay with that.

It's been a while since Stacy and I split up, and I think it's high time I started to move on. Samantha's pregnant, and that's as good of a sign as any that it's time for me to start looking ahead. To the future. *Our* future, together. Whether or not Sam wants to start a family with me. No matter what form, I'll always be there for her. Whether it's a car ride or a phone call away, I can promise her that I'll always be around.

I'm distracted, sick to my stomach with longing and desire that I haven't felt in a while. And I know Samantha's the only cure. I won't admit any feelings to myself just yet, but I know the sentiments are there. No other girl could fix what Sam brought on to me.

The four-letter word creeps up to the forefront of my mind,

and I'm startled with the thought of experiencing a love this early on. As dark and grim as it sounds, I know I have to protect both Samantha and myself from those feelings early on. Heartbreak's only around the corner, and I've been on this rodeo once before. It didn't end well, to put it lightly. And I'd never be able to live with myself if the same thing happened to Sam and I now. I have to remain cautious, stay safe. Keep my head screwed on tight, do my best to keep my cool as I remain as level-headed as possible.

Now that I'm back in D.C., I don't have any reason to skip work. My office is just down the street from my three-story colonial house, but I don't see any reason I need to go into work this week. It's not like my work's going to single-handedly keep the company afloat, that's thanks to the workers on the bottom rung of the corporate ladder.

As I sit on my front porch, watching the suburban D.C. traffic head to work for the day, I can't help but feel incomplete. Like I've never been so lonely in my entire life. I check my watch, it's only ten-thirty in the morning. But I *have* to call Sam. I need to hear her voice, make sure I'm still alive. *She* makes me feel alive. I pull out my cell phone, punch in her contact. I dial her number, holding the phone to my ear expectantly as I wait for her to pick up. She's probably still in the middle of the workday, but I don't really care. I need her, and that's all that matters.

Sam picks up on the first ring, and I can instantly tell something's off.

"Hello?" her voice is nasally, clogged. She sounds exhausted. I can hear it in her voice with just one word: she's sick today.

"Hey, Samantha. How's it going?"

She groans, and I can hear her wincing over the phone. "I've been better. I think I'm just a little under the weather today, that's all."

"Yeah, I can tell. Anything I can do to help?"

"Oh, *God,* no."

I'm taken aback for a moment, reeling at her comment until Samantha explains further: "Look, I know you're all the way in

D.C., and I couldn't ask you to drop everything and rush over to me. That would be extra crappy of me."

I shrug, and then realize Samantha can't see my gestures. "It's no problem, really. I'm not going to have any more work to do this week. You might as well let me help you out. It's the least I can do."

"What does that mean?"

"It means, I don't think you contracted that sickness from our date at the museum. I would've fallen ill, too. I think it's something else."

"You think it's the pregnancy?"

"Not a doubt in my mind. I've heard about this happening before. And I have just a little bit of experience to go off of. Don't worry, I'm not hiding a kid or another family from you. It's just a feeling I've got. Sometimes it's worse than what you're used to, the pregnancy nausea."

"I figured that was it," she says. "I knew the morning sickness was coming, I had it back in Morocco when I found out—you know. But today's different. It's like a thousand morning sicknesses at once. I feel like I'm being struck by lightning or something. It's weird, you know?"

I do know, in fact. I can't help but feel totally sorry for her. After all, *I'm* the one who put her in this position. And I'd like to do whatever I can to help her get through it; it's the least I can do, to put it mildly. And I've seen this happen before, and I know just how bad it can get at times.

"Look, if you don't want me to come over, I can still help you. I've got nurses, stay-at-home care physicians on call. My father needed them when he got really sick, I still have them on-call. I can have one sent out to you, if that's alright."

"I don't want a stranger coming here," Samantha groans. "I'm sorry, Alistair. I'm just a wreck today. But you're really sweet."

I pause for a moment, weighing my options. "Then can I come over?" I ask.

She pauses for a moment, too. "Sure," Sam says. "I could use the company. Just don't freak out when you see me. Like I said before, I'm a mess today."

I grin. "You couldn't look like a mess even if you tried. I'll be over there as soon as I can. Just need to get the plane warmed up first."

"I'll see you soon, then."

After we hang up, I call Kennedy, tell him to come pick me up from my home. We're making an impromptu visit to the heart of Virginia, and every second counts.

Kennedy gets me to the D.C. airstrip as fast as he can, and I take my private plane to Richmond, Virginia as my driver rides along with me. When we disembark, a rental limo's already waiting for us. Kennedy takes me in the direction of Samantha's, but we make a quick stop at the pharmacy on the way. I know exactly what Sam needs to feel better, and I grab a packet of the anti-nausea powder that I've used before myself.

After the pharmacy, Kennedy rushes me over to Samantha's house, quick as lightning. By the time we're parked outside, it's been an hour and a half since our phone call had ended.

I bid my driver goodbye, telling him to enjoy the rest of the day until we need to get back to D.C.. I step up to Samantha's front porch, medicine in hand as I knock on her door.

She answers, and I can see she's a total wreck today. Not that that's a bad thing, but I can tell the morning sickness has consumed her entire day as is. She's wearing a bathrobe, loosely tied over a tank top and baggy grey sweatpants with holes in them. I know it's strange to say, but she's pretty hot right now. It makes her look imperfect, reminds me that she's human, too. Just like me.

I hold up the bag of medicine, grinning like an idiot. "Special delivery."

Samantha opens the door wide. "Come on in," she says. "And I hope whatever you have can fix this. I'm sick of this sickness already."

I step inside Sam's house, looking around. It's a standard two-story house here in Virginia, I'm vaguely familiar with real estate trends. There's an old felt couch, a flat-screen TV, coffee table, nothing out of the ordinary. I can see a kitchen up ahead, a dining room to my right. There's a flight of stairs in front of the door, going upwards to where I assume Samantha's bedroom is. It's a cheaper place, by my standards, but obviously I'm not going to hold it against her. It's not like she's got a billion dollars lying around like some of us do. The class difference between us is immense, and I wonder what kind of shock Samantha's going to get when she sees my place. I know it'll stun her, to say the least.

I head into the kitchen, grabbing a glass from the pantry just above the sink. I set the bag of medicine down on the counter, pulling out the anti-nausea powder I'd bought at the pharmacy down the road. The powder comes in packets, and I rip one open as I shake the dust into a glass of water, stirring it with a spoon I find in a drawer of silverware. I return to the living room, glass in hand, as I sit down next to Samantha on the couch.

"What's this?" she asks. "Just water?"

"No, no," I chuckle. "Although fluids *do* help. But this is an anti-nausea powder I'd used myself out in the desert, as your body gets sick when the temperature rises and falls quickly. It's nature's equivalent of morning sickness, and this'll help you with that. Go on, drink up."

Samantha shrugs, but still takes the glass from my hands as she drinks. She finishes the medicine in one go, setting the empty glass down on the coffee table in front of her.

"Now what?" she asks, looking at me with a smile on her face.

"We wait for you to get better," I beam back. "It's been a while since I've done a sick day. What *should* we do? Watch TV?"

Sam giggles. "What, they don't let you take sick days at Pemberton Computers?"

I shake my head, laughing. "No, it's not that. I don't get sick that often, really."

"You lucky duck. You think the little one's going to get that immune system of yours, then?"

"Let's hope so."

"Did your wife ever get sick?" Sam asks, and I freeze up in fear. *"What?"*

"Your ex-wife, I mean. Did she ever get sick when you two were...?"

I nod gravely, choosing my words carefully. "How did you know about her?"

Sam chuckles darkly. "You're Alistair Jensen. Your personal life doesn't elude the gossip columns. And a girl likes to Google her prospective dates, no matter how famous they are. I'm sorry, I didn't mean to push. I just read some stuff online and got curious."

"What did you read?" I'm nervous, petrified. I don't know how much Sam knows, and we're in uncharted waters here. I'm afraid she's going to pry, find out more than she needs to know right now.

"That you two were happy," is all she says. "But you guys ended things, what? Five years ago?"

I nod. "That's correct, more or less." Hopefully that's all she wants to say on the matter, and I feel my heart leap into my throat when Sam asks her next question.

"What happened?"

"Sam, I don't know if that's a good idea—"

"What happened between you guys?" she presses me further, and I know I don't have any out. I owe her an explanation after all we've been through already.

I take a deep breath. "I don't know if I want to get into that right now," I tell her. "It's...a lot. And I don't know how you'll react to the truth."

Sam scoots a few inches closer to me on the couch. She places a hand over mind, clammy and cold. But the gesture's still appreciated, and as she looks up at me with those bright blue eyes,

I can feel myself letting my guard down.

"Try me," she says. "I can handle it."

Okay, then.

Here goes nothing.

I take a deep breath. I hear my voice start to shake, and I drop my voice down to a half-whisper. "My ex-wife, Stacy, got pregnant right after our three-year wedding anniversary. We were happy, ecstatic. I couldn't have been more excited for us. We made plans for everything, made up the baby's room just right. Life was good. We had everything ahead of us, nothing in our rear-view mirror to give us pause."

Sam looks at me with sympathetic eyes. I'm sure she already knows what's coming next in my tale.

I take another shaky breath, and I hear my voice crack. "We even picked out a name. Annalise. She was just a little girl, precious and innocent. But Stacy's body couldn't bear the weight of pregnancy."

Samantha looks down at the floor, her hand still holding mine. Her grip tightens as I feel a frog slip in my throat. I haven't thought about this in years, and I thought this business with Sam would let me forget, but…" I sigh, trailing off. This is always the hardest part.

"She couldn't carry the baby to term," I finish quietly.

And the pain's still as real as the day it happened.

"I'm so sorry," Samantha says quietly.

We sit together in silence for a minute as I choke back the tears that threaten to sting my eyes. I can't believe I'm still a wreck over this. I thought I'd gotten better, the years of therapy behind me, but I can tell I'm still tender at the thought of the subject. Maybe this is how it'll always be. I'm scared to look over at Sam, worried she's going to think I'm less of a man for holding back tears in front of her. But it's the truth, she wanted to know my story. Well, there it is. Warts and all.

"Are you…worried that it's going to happen again?" Sam looks up at me with wide eyes. "Because I want you to know that it won't. This time it's different. I'm not Stacy."

"I know. But that doesn't make the hurt go away."

Sam runs a finger over my hand. And to think that *I'm* here to take care of *her.* Now she's the one coddling me, and I couldn't feel like less of a man in this moment even if I tried.

"Alistair, I wish there was something I could do to take the pain away from you. I'd bear it all myself if I could."

I look over at her, and our eyes lock.

"You would?"

She nods, sighing. Her voice is shaky, her breath bated. "We can't do anything about the past. All we have is each other, right here, right now. And the future ahead of us. But I know we'll do right by each other, Alistair. Because I've seen the hurt we both can cause. And if that's anything to go off of, I know we'll be able to make each other feel good, too. If we can dish out pain, who says we can't dish out the opposite?"

I smile. It's a kind gesture, her words to me. I don't know what to say back, so she continues:

"All we can do is prepare. Prepare for the future; the good, the bad, everything in between. I know if we work together, we can handle anything that life throws our way. Even if history repeats itself."

I nod. "I'm sorry I dumped all that on you today. It wasn't fair of me to do so."

But Sam shakes her head. "No. I asked you to open up. If anything, that's on me. You didn't do anything wrong, Alistair. I know you're a good man, deep down."

I smile, gazing past Samantha to look out the window. It's a gorgeous day outside, the trees are in their full green bloom. The sun is shining, birds are chirping. I know if misfortune befalls us, Sam and I could bounce back. Stacy and I never experienced troubles together, and when the going got tough, Stacy got going. I don't think Sam'll ever do that to me.

It's a new day, a new future. One that Sam and I can face head-on.

She grips my hand tight in hers, inching closer to me.

"How's the nausea?" I ask.

She smiles up at me. "It's better," she says. "Now that you're here."

I lean down, kissing her softly. It's short, sweet, to the point. But I hope she gets the message, that I care about her more in this moment than I've ever cared about anything or anyone else. The kiss is slow, steady. When we both pull back, I can see Sam's got a massive grin spread across her face.

She leans over, resting her head on my shoulder as we take in the peaceful afternoon. I don't ever want to leave Sam's side, I don't ever want her to think I'd abandon her ever again.

I never want this moment to end.

FOURTEEN
Samantha

Unfortunately, our perfect day together has to come to a close. Alistair gets a call from his secretary, the office needs to go over earnings report for next quarter this week. And they'll need the CEO to mobilize the workers, keep them organized and in line.

Alistair bids me goodbye, telling me to get better soon as he steps outside and heads to the limo that's waiting for him on the curb. I take a look around outside, the sun's going down over the tree line just ahead of me. The night's growing cold, and I can feel a chill coming on. I step back inside, feeling rejuvenated and reinvigorated after Alistair's visit. I'm sure the medicine he brought helped, too, and he left the box of anti-nausea packets on my counter for me to use whenever I need.

What a gentleman. Seriously.

I was wrong about him, back in Dubai and in the restaurant *Retrait.* He's a sweetheart, really. When a caring man like Alistair's been hurt before, it's normal for him to lash out when things look tough. Now that we're on the same page, I feel like nothing can stand in our way.

We're becoming whole. For the first time. And it's a wonderful feeling, that.

I check the clock, it's already half-past ten. If I'm planning on going back to work tomorrow, I'm going to need some shut-eye.

◆ ◆ ◆

When I head back to the Langley Office the next morning, I can feel the pregnancy nausea rescinding. I've gotten over my sickness, and it's onto the next assignment on my docket. And I know I'll see Alistair again soon, I just know it for a fact. Nothing can pull us apart. Nothing.

When I step inside the office, however, I can already see that my entire department's practically on fire.

There's a crisis happening, everyone's firing on all cylinders. I hear phones ringing, calls being answered, keyboards clacking. I scurry over to my desk, wondering what on Earth's going on.

Tracy's hunkered over her keyboard, focused intently on what's on her computer screen. She doesn't even look up when I plop my stuff down on the desk next to her.

"Tracy?" I ask meekly.

She holds a finger up to me—*hold on a sec*, it says. I nod, sitting down at my computer as I log in to the CIA mainframe with my credentials.

"Samantha, you're not going to believe this," Tracy says.

I swivel in my chair to face her. "What's going on?"

"It's Alan. He found the Malstrom safehouse in Spain."

"Where was it?"

"Just outside Madrid, close to historic Toledo. I know. I can't believe it either. It was so close, we must've skipped right over it before."

"What's going on, Tracy? It looks like everyone's on double-time. Did the whole office take a sick day yesterday, too?"

Tracy just shakes her head. "No, Sam, it's worse than that."

"Then tell me what it is, already. Before the stress puts me into early labor."

Tracy sighs. "Alan's gone missing. He checked in last week, Friday, to be precise. And today's Tuesday. He's been at that safe house for three days, not a word."

"You never know. Maybe he's busy with something. Or maybe he needs to lay low for a few days, keep Malstrom's goons off of his back."

"No, Sam. You really don't get it, do you?"

I shake my head, confused. There must be something I'm missing.

Tracy explains: "Alan always checks in with our department. You know how strict he got with you in the field?"

I snicker, remembering my forced check-ins with my supervisor before. "Yeah. He'd ask me to call in to the department every hour, on the dot. Exactly. Or else he'd freak and spam my phone with calls and texts, worried I'd gone missing."

"Yeah, that's for a good reason, Sam. Alan *always* checks in every hour. Now it's been seventy-two since his last update. We're just a little worried about him because of that."

My eyes widen. When you put it like *that,* I can see why there'd be an issue.

"So what are we supposed to do?" I ask.

Tracy shrugs. "Whatever we can," she says. "I've started running through recent arrest records in all of Spain—I'm starting in Toledo, working my way to Madrid, then north from there. I'm sure we're bound to find something. Someone related to Malstrom. Someone who works for him. Or, if we're especially lucky, maybe Alan just got arrested. But I highly doubt that one."

"No, Alan wouldn't get arrested working on foreign soil. The man's practically a diplomat."

Okay. *Now* I'm worried.

"Tell me what you need me to do," I say.

Tracy nods. "Come here. I'll show you how to access the Spanish database. Might have to use a translation software, but it's a start."

I wheel over to my deskmate's computer as she shows me the login process. Honestly, I can't believe today's happening. Alan was always the careful supervisor, the one who never wanted to take risks. And he'd never send an agent out into the lion's den alone. But that's exactly what he's done to himself—he's alone. And the team of people working for him have no idea where to find him.

I just hope we find a lead, and soon. Because I have no idea what to do if we don't.

◆ ◆ ◆

After digging through the Spanish Police database for the better part of the morning, Tracy and I finally find a lead.

It's Randall Friendly—yeah, that's his real name—one of Terrence Malstrom's most trusted associates. He's more than just a loyal goon. Friendly could be Terrence's right-hand man, for all we know.

And he's been arrested. Today, in the outskirts of a Madrileño neighborhood.

We have to get to the bottom of this.

I print out the rep sheet for Friendly, and I scurry over to the printer as I collect the sheets and run them over to our new supervisor's desk. I'm sure Paul will want to know about this, especially because he's the one filling in Alan's position at the moment.

But Paul isn't at his desk. I rush over to my computer, pulling up the corporate schedule. And it looks like Paul's in a meeting for the rest of the day.

I look over at Tracy with dismay. She stops what she's doing, cocking her head in confusion. "What's up, Sam?"

"Paul's out for the day."

"Jeez. *Really?*"

"Yeah, really. We're dead in the water without a supervisor. We can't send any agents out to check on Randall Friendly. Find out what's going on."

Tracy nods gravely. "Yeah, figured as much. The red tape here is fucked."

I stifle a gasp, covering my mouth with my hand as I reel

back. It's not like Tracy to swear, and I know she *loves* her job here. If *she* thinks a situation's fucked? Then it's *royally* fucked.

"What do you think we can do?" I ask.

Tracy shrugs. "Not much we can, if we're abiding by regulation. We need a supervisor's approval before sending a field agent to check in on Friendly. And I guess that's not happening today."

"So, what, we just have to wait around to find out if Alan's alive or not?"

"I guess so. What else would you do, Sam? Go out there yourself?"

If I wasn't pregnant, you bet your ass I would. In a heartbeat. But I know Alan would just get upset with me, demand to know why we couldn't send someone else in my place. It's not that he doesn't trust me. The CIA doesn't want to put me in any danger, now that I've officially spoken out about my pregnancy.

"We both know that's not going to happen, Tracy. What else can we do?"

"Like I said, the red tape's fucked. We're probably not going to be able to cut through it in time. Even if we could get an agent out there *today,* they wouldn't be able to get in contact with Friendly for at least a few days while Spain goes over their legal proceedings. By that point, I'm sure Alan'll be accounted for. He's going to check in eventually, Sam. I just know it. We'll find him. Don't worry."

But how can I not worry? It's the one thing that's telling me Alan's still alive. I'd hate to admit how much I believe the opposite is true; I'm terrified that our supervisor's befallen a terrible fate, and we're all stuck in an office as we worry about how quick we can get to him in time.

I'm almost certain things are worse than they seem. But to admit defeat now would just be giving up, and I know one thing: the CIA doesn't give up easily. They don't give up on their country, and they certainly won't give up on one of their own. Not without a fight, at least.

I know we're going to find Alan. I'm just worried it'll be too late when we do.

I put my head in my hands, defeated. I don't know what else I *can* do, sitting here behind a computer screen.

Were I still out in the field, I know I'd be the first one to go after Alan. But things have changed, I've been pulled out of the field for medical reasons. The CIA's not going to send me back out there anytime soon, and I doubt it'll be easier to get back to the field after the baby's been born.

I've accepted my fate, however terrible it seems. I have an obligation now, to Alistair and our baby. I'd never do anything to jeopardize it, but I know Alan's not going to come back home without help.

I don't know what to do.

As I sit behind my desk, feeling more hopeless than ever, I can't help but worry that things changed on me too quickly. Now I'm going to pay the price for it. Alan's already paid the price, it seems like. He hasn't checked in with our department in seventy-two hours.

I *want* to serve my country, get back out in the field. But I can't.

I'm helpless, frozen in place.

I have no idea what to do.

FIFTEEN
Alistair

It's been a long, long night at the office, and I can't help but feel like this week's already fucked beyond repair.

The earnings report came up in the red, Pemberton Computers isn't doing so hot after the move into the Burj Khalifa. We'd spent more than we were able to make up for last quarter, and investors are getting antsy. Wanting to sell their stock. On the report, I had to qualm the nerves of every higher-up and manager that felt the need to panic sell. We're going to get through this, I told them, but even I didn't believe it at times.

But it's over now. The investors are settled, and the company's back to the old operation, day-in and day-out. I've been putting in some extra hours at the office, extending my usual ten-hour workweek to an even twenty. It's not much, but when the CEO's doubling his hours you know you're in uncertain times. Financial trouble isn't something to sneeze at, and I've seen lesser companies go down in flames with less issues than we're having right now.

As I work late, sitting behind my freshly-cleaned desk, I can't help but think about Samantha in all this. What she's up to. How our baby's doing. I know she's a couple hundred miles away, but there's nothing I'd rather do tonight than see her.

I swivel around in my chair, taking a look at the skyline behind me. Washington, D.C. is an elegant place, don't get me wrong, but sometimes it's old hat to me. I can do without the monuments, the museums, the bustling city streets. Honestly, I'd kill to be working somewhere peaceful. Quiet. And I'm missing Sam's quaint home outside of Richmond right about now. Something about that place puts me at ease. If I could just work there, in her home, I know it'd be easy enough to handle. It's too loud in my townhouse in D.C.. But what an odd request that would be, right? *Hey, honey, how's it going? Hey, can I move my office into your upstairs guest bedroom? I hope you don't mind, I really like how peaceful it gets in your area. I'll be quiet, I promise.*

I mean, come on. Anyways, I have a lot of things on my mind as of late.

But all those thoughts slink away as I see my cell phone light up, it's an incoming call. Samantha's calling me; I'd given her my number after our time together on Monday. I told her to call me whenever, day or night, and I'm overjoyed to see she's already taken me up on that offer.

I pick up my phone, answering it without hesitation. "Hello?"

"Alistair? It's Samantha."

"I saw you on the caller ID. What's going on?"

She sighs, and I can already tell something's bothering her.

"Work going okay?" I ask, probing her.

"No, it's not. Alistair, I'm sorry to dump all this on you, but I've got to talk to *someone* about this. If not you, then a therapist."

I cock my eyebrows in surprise. "If you'd like, I've got a few therapists on-call I can recommend, if that's what you're—"

"I'd rather just talk to you, if that's okay."

"Sure. Anything you need. What's up, Sam?"

She sighs again. "Work's getting crazy. It sucks, having you be so far away from me when shit hits the fan. I'd kill to see you tonight."

"I know. I feel the same way, Samantha. But I'm busy with work at the moment, I can't get away from the office this week. You'll have to tell me over the phone."

"That's fine."

"What happened?"

"You know I got pulled from the field after I got pregnant,

right?"

"Of course. It's why you're not country-hopping all over the world."

"Right. Well, my supervisor grounded me. But we'd been chasing Terrence Malstrom, I've just been a desk jockey in the hunt for him. Well, we found something. A safehouse in Spain, and his right-hand man's just been arrested in Madrid. Guy by the name of Randall Friendly."

"That all sounds good," I say. "What's the issue there?"

"My supervisor, Alan, put himself back in the field. He went to Spain to check things out, but we haven't heard from him in almost four days now."

"Let me guess," I say. "He's the type who wouldn't go more than a few hours without checking in."

"Right. When he was in charge of me, anytime I'd go more than an hour without dropping him a line he'd blow up my phone. This is bad, Alistair. And I have no idea what to do."

"I don't think there's anything you *can* do," I reply, pressing my phone up to my ear as I swivel around and stare out the window. "He's missing. You're not in the field anymore, Samantha. I'm sure the CIA'll send someone to check in on him eventually."

"Yeah, but we can't even get approval to send an agent after him. That's up to the supervisors here, and the backup's been gone with meetings. We're dead in the water here, Alistair. I have no idea what we can do."

I know what she's thinking, and she's expecting me to say it first. Make it seem like it was my idea, not hers.

Samantha wants to go after her supervisor herself.

"What do you want me to say, Sam?"

She sighs. "I don't know. Really. I just needed to vent, I guess."

"Vent away. As long as you aren't looking for me to give you permission to do something stupid, I suppose."

"What's *that* supposed to mean?" Sam's tone shifts, becoming harsher than I'd expected from her. It's like we're back in *Retrait*. Arguing again. I don't like it one bit.

"It means I know what you want me to say, Samantha. I know

you want me to give you my blessing, tell you to run out after this guy. But that's wrong, Samantha. I'd never want you to put your life at risk again. Not when you're pregnant."

"That's not your call to make, Alistair."

"Why not? I'm a parent now, too. We have to put ourselves second when it comes to these matters."

"Bullshit. I'm not doing this for me, Alistair. I'm doing this for my country. For my supervisor, a man I'd consider a friend even on the worst of days. I know he'd go after me in a heartbeat if the roles were reversed. I have to do the same for him, Alistair. I wish you'd see that for yourself."

I sigh quietly, rubbing my brow with two fingers. "Sam, you'll never get my blessing. Not for this."

"Well, who says I need it?"

There's a pause that hangs in the air, and I feel sick to my stomach. I wish I'd kept some of that anti-nausea powder for myself.

"Sam, don't do this. Don't risk your life on a bad bet. Just… just calm down, okay? We can figure this out, I promise. Things just look bad now. I need you to stay calm, alright?"

Wrong choice of words. Sam's tone is cold, quiet. She's not raising her voice. But her words still cut deeper than any knife ever could.

"I'm going to do this, Alistair. With or without you. You can help, or you can sit on the sidelines. Your choice."

"Sam, I—"

"What? You're going to tell me you don't approve. Is that it?"

"…No. It's not the nineteen-fifties. You can do whatever you want, Samantha. And I can't force you to do otherwise. I'm just asking you to slow down, think things over. Is this really worth the risk?"

She pauses, mulling my words over.

"Yes. It is worth the risk."

I sigh, loud enough for her to hear. "Then I can't say anything else, Samantha. I can only request you stay home, rest up. Get ready for the baby."

"I guess you *really* can't say anything else. Nice talking to you, Alistair. I feel *so much* better now."

Sarcasm. Not my first trip 'round the block there. But I can tell she's upset, that she just wants to feel better in a time like this. But I'll never give my blessing for her to run off on some crazy half-baked scheme. It'll just spell trouble for us and the baby.

"Sam, please don't—"

"Goodbye, Alistair."

She hangs up suddenly, the line going dead the moment she's finished.

And I'm left alone in my office, terrified for the future. I don't want her to risk her life, but she's going to do what she wants at the end of the day. And she wants to do the right thing. It's noble, I'll give her that.

But I can't imagine losing another child.

It'll hurt beyond belief. Possibly even beyond repair.

My head in my hands, I turn back to my desk, defeated.

I feel like I've already lost her.

SIXTEEN
Samantha

I hang up, disgusted and angry at Alistair's analysis of the situation. *How can he be so dense? Especially when he knows how much this means to me.* But I can't fault him for wanting to keep me safe. After he'd opened up to me about Annalise, I'm not surprised that his primary goal as a father would be to keep me as safe as possible until the baby arrives. But this job, this *mission,* is important to me. And I wish he'd see that himself, instead of me having to explain every little detail to him.

I throw my cell phone down, flopping over on my couch as I recoil after tonight's events. I'd been home for the past few hours, working up the nerve to call Alistair to talk to him about my work issues. And he pretty much threw it all back into my face, ignoring my hints.

That phone call got ugly. I'll admit, I'm probably to blame. The hormones form this pregnancy are starting to really mess with my head, and I doubt I'm able to think straight right now with all the emotion from Alan's disappearance. But I know what I want, and Alistair tried to stifle that, even if it was inadvertently. I can't let him control me, not this early on in our relationship. He wants to 'request' that I stay home? Well, what if *I* don't want that? What about what *I* want to do? I'm not the one who decided to get pregnant. If anything, *he* should feel responsible for putting me in this situation.

Whatever. What's done is done, and words spoken can't be unsaid.

We'll just have to agree to disagree.

I sit back, taking in my world around me. The sun's set, the TV's flicked off, and I've never felt more alone in my entire life. I don't know why I feel this way, I'm conflicted and angry. But I know I'm right, and I'm not going to give up on Alan just yet, not when it seems like everyone else has already done so.

Angrily, I trudge upstairs, head into my bedroom. My room's been nothing short of a mess ever since this all started, and I haven't had the strength to clean up ever since I discovered I was with child. But now's as good a time as any to start, right?

I pick up my clothes, sifting through clean and dirty laundry as I toss piles of fabric into the hamper next to my door. I dust the countertop of my makeup stand, organizing my dresser as my clean clothes take up what little space I've got left. I grab glass cleaner from my bathroom, squeegee the mirror that sits atop my dresser. I make my bed, folding clean sheets over the mattress, and I flop down atop it when I'm finally finished.

I take another look around. I've managed to wrangle this mess, and it took a hell of a lot less effort than I'd anticipated. I was ready for a whole ordeal, getting this room in order. But when I finally bit the bullet, got started, it wasn't half bad. Really.

If only life could be so simple.

I wish I could call Alistair, tell him how sorry I am for my attitude. I'm willing to bet he wouldn't answer a call from me right now regardless, he's been putting more hours in at work and I'm sure the life of a CEO doesn't have much room for preg-nant-girl drama. Which is what I am. Drama.

I groan, rubbing my eyes with the palms of my hands. I feel light-headed, dizzy, and I take deep breaths to stave off the wave of nausea that washes over me. It's all so much, I can hardly han-dle it. The nausea subsides for a brief moment as I exhale a sigh of relief. Then it all comes back, stronger than ever. I rush up from my bed, scurry to my upstairs bathroom as I fling the door open and lean over the toilet seat, gagging.

Fucking *Christ.* I can't wait until this shitshow is over. I want this baby *out.*

The gagging doesn't help, and I still feel sick to my stomach. I can't get this feeling out of me, no matter how hard I try. I gag again, reeling back as I lean up against the bathroom wall. I take deep gulps of air, trying my best to stabilize myself.

It's no use. I gag again, but stand up as I clutch my stomach.

I trudge downstairs, head to the box of anti-nausea medicine that Alistair left for me. I take out a packet, pour myself a glass of water as I empty the white powder inside. I mix the water with the medicine, stirring the glass with my pinky finger before drinking it down in one go.

Immediately I start to feel better. Alistair wasn't kidding about this stuff. I take a look at the box, the label reads *B12-C33*. Fancy name. Looking at the side of the label, I can see the label advertising it's perfectly safe for pregnant women to use. Thank God. I don't know what I'd do if this was unsafe to take in my current state.

I feel the wellness washing over me almost instantaneously. I send out a silent prayer of thanks to whatever God might be watching over me, another silent thank-you goes out to Alistair himself. I know I've been giving him shit since we met up in Dubai, and he's a real champ for sticking with me throughout all this. I owe him the world. I really do.

I want to call him, tell him how sorry I am for snapping at him earlier. But I know he's busy, so I elect to head upstairs, take an early night of rest. It's not even nine o'clock, but I'm exhausted. Drained. And I know the baby'll need as much rest as I can get.

As I curl up underneath my fresh bedsheets, I can't help but feel like we've turned a page tonight. If we can make it through this, Alistair and I can get through *anything*. And our baby's going to be better off in the long run if the parents have been through hell and high water together.

Let's just hope we'll be able to bounce back from this. I'm sure we will, but I know Alistair's probably getting tired of me starting all these spats. I know I am.

I shut my eyes, drifting off to an early sleep.

When I dream, I dream about Alistair. Those sculpted muscles of his, chiseled to perfection. That jawline, headstrong and powerful. That adorable smile of his, the perfect combination of cheeky and inviting.

And those eyes. Those stunning, piercing brown eyes.

I can't stop dreaming about them.

◆ ◆ ◆

I wake up early the next morning, a fault of mine for going to bed so damn early. I'm up at four-fifteen, the earliest I'd ever been up since graduating from college. But I don't feel any morning sickness, and I count that as the blessing it is.

I get up, throw on my bathrobe as I trudge downstairs. It's early, too early. But I find it impossible to go back to sleep once I've woken up, and I figure I might as well take advantage of the early rise. I flick on the TV, fill up the kettle for some non-caffeinated green tea to help me start my day.

The kettle screams, and I pull it off the element as I pour myself a mug. I take the tea, piping hot, into the living room. I set the mug down on the coffee table, start scrolling through the endless TV stations I've got available.

Nothing's on. Well, that's not *entirely* true, but you know how TV is. Boring as shit when you've got nothing else to do, enthralling when you've got other plans for the evening.

After I scroll through nearly every channel available to me, I finish off my decaf green tea and take my mug into the kitchen, depositing it into the sink next to my other dirty dishes. I'll get to those later, I swear. Not this minute, but eventually.

I head back into the living room, tap on my phone's screen to wake it up. Five-thirty.

I don't know if he'll be awake this early, but it's worth a shot.

I pull up my contacts, scroll to Alistair's name. I call him, taking a total shot in the dark as I place the phone up against my ear.

◆ ◆ ◆

"Samantha? Is everything okay? You're up early."

Thank *God* he picked up. Honestly, I don't know what I'd do if he didn't.

"Yeah, I'm fine. You awake?"

"I am now," Alistair says. I can hear tiredness in his voice, I can tell he's exhausted. But I need to talk to him, I need to get a few things off my chest after last night. I can't leave things the way they are between us.

"Hey, I'm sorry about last night."

"Don't worry about it," Alistair yawns. "I'm not mad. Nothing's changed between us. Sometimes...pregnancy can make you a little forward. I don't blame you at all, Samantha."

I smile. "That's good to hear. Still, I wanted to talk to you about the situation overseas. The issue in Spain. I want to hear your thoughts on the matter. What you think I should do."

I hear Alistair sitting up, bedsheets moving aside as he yawns again and stretches out. "I think you have to stay safe, Samantha. I know how hard it is for you to hear that, but there are things bigger than you at stake here."

"Such as?"

"Our future. The baby, their safety. Don't you think that's important?"

"Of course I do. But I'm also willing to admit that the CIA needs my help. I'm the only one who's going to be able to go after Alan. Even you know that."

"Why do you feel like you're the only one who can help him?" Alistair asks. We've come full-circle, debating over the same question as last night.

I can only hope it stays civil this time.

"Because I *know* I'm the only one who can help him," I reply. "I'm the most experienced field agent in the department, second only to Alan himself."

"And *he's* gone missing," Alistair says. "If you say you're second-best to him, what makes you think you're going to have any better luck than he did?"

I sigh, already exasperated. "I just know it, okay? It's one of those things. My gut says so, and that's all I need to go off of."

"You have to think with your gut, yes. But it's more than that, Samantha. It's about keeping what's *in* your gut safe."

"If I can't defend my country from Terrence Malstrom of all people, then what's the point in having the baby?" I blurt out. "We're the last line of defense to our national security. Alistair, you have to understand. This could get bad. This isn't going to stop with one agent."

"Right. And I'm worried the next one'll be you, if you aren't careful."

"You're saying I'm incompetent?" I blurt out. Great. Here comes the nerves again. I'm starting to think it's not just the hormones keeping me like this. It's passion, real and unrequited.

"No, Samantha, let's not get ahead of ourselves here—"

"The only one getting ahead of themselves here is *you*," I retort. "This is about doing what's right for my country and all the families who live here. That's it."

There's a silence that hangs in the air between us, and I'm terrified I've just said something I'll never be able to take back.

"Okay, then. You win, Samantha."

"What?"

"You're right. I can't stop you. I can only do everything in my power to keep you safe. If that means watching you go abroad, then so be it."

"Really?"

Alistair sighs. "Yeah. Like I said, I can't stop you. I can only offer my help."

I grin. "I'm glad you came through, Alistair. It means a lot to me, really."

He pauses. "I'll help you, but on one condition."

"What's that?"

"I'm coming over to see you today," he says. "You can take the day off from work or not, but I'm going to see you before the day's ended."

I nod. "Works for me. I have to go into the office today, see if we've got a lead on Malstrom. Or Alan. I'll be home a little after five, you can come over anytime after that."

"I'll be there," Alistair says.

And just like that, we're back in business.

◆ ◆ ◆

The work day goes by in a total blur. All day, Tracy and I re-route calls from different departments, all of us working together to help locate our missing supervisor. We hear from IT, Intelligence, Field Work, the whole nine years. And our department of agents are busy as hell, up to their necks in paperwork and filing in our supervisor's absence. Things look bad, and we're not able to find a lead at all on Alan today. I can't help but feel like I've wasted the entire day, but I know I'm going to see Alistair tonight to begin to make things right.

After I get home, I'm on the couch for no more than ten minutes when I hear a knock at my door. I hop up, flinging the door open to see Alistair Jensen on my front porch, waiting for me. He's dressed casually, a button-down shirt over a plain grey tee. Khaki pants, and I can see the limo parked out on my street behind him. He looks tired, exhausted, but I know tonight's going to be worth it in the end. And compared to my bathrobe and sweatpants, he looks like a dream come to life. Compared to my messy sloppy self.

"Come on in," I tell him. "The flight here go okay?"

Alistair shrugs. "You know. The usual."

I grin. "Actually, I don't know. I'm not fortunate enough to own a private plane of my own."

Alistair chuckles. "You'll take a ride in it one day, I promise. This'll all be over, and we'll take a vacation overseas. No agents, no missions, no assignments. Just the two of us," he says, looking down at my stomach, "and maybe a third in tow if we'll let them ride along."

I smile. It's nice having someone map out your future. But that's not why I called Alistair to come see me tonight.

"Driver waiting outside?"

Alistair shakes his head. "Nope, he's going to cruise around town for a while. I gave him a wad of cash, told him to treat himself while I was over here for the evening. He told me he's going to get a tattoo. One on his face, he says. God, I *really* hope he was kidding about that."

I chuckle. "Yeah, let's hope not." In all honesty, I have no idea what a bearded Kennedy would look like with a face tattoo. I hope for Alistair's sake that doesn't happen.

I lead my date to the dining room, a table with four chairs in the room adjacent to my living room. Alistair and I sit across from one another, hands folded like we're about to sit down for a job interview.

"So, you wanted to see me?" I ask cheekily.

Alistair nods. "Yeah. I wanted to talk in person. It seems like we were running in circles, talking on the phone. And it's easier for me to come to you, anyways."

I smile. "I appreciate you coming. And I'm glad we got to sit down, hash this all out like adults."

"I guess there's no convincing you not to go, right?"

I grin. "Now you're starting to get it."

Alistair sighs. "Okay, then. Then let's talk this over. Figure out how to make this work."

"Sure. Let's put our cards on the table: I'm not even one month along. Before the three-month mark, I'm going to start showing. And then people are going to start asking questions."

"Questions, like…?" Alistair looks confused, and I chuckle.

"Questions like, *who's the father? How far along are you, and what are you going to do when the baby comes?* Those things."

Alistair nods. "Yeah, those seem pretty important. Well, I guess let's start with the first question."

"Uh-huh."

"There's not a doubt in my mind that I'm the father," he says. "But I guess the real question is…what are we?"

"What are we, relationship-wise?"

Alistair nods again.

"I…I haven't given it that much thought," I reply. "I'm sorry if that upsets you. I just didn't want to make any assumptions."

The billionaire sitting across from me nods. "No, you're right. I'd have been upset if you went to the gossip columns without telling me first. We can figure that one out later. Skip the labels for now. But you're the only one for me."

I beam, feeling my face flush. "You're the only one for me, too. I guess we've cleared that one up. What's next?"

"What we're going to do when the baby comes."

I pause, sitting back in my chair as I weigh our options. "Well, there's a few choices, I guess."

"You go first," Alistair says. "I want to see your thought process."

"We can give the baby up for adoption. That's one choice. Or, the other, the one that's all the more terrifying: we keep the baby, raise them as a family. Together."

"What would you think of that?" Alistair asks. "Of us. Being a family."

I'll admit, it's a lot easier to picture now than it was back at *Retrait.* Now, I can easily see myself spending my life with Alistair. I'll admit it. And I know—I *hope*—that's what he still wants, too.

"I'd like that," I reply.

Alistair grins. "I'd like that, too. Well, then that's settled, I guess."

"What's next?"

"My ultimate question, I suppose. How you're going to find your supervisor. And how you're going to stay safe, for your sake and the baby's sake. And mine, too, I guess."

I hadn't thought that far ahead, to be perfectly honest. I'd just assumed I'd play this one the old-fashioned way: work in the field until the job's done. But now I'm no longer an individual alone—I'm eating, sleeping, resting and living for two right now. And that's something to consider when you're putting yourself out in the world, right smack-dab in the middle of an international conflict.

"Well, I was thinking I'd just go it the way I'm used to. I don't know. I wasn't really thinking about a game plan when I told you I wanted to go after Malstrom, find Alan myself."

Alistair nods, scratching his chin stubble. "Then we're going to have to take things from the top. Tell me everything you know about this Malstrom. We'll see if I can bring anything new to the table."

I take a deep breath. "Terrence Malstrom is the worst of the worst. He used to be a hedge fund manager, made off with a bunch of executive's money. When the feds came, knocked on his door, he bolted. Ever since then, he's been racking up crime spree after crime spree. You name it, he's probably wanted for it. Arson. Embezzlement. Identify fraud *and* theft. He's the number one most wanted criminal in the USA, and I intend to bring him to justice."

Alistair takes it all in, pondering while deep in thought. "Sounds like a bad guy."

"He is. If I can just check out the safe house that Alan saw, I'm sure we'd find a lead. I bet that's what happened to my supervisor. Got too close to finding Malstrom."

"What happens if they find *you*?" Alistair asks, concerned. "With you being pregnant and all, I can't imagine they'll go easy on you if they think you're meddling in their enterprise."

"No, they won't. That's why I'm not going to get caught."

"Easier said than done."

"Alistair, I *have* to do this. You know I do."

He leans forward in his chair, determined as ever to prove me wrong. "But do you *really* have to? You've told me it's for your country, and I respect that. Keeping American families safe is my priority, too, but that includes *our* family. The one you just agreed you'd like to maintain."

He's right. I know he's right, and I hate feeling like I'm in the wrong. But this is bigger than us, and I need Alistair to understand that.

"You'd do anything for your company, right?" I ask, probing my date.

"Right."

"Even if that meant removing yourself from the equation."

"Correct. If it was in Pemberton's best interest, I'd step down as CEO."

"Well, I'm willing to do the same for my job and country. I'm ready to get fired for this, Alistair. Hell, the CIA has a pretty nifty severance package, doubly so for newly expectant mothers. If you can understand that, I don't see why you couldn't understand why I *have* to do this."

Alistair sighs. "Okay," he says.

"Okay?"

He nods. "If you have to do this, then you have to do this. But I'm going to help you do this."

"Really?"

"Really. I'll move some money around, divert our resources elsewhere in the company. Pemberton Computers is going to help you in every way it can. Anything you need, we'll provide. Cash, cars, planes, trains. You name it, it's yours if we've got it."

I beam. "Alistair, you have no idea how much this means to me."

He returns the smile, reaching across the table to take my hand in his. His grip is gentle, yet firm, and I know he's fully serious in his support of my endeavor.

"I'll do anything I can to keep you safe," he says. "And if you're dead-set on hunting this Terrence guy down, then I'm going to help you do it."

We sit there, peaceful and silent for the longest of moments. His thumb strokes the palm of my hand, and I feel like we've never been stronger together.

This bond's never going to get broken.

We're never going to fight again after this, something tells me. This has *got* to be the biggest obstacle we've ever faced, and now Alistair and I are going to tackle it together, head-on.

Together.

SEVENTEEN
Alistair

Samantha and I spend the next few hours going over her case files from memory as she recants to me the extent of the investigation into Malstrom. He's a bad guy, I'll give her that. I'd like nothing more than for Samantha to catch this guy, find her supervisor and come home safely. And that's going to take a hell of a lot of effort to pull it off, but I believe we can do it.

Samantha and I pull up a map application, checking out the city streets of Madrid, Spain. Sam shows me the jail where Randall Friendly is being held, Terrence Malstrom's right-hand man. If she can get there, talk to Friendly before anyone else gets to him first, we'll have a lead on her supervisor Alan. And from there, she'll work her usual magic. Swoop in, save the day before anybody else even notices something's amiss.

As she explains her plan to me, I can't help but stare at Samantha in the low light of the evening. She's passionate, caring. She knows what she wants out of life, and I feel truly sorry for anyone who stands in her way. As we pour over the files, copies Sam had brought in from the office, I keep stealing glances, checking her out. Honestly, she's fucking *sexy.* And I know I'm getting turned on as she explains to me the international judicial processes of capturing a wanted fugitive.

After a while, I lean back in my seat, rubbing my eyes. I'm exhausted, and I know I've got a long flight back to D.C. ahead of me tonight. Not that I've got any pressing matters to attend to, I just don't want to impose on Samantha while she's determined and hard at work.

"How're you holding up?" Sam asks me from across the dining table. She's still pouring over her notes, reviewing case file after case file. I can tell she's going to be hard at work on this long after I'm gone, and I can't stop her from pursing the justice she believes the world's sorely lacking.

"Fine, I'm just burnt out," I reply. I chuckle. "This is a lot more work than I'm used to. Usually I cap out at an hour or two a day. This is...this is beyond me," I reply. "I can't believe how dedicated you are."

Samantha shrugs. "All part of the package deal," she grins up at me. "You'll like it after the baby's born. I'll get *really* into finding them the best schools, the best healthcare. You know it's only going to get easier after this is all said and done."

I nod. "Still, it'd be nice to have the guarantee that you're going to make it out safe. I'm just worried about you, is all."

She stacks the papers she'd been reading, rifling through them as she sets them back down on the dining room table. Samantha leans back in her chair, rubs her eyes as well.

"No, you're right. This *is* exhausting," she laughs. "I still have to call into work, take some time off. I'll do that in a little bit, I'm positively burnt out."

I stand up, stretching my arms and legs as I hear my joints pop. "How about a drink, then?" I ask, heading into the kitchen. It's pristine in here, clean as can be. It's an average kitchen, a fridge, oven, range. Stacks of plates and cups in the pantry. I lean back, hollering into the other room: "Can I get you anything?"

"Just some water, thanks," Sam calls back.

I reach up, grabbing two plastic cups from an open-plan cupboard as I run the tap, setting aside the glasses of water for us. I pick them up, carrying them into the dining room as I watch Samantha pack up her case files.

"Finished?" I ask, handing her one of the glasses of water. She takes it, chugging it down in a flash. She sets the cup down on the table when it's empty.

"Yeah, I think so. My brain's gone kaput on me," she chuckles. "I can't believe how long we've been at it."

I nod. "I don't know about you, but I'm going to need a rest before I get started back to D.C.." I head into Sam's living room, plopping down on her couch. It's nice here, and I feel like I'm finally able to fully relax around Samantha. She follows me into the living room, sits down next to me on the couch with only a few inches between us.

"How're you feeling?" I ask. "The pregnancy and all, I mean. Any more nausea?"

Sam shakes her head. "I've never felt better. And thank you. For sticking around, for the medicine last week. For everything, really. I owe you a lot, Alistair."

Her face is open, inviting, and her smile's infectious. I return the gesture, inching my hand closer to hers. "It's no problem, really. Anything to help."

"Well, you didn't have to agree to help me," she replies, looking down at our hands, only mere centimeters apart. She places her hand atop mine, warm and safe. The clamminess is gone, her pregnancy sweats temporarily over. I smile up at her, rotating my hand to grip hers, stroking the palm of her hand with my thumb.

Sam inches closer to me, leaning her head on my shoulder. It's a kind gesture, one that makes me feel accepted. Loved. Cared for, even when Sam's indisposed with her pregnancy.

I don't feel as alone as I used to anymore.

"Hey," she breathes, looking up at me from her spot on my shoulder. "Do you *really* have to be back in D.C. tonight?"

I grin. "Not particularly."

"Then why not stay here? Just for tonight, Alistair."

"I think we could manage that," I chuckle. "Gonna blow up an air mattress for me on the floor?"

Sam grins. "No."

Well, that's that, then.

"I guess we'll have to figure out sleeping arrangements, then," I whisper, leaning down to kiss Samantha as her head rests on my shoulder. The kiss is warm, inviting, telling me to stay the night. And I want to. *Boy*, do I want to, nothing would make me happier. She returns the kiss passionately, wrapping an arm up and around my neck as she pulls me in closer to her.

I've never felt more wanted in my entire life. And I know that for a fact.

Sam pulls back suddenly, her arm still clutched tight around my neck. "Do you want to go upstairs?" she breathes sultrily, flashing a cheeky smile up at me.

"Where else?"

I stand up, Sam's arm still wrapped around my shoulder as I place my other arm underneath her waist. I pick her up, straining only lightly as she readjusts her weight for me to carry her upstairs. Samantha giggles, and so do I when her legs flop around wildly as we spin over to the staircase. I start carrying her upstairs, one step at a time, as I hold onto her for balance and for dear life. Sam's gripping me tightly, nuzzling her face into my neck as I hoist her upstairs.

When we reach the top, Sam looks up.

"My room's that one," she points to the door down the hall to our left. I nod, stepping carefully to pivot so Sam won't hit her head on the wall as we enter the doorway. She grabs the doorknob, flinging her bedroom door open as I carry her inside over the threshold.

Her room's exactly what I'd pictured. Standard bedroom, a queen-size mattress on a frame. Dresser with a mirror atop it for applying makeup. There's a bathroom down the hall from her room, the second door inside her room opens to a walk-in closet that I could never fill with my clothing alone. Sam's got posters on her wall, old punk bands from her college days, movie posters from blockbusters six years past their prime release.

"What do you think?" Sam asks.

I grin. "It's perfect here," I reply.

I set her down on the bed, gingerly and carefully. She keeps her arms wrapped around my shoulders, pulling me down on top of her as I flop onto her bed as well. She pulls me in for a kiss, one that's more passionate than any other we'd shared before. Hell, not even our night in Paris felt like this. The feeling between us is different now, I can't explain it. But she knows I feel it, too.

I lean up, pulling back from Sam's kisses only momentarily as I start to unbutton my shirt, tossing it aside when I've gotten it loose. I pull off my undershirt as well, and Sam looks down at my bare chest with admiration, running her hands over my muscles as she sits up.

"*Jeez*," she breathes. "How long have you been hiding *this* from me?"

I laugh. "I remember you saying the same thing back in Paris," I reply.

Sam giggles, leaning up to kiss me again as she starts to wriggle out of her sweatpants. I help her out of them, tossing them aside once her legs are free. I lean back down over her, and she brings her legs up to wrap them around my waist, pulling me in close.

"Is this what you wanted?" Sam breathes between kisses.

I nod eagerly. "That, and more," I tell her.

She pulls back, grinning devilishly as she grabs the bottom of her tank top with both hands, pulling it up over her messy blonde hair. She undoes her ponytail, letting that golden hair fly as she shakes her head and giggles. She unstraps her bra, letting it slide to the floor as she sprawls out in front of me, naked and ready for me to return the favor.

"Well, come get it, then," she winks up at me.

I don't hesitate for a second.

I rush to the side of the bed, unbuckling my belt as I slide it off the loops. The pants go next, underwear, too.

I jump up on the bed, pressing my weight down on Samantha as she wraps her legs around me once again. She moans my name in pleasure as I start to kiss the soft underside of her neck, working my way up to the tender part just below her earlobe.

"*Alistair, Alistair. Don't stop*," I hear her voice, shaky and rife with pleasure. She reaches down, grabbing me as I shift my weight to get a better angle.

She gasps when I enter her. It's sudden, quick, but she pulls me closer with her bare legs, writhing with happiness as I thrust.

And from there, we envelop one another.

The curtains gently move in the cool air of the evening, and I've never asked for a better night. Or a better partner to spend it with.

The night comes fast, and so does Samantha.

◆ ◆ ◆

We slink back, propping our tired heads up on stacks of pillows as our panting and heavy breathing comes to a standstill.

Sam looks over at me, grinning, still naked from our shared endeavor. Her breath is stifled, her panting still heavy as it was just a few minutes ago. I've got my arm around her, pulling her close to me as she moans happily.

"I've never wanted anyone as bad as I've wanted you," she whispers.

I run my fingers through her hair. "And I you," I smile back down at her. She leans up, kissing me quickly. Softly. It's the perfect closure to the night's end. "Still okay if I stay here tonight?"

"Of course," Sam beams as she rests her head on my bare chest. She runs a finger up and down my torso, lightly playing with the tufts of my body hair. "I'd be a little upset if you up and left."

"Just like Paris," I sigh heavily.

"Just like Paris," Sam nods. "I think we should just put all that behind us. Let the past stay in the past. What do you say?"

I chuckle. "I'd like nothing better. I wasn't happy then, not like I am now. I treated you like garbage in Dubai, and that was just indicative of a bigger problem. And that's all changed now that you and I are..." I trail off, staring out the window, past the gently wafting curtains.

"Are?" Sam asks.

I smile back down at her. "Now that you and I are together," I finish.

She leans up, kissing me one final time before we flop back down and close our eyes.

We fall asleep in one another's arms, each cradling the other as we shield ourselves from the outside world, if only for just one night.

EIGHTEEN

Samantha

The gentle sunlight wakes me up in the morning. Warm sunbeams splash across my face, tracing a route from the half-opened window as they dance across my cheeks. I open my eyes, grinning eagerly at the day ahead of us.

Alistair's in bed next to me, utterly passed out. There's no waking him, I can tell as I gently rock him back and forth. Well, no matter. I'm sure last night wore him out, too, and a man as strong as him is going to need that rest before we face the day today.

I get up, trudging out of bed and into my hallway, ducking into my bathroom. I get washed up, taking a quicker shower than I'm used to. I dry off, head back to my room and get dressed; I've elected to put on something casual today, a change of pace from my usual sweatpants and tank top that I'm usually decked out in when at home. I throw on a sun dress, a yellow garment with a sweet floral pattern stretched across the midsection.

I hear grunting coming from my bed, and I peer over and watch as Alistair wakes up, looking around my room in a half-groggy state.

"Wha—Where…oh, right."

I laugh as I adjust the straps on my sundress. "Having trouble with your memory?"

"No," Alistair moans sleepily. "Sometimes I wake up, forget where I am for a half-second. Side effect of traveling all the time. I'm sure it's happened to you, too, out in the field."

I nod. "Oh, yeah. It's just funny to see someone else going

through my old daily routine."

Alistair sits up in my bed, wrapping a bedsheet around his exposed midsection. "What's the craziest place you've ever woken up in?"

I chuckle. "You don't want to know," I reply as I sit back down next to him on my bed. I reach a hand out, stroking his thighs as I grin at him devilishly.

"Yeah, I do."

I chuckle again, ready to indulge Alistair. "Okay, then. I woke up on a train, in transit halfway between Milano and Florence. I don't remember how I'd gotten there, until I finally remembered the fuzzy details of my work assignment. I'd say a moving train has to the strangest place I've ever woken up in. What about you?"

Alistair laughs. "Shit. Well, since you asked...I woke up on a plane. That I'd bought myself. And I had no recollection of ever making the purchase."

I blow hot air out of my nose, surprised as hell he'd ever admit something like that to me. "Seriously?"

He nods. "Hey, you asked."

I laugh, and Alistair grins as he starts laughing, too.

He gets up out of bed, still stark-naked. "Bathroom?"

I grin, eyeing his muscular physique up and down as I point outside to the hallway. "Last door on the right. Don't take too long," I smile devilishly.

Alistair nods, his hazelnut eyes shining as he walks out the bedroom and into the hall.

I lean back in my bed, sighing a pleasurable breath of relief. I'm happy he's here. And we don't have anything on the agenda, as far as I know. I grab my cell, call into work; I'm taking a sick day today, I tell HR. Pregnancy troubles, nausea, the usual. The rep on the phone tell me it's no problem, that I can come back to work the next day when I'm feeling better.

And just like that, I'm free for the entire day.

Alistair re-emerges into my bedroom, drenched from a quick shower. He finishes drying off, gets dressed in his clothes from yesterday as he tosses the used towel in my hamper. He shoots me a glance, lifts up his shirt and smells it as I laugh heartily.

"Smells fine to me," he says. "Okay. Now what?"

I grin. "We've got all day together," I say. "Do you have any pressing CEO matters to attend to today?"

Alistair shakes his head. "Just a conference call at noon, but I can push that back. I'd rather spend today with you. D.C. can wait until tomorrow, I think. They won't let Pemberton Computer's stock fall off if the CEO takes a personal day."

I want to jump for joy, but I stifle the response as I keep beaming up at Alistair. "Then we're free to do whatever we want," I say. "What did you have in mind?"

Alistair nods, looking around my room while he ponders his response.

"How about breakfast?" he says.

"That's as good as a start as any."

We throw together a simple breakfast in my kitchen: a classic, all-American plate of bacon, eggs and toast, just the way it's meant to be. We eat in the dining room, sharing the peaceful morning together as we prepare ourselves for the day ahead of us.

The world's our oyster, and today's the pearl. It's a day I've sorely needed, a break from all the hubbub in the office and the exhaustion of modern pregnancy. It's been so much, I can't believe we've finally got a day off together.

Alistair finishes his plate as I scrape the last of the bacon into my mouth with a fork. He laughs, standing up as I hand him my plate sweetly. He runs them into the kitchen, I can hear running water and the clack of plates arranged on the drying rack. Alistair returns to the dining room, sits down across from me.

"Now," he says. "Now what?"

I grin. "I know there's a farmer's market here in town," I tell him. "I almost went with some friends from work a few weeks back, but I never got to go."

"Aren't those usually only open on weekends?" Alistair asks.

I nod, pulling out my phone. I check my social media feed, checking to see if anyone else in town's been to the market recently. Surprise, surprise: I see an old acquaintance from high school's been to the market this morning. They're still open, I can see from their post.

"I think we're good," I tell Alistair, showing him the social media post. He nods, shrugging.

"I'm game if you are," he grins.

"Then let's get to it," I reply. "Why don't I drive us? My car's just outside, I don't know if your limo's—"

Alistair's eyes widen suddenly. *"Shit!"* he exclaims, hopping up from my dining room table as he yanks his cell phone out of his pocket. "I can't believe I spaced on that," he says frantically.

"What's the matter?"

"I forgot about Kennedy," he groans as he dials a number, holding his phone up to his ear.

I giggle. "No, seriously," Alistair says. "I totally fucking forgot to tell him I'd be spending the night here. I gave him a wad of cash, told him to wait in town while I met up with you—"

"So, what's the problem?" I ask, confused.

Alistair groans, the phone still ringing against his ear. "He said he was going to get a face tattoo. I seriously *cannot* imagine what it's going to be."

I cover my mouth, stifling a laugh. I'm sorry, but it's funny. Alistair's sweating bullets. And it's all over a face tattoo his driver probably joked about getting.

Someone must've finally picked up, because Alistair perks up as he starts talking. "Hello? Kennedy? Yeah, look, I—yeah. We spent the night here. No, we're okay. No. No. *No. You didn't."*

My eyes widen. *Did he?*

"Fine. Well, we're going to stay in Richmond today. Come

pick us up from Samantha's as soon as you can," Alistair says into the phone. "We're going to a farmer's market. Don't...don't tell me you actually got the damn thing. *Please.*"

I laugh again, covering my mouth with one hand. His driver most *definitely* got a face tattoo while in town.

"Fine. We'll be ready," Alistair says. He hangs up, shooting me a look of dismay.

"So, he got a tattoo—?"

"Don't start with me," Alistair says. I can't help but laugh again. It's all just so funny to me, seeing him get anxious over his driver's tattoo. I can't help but wonder what kind of parent Alistair would make—would he be *this nervous* if our child went out with their friends for a night? I have no idea, honestly. Maybe it's different when Kennedy's on his payroll, I tell myself.

"So, farmer's market?" I ask, changing the subject. Alistair's face lights up, and I can tell he's eager to get off the topic of his driver's choice of permanent facial expression.

"Absolutely," he breathes, sitting back down across from me at the dining room table. We take a moment, look into one another's eyes. I'm positively addicted to those hazelnut irises of his, and I feel like I could get lost in those for hours if he'd let me. Maybe one day he will, who knows?

"Now what?" I ask.

Alistair grins. "Now, we wait. And wait to see what kind of fuckery my driver's gotten up to in the past twelve hours."

I honestly can't wait to find out.

A little while later, we hear a car pulling up to the curb outside. Alistair and I get up off the couch, flick off the news channel we'd been watching on TV as we grab our jackets and step outside.

Alistair stares down the limo from my front porch as I lock the door behind us. "He's in there," Alistair says. "And he might have a fucking *face tattoo.*"

I laugh again. "Come on, it can't be that bad, right?"

We head to the limo, and Alistair walks around to the driver's seat, knocking on the window. I follow after him, standing closely behind. I wouldn't want to miss this for the world.

"Hey guys, have a good night last night?" The window rolls down, and Alistair's driver Kennedy waves at us cheerily from behind the steering wheel. Alistair gasps, and I lean over his shoulder to get a better look.

Yeah. He got a face tattoo, and Alistair looks like he'd just taken a bite out of a rotten apple.

Kennedy's got a barbed wire streaking across his forehead, and I burst out in laughter at the overall ridiculousness of the situation. Everything else is the same; his beard is still thick and bushy, Alistair's driver is still grinning his usual smile. Kennedy laughs along with me as Alistair shoots us both dirty looks.

"This isn't funny," Alistair says to both of us. But he turns around, gets in the backseat of the limo regardless. I follow after him, sitting down next to Alistair as I close the backdoor behind me.

"Everything good back there, boss?" Kennedy calls from the front seat, taunting Alistair through the partition window.

Alistair groans. "It's fine, Kennedy. Get us to the market and we won't have a problem." And with that, he rolls up the partition window, giving us the well-needed privacy we need to talk about what on Earth just happened in the front seat.

"Are you...okay?" I ask Alistair. He's really worked up about the tattoo, I can tell.

"Fine," he says. "I'd fire Kennedy on the spot if he wasn't the best damn driver I've ever had."

I nod. "Sounds like you're stuck between a rock and a hard place. Except the rock is finding a new driver, and the hard place is that face tattoo you seem to be up in arms over."

Alistair laughs at that, and I know he's already over Kennedy's stunt from before. We sit next to each other, staring out the window as Kennedy pulls out to the street. He drives ahead, turning around in the cul-de-sac just a few blocks north of my house. After that, we're on the road.

I grin over at Alistair, and he returns the gesture.

"Hey," I say.

"Hey," he beams back at me.

"We're going to have a good day today," I tell him. "And I'm grateful to be spending it with you."

"And I with you," Alistair says warmly.

We watch from the window as Richmond blurs past us, on the road to adventure ahead.

I couldn't have asked for a more perfect day.

We reach the farmer's market in just under half an hour, and Kennedy parks the limo just outside the square where all the booths are set up. Alistair rolls down the partition, relaying a message to his driver.

"We're going to spend the day here, as long as we want," Alistair calls up to the front seat. "We'll call you when we're ready to head out. And please, for the love of God: no more fucking tattoos. Got it?"

"You got it, boss. I've got plenty already."

Alistair groans, shooting me a half-hearted chuckle as we step out of the limo and into the warm light of the afternoon.

The market's spread out, using an old basketball court as a foundation for the booths and stalls to operate on. I can see countless customers, perusing the isles of the market as they inspect the goods offered to them. There's bright red tomatoes, apples that have never looked more crisp. I can see stands full of rows of lettuce, cabbage, celery stalks. Customers carry plastic carts under the crooks of their elbows, some wheel carts between stalls. The air smells clean here, pure. Like nothing could touch it, without a hint of pollution to account for.

Alistair grins, taking my hand in his as we start heading to the market. I grab a basket, tucking the handle in the joint of my elbow. We walk slowly, deliberately, as Alistair and I check out every booth we can possibly imagine. There's endless possibilities here, and I can't help but feel content with Alistair by my side. I feel like we can accomplish anything, that anything the universe throws our way would be just another speed bump in the road. Just another obstacle to get over.

We stop in front of a booth selling the longest carrots I've ever seen in my entire life. The sticks are bright orange, a vibrance you'd never see in the local grocery store, and an old man with a straw hat inspects us as we peruse the selection. I'm a fiend for carrots, my pregnancy cravings spiking as I look to Alistair eagerly.

"Why don't we get some of these?" I ask.

Alistair nods, reaching into his pocket to pull out his wallet. I stop him, taking out my snatch purse as I unclip some money from my wallet.

"How much?" I ask the vendor, signaling for Alistair to put his money away.

"Three-fifty for a bunch of ten," the man behind the counter says. His straw hat bobs when he talks, and I can't help but giggle at the notion that the hat might be doing all the talking for him.

I reach into my money clip, pull out a $5 as I hand it to the vendor. "Keep the change," I tell him. I grab a rubber-banded stack of carrots, the perfect selection as I throw them in my basket. I look up at Alistair, who's beaming down at me, happy as a clam.

"What?" I ask.

Alistair shrugs. "I'm just glad to be here with you, that's all."

I return the smile, grinning up at my date for the afternoon. For all time.

"I'm glad to be with you, too."

We get back to walking, checking out the rest of the booths on offer at the farmer's market. Everything here is so bright, so colorful. And I swear I've never had as much a craving for broccoli as I do right now. We stop by the booth, grabbing a massive stalk of the green unmentionable and throw it in the basket after paying the vendor. We grab a few other things while we're at it, too: a head of lettuce that's greener than my face in my nausea-induced mornings, a stalk of celery. Some organic peanut butter, manufactured locally. After the basket's stocked to the brim, Alistair and I agree to head out for the day. He reaches into his pocket, dialing his driver's number as we head to the entrance.

Kennedy's only a block and a half away, and the limo's waiting for us by the time we're able to cross the street over to him. Alistair and I hop in the back seat, placing our paper bag of veggies on the floor between us.

The partition window rolls down, and Kennedy sticks his tattooed face into the rearview mirror as he calls back to us. "Everything go alright?"

"Yeah, everything's fine," Alistair says. He turns to face me, his hazelnut eyes aglow. "You done for the day? Because I'm not," he says.

I shake my head. "It's only the middle of the afternoon," I reply. I call up to the face-tatted driver. "What are we close to, does it say on your GPS?"

Kennedy nods, taking a look at his onboard navigation. He pauses, scrolling through a list of attractions and hotspots available in town. "No, here's something," he says, trailing off. A moment later he finishes his thought: "There's a movie theater just a few blocks south of here. And…there's a tennis court on the other side of town. That's what we've got to work with."

I smile at Alistair. "How about a movie, then?"

He nods, leaning to call out to Kennedy. "Take us to the theater, Kennedy," he says. His driver nods, rolling up the partition window without another word.

We pull out from the curb, merging into traffic as our day

continues.

◆ ◆ ◆

The movie theater, the *Plexicon*, is an old run-down mill of a place. But Alistair and I don't care much about that, and we duck inside after hurrying to buy our ticket to the afternoon matinee. I don't even catch the title of the flick, I'm just happy to be here with Alistair.

We duck inside the theater, finding the audience to be sparse. Rows and rows of open seats available to us, we elect to sit down in the back of the room, close to the projection booth. The movie's old, black-and-white, and the ticking of the old film reels gives the whole place an old-Hollywood vibe that's been lost to Father Time.

The movie's alright, I guess. Again, never caught the title. But it's an old show, a movie about a married couple who have to tap-dance their way through a talent show in order to prove their love to each other and win the top prize. Simple enough. The movie's got a *ton* of dance numbers, old-Hollywood tap moves that are pulled right out of the 1930's. It's all in good fun, and the movie's over in less than an hour. The lights come up, and Alistair and I head back out into the waning afternoon of the day, our fingers interlocked with one another as we wait for Kennedy to come pick us up.

I look up at my date, having spent a day in total bliss together.

"I'm glad you stuck around," I say, holding his hand tight in mine.

He nods, grinning. "I'm glad I did, too."

"What'd you think of the movie?"

"You first," Alistair chuckles.

"What, you didn't like it? Well, I sure did. I used to *hate* romance flicks."

"Used to?"

I smile up at him. "Yeah, used to. Not so much anymore. I can pretend that's us on the screen. It's weird, I know, but I had a good time. I liked it. I like hanging out with you, no matter what we're doing."

"Well, I liked it, too. And I'm never one to shy away from a sappy romcom," Alistair laughs. I laugh, too, and we hold one another's hand a little bit tighter.

We stand out there on the curb for a while, completely ignorant to the world around us. Pedestrians stroll by, some of them ducking into the movie theater we'd just left ourselves. All I need is Alistair, and I've got him on lock.

A little while later, Kennedy finally pulls up in his limo. I'm half-expecting Alistair to knock on the driver's side window again, check to see if his driver's gotten any more unmentionable tattoos. But he doesn't, and we slink into the backseat together as Alistair tells Kennedy to take us back to my place. The evening's upon us, and I know my date's probably got to head back to D.C. eventually. I just wish today would never end, in all honesty. It's been perfect, spending today with Alistair, and I don't know how I'm going to go back and face reality tomorrow morning without him.

The city of Richmond, Virginia, passes by the window in a blur. I'm exhausted, spent from the day walking outside. And I know the baby's going to appreciate the rest; I sure know I'm eager to kick off these shoes and unwind on the couch after all the hiking today. I don't know about Alistair, but I'm glad today's finally ended. I only wish we'd have the same day tomorrow, and the next day, and the next day. But I know that's not possible, not for the way our lives are going. I'm not sure when we'll be able to see each other again, with my trip to Spain coming up so soon.

After the long drive back home, Kennedy parks the limo on the curb just outside my house. I look over at Alistair, grateful for the day we'd spent together.

"So, when are we doing this again?" I ask, beaming.

Alistair grins. "Whenever you want," he says. "I knew today was special. And I'd pay all the money I had to re-live it all over again."

I lean over, kissing him softly on his lips. It's short, sweet, and hopefully leaving him wanting more. He wraps his arms around me, kissing me back as we say our goodbye.

"We're going to find him," Alistair says once I've pulled away. "Your supervisor. We're going to do this, I promise. And you're going to bring him back home safe and sound. That goes for you, too. Safe and sound."

I nod. "I wouldn't have it any other way," I reply. "And I know I couldn't have done this without you."

"And I wouldn't have done it had you not convinced me otherwise," Alistair replies. "I'll see you soon, I swear. Keep in touch?"

I smile, grinning like an idiot from ear to ear. "Yeah," I say. "Keep in touch."

And with that, I step out of the limo. I close the door behind me, waving as Alistair rolls the window down to say one last good-bye. Kennedy stars the engine back up, the limo roaring to life as it pulls ahead, driving down my street to loop around in the cul-de-sac ahead.

I wave one final good-bye as I watch the limo careen back around, driving past my house as it disappears onto the main road outside my neighborhood.

And with that, I head back inside, the day of bliss finally coming to a close.

I'd do today all over again if I could. And I know Alistair would, too.

We'll just have to see each other again soon. I don't know how long I'll last without him by my side.

Home, sweet home. I unlock my front door, stepping inside as it closes shut behind me.

NINETEEN
Alistair

I had to fly back to D.C. after our day together, and I don't think I could miss a person as much as I miss Sam right about now. Back in my office, I can't help but worry about her. She's in such a vulnerable position, eager to be back out in the field. But the pregnancy worries me, I'll admit it. I've been around the block before, I know how sensitive women get when they're with child. Not that I'm going to back out of our arrangement to help her get to Spain; that's not what I'm getting at. I'm just afraid. For her. For her safety. For the safety of our child, the one that we might still have a shot at raising together. Only if she'll have me, of course.

It's all so much, weighing heavily on my mind.

I can't focus on work. It's been a few days since I left town, and the weekend's almost here. I know Sam's going to be eager to take her trip to Spain sooner rather than later, and I'm powerless to stop her drive. All I can do is make sure she's out in the world, safe as can be.

And that's why Pemberton Computers is going to help her out.

I've spent this week making arrangements, calling different departments to help line up our story for Samantha.

Pemberton is going to bankroll the entire operation. After all, the CIA sure isn't going to send Samantha out into the field, not in her current state. Which is where we come in. The company is going to buy the plane tickets, reserve the hotel rooms she'll need while traveling. It's all under the guise of corporate expansion, I've told my higher-ups that we need to look into relocating into Spain. They sounded agreeable enough, and the Board of Directors gave me the green light to start investigating into such matters myself.

I know the trip's going to happen soon, and I need Samantha to know that she won't be alone out there. When push comes to shove, Pemberton Computers and I are going to make sure she's protected. It's the least I can do.

Friday night finally rolls around, and I'm sitting behind my desk, holed up in my office while I listen to my employees punching out for the weekend outside. I rub my brow, my head in my hands. I've been weighing my decision this past week, wondering if I'm doing the right thing with my support of Samantha's endeavors. But I know if the tables were turned, if she were the one in my position? She'd do everything in her power to see the job through to the end, make sure all parties come home. Safe and sound.

I just need to hear her voice, make sure she's doing alright. Anything to calm my nerves. If I had one, I'd be sipping on the stiffest of drinks right about now, but that luxury's only waiting for me at a local bar, should the occasion rise. I pull out my cell phone, dial Samantha's number as I hoist the phone up to my ear.

"Hey," she beams. I can hear her smile through the phone.

"How's it going?" I ask, curious. "You still hard at work on those case files for Terrence Malstrom's safe house?"

"Yeah," she sighs. "It's so monotonous, I'm ready to jump out of a window at this point. But I know it's all going to be worth it in the end. I can't thank you enough for helping me with this, Alistair. I owe a lot to you and Pemberton."

"Don't worry about it," I tell her. "We're happy to help. And it's not like the rest of the company knows about the trip anyways. They think we're looking to expand into Spain, that's the guise I'm filing this under, anyways."

"That's good," Sam says. "We wouldn't want your Board of Directors getting you into trouble, would we?"

I chuckle. "Only if you get hurt out there. Which isn't going to happen."

"No. We'll be perfectly safe, Alistair. *I'll* be perfectly safe, I mean."

"About that," I start, trailing off.

"Yeah?"

I sigh, taking a deep breath. "I want to go with you, Samantha," I tell her. "Look, it's not that I don't trust you. In fact, on the contrary: I believe you're the best person for the job. Seriously. I don't know your department in the CIA, but I know that you're the most qualified person to go after your missing supervisor. After everything you've told me about your experience in the field, after listening to your briefings on Malstrom? I want to be a part of this, Samantha. It's dangerous out there. If something happened to you or our baby, I'd never be able to forgive myself. Which is why I'm coming with you."

Sam takes a long pause, the longest moment of silence I think we've ever shared. I can tell she's mulling things over, weighing her options.

And then I hear her sigh, and she speaks up: "Alistair, I don't want you getting hurt. There's a lot of dangerous people out there, and one wrong move can—"

"One wrong move can kill you, I get it," I say, cutting her off. "But let me offer a counterpoint of my own. You say there are men out there that can kill me, and that's true. But I've never met someone who wasn't loyal to money. The pressure of money, and a lot of it, can supersede loyalty to any country. Any cause. I'd be willing to bet if your skills fail, for whatever reason, then money can answer the question of staying alive for just another hour longer."

Sam pauses again, and I know I've got her on the ropes.

"But I wouldn't," she says.

"Wouldn't what?"

"I wouldn't sell out my country, not for all the money in the world."

I nod, shrugging to myself. She makes a good point there.

"But you're not everyone else," I tell her. "You're unique. Your morals just happen to line up with the CIA's. Not everyone else can say the same thing. For every loyal agent in your department you can show me, I'll show you a hundred men that would *easily* turn on their boss for a bigger paycheck. You're outnumbered, Samantha. But you don't have to be, not out there. Not when it counts. When shit hits the fan, you won't be alone, not if I can help it."

"Fine," she sighs. "You can come."

"Good," I smile. "And for the record, if you'd said no? I wouldn't have changed a thing."

"I'm glad to hear that," Samantha says. "Really."

"How's the pregnancy?" I ask, changing the subject.

"It's okay, I guess," Sam says. "No nausea today or anything. I guess that's enough to make me worry, I guess."

"No need," I reply. "Stacy had the same issue when she was in the first trimester." I'm shocked to hear the words coming out of my mouth; usually I require coaxing to talk about my ex-wife or the child we'd lost. But now it's old hat, simple advice for me to give to Samantha on her journey. "We went to the doctor's after she'd felt the same way. Worried that the nausea went away."

"What happened?"

"Doctor took a look at her, said there wasn't anything he can do. Sometimes nausea is caused by other factors during pregnancy. Stress, uncertainty of the future. Work. Home-life balance, if it's an issue. It was for us," I reply.

"What...what else happened?"

"Not much, but I know the nausea or lack thereof didn't cause her to miscarry." I hope Sam doesn't probe me further, I'm not eager to talk about Stacy and Annalise just right now.

But that's enough for Samantha. "Okay," she says. "Then I won't worry. I trust you, Alistair."

I smile. "I trust you, too."

"So, got your bags all packed?" she asks. "If you're coming with me, I guess you're going to have to be ready for an extended vacation."

I grin. "Haven't packed just yet, but I'll get on it tonight.

"You better," she says. "Or else I'm going to leave you in the dust if you can't keep up."

"Well, I better get on it, then, shouldn't I?"

"As you should," Sam giggles. "I'm ready to go when you are," she says.

We say a quick goodbye, and I hang up the phone as I turn to face the cityscape behind me. Washington, D.C.'s an elegant city, one rich and full of history. I know I'm going to miss it here, oddly enough, but I'd rather be with Sam. Especially since she'd agreed to my tagging along.

I guess I've got to get packed, then.

I call Kennedy, telling my driver to come get me from the office. I need to get home, right stat now.

I've got work to do.

When I finally make it back to my house, I rush upstairs, throwing open my closet door as I inspect the rows and rows of formal suits, clothes, pants, shoes. It's a lot, and I don't even know where to begin with the packing. Are we going to play dress-up, make pretend we're international assassins? Or are we going to try to blend in, play it casually? I don't know how the people in Spain even dress, I'm sure the rumors of them wearing all-black all the time are misguided.

I pull out a row of suit jackets, sorting through them as I pick out the best selection. I throw my final choices on my bed, placing the rest back on the rack. I go back into the closet, pick out a couple of tee-shirts, throwing them onto the pile as well. Pants come next, khakis and jeans, a pair of running shorts just in case. Socks, underwear, a few pairs of shoes built to run in, should worse come to worse. I grab a leather-bound suitcase from the back of my closet, stuffing my clothes inside. After that, I bounce over to my bathroom, collecting my toiletries in a bag and shove them in the suitcase.

And just like that, I'm ready to go.

I know it's still a few days before Sam's set to leave for Spain, but it helps me to get ready as soon as possible. I head into the bathroom, making sure I haven't left anything behind. Nope. Toothbrush, comb, hair gel, all accounted for. I'm good to go whenever she needs me.

I look up, and I see my face in the mirror.

I hardly recognize myself anymore. Sure, it's *me,* but you know what they say—every cell in your body regenerates every seven years. I'm not the same person I was seven years ago, not physically. Emotionally too. All that pain, all those years ago, have been washed away like dead skin cells on a hand.

And for a moment, I genuinely can't believe what I'm doing.

I'm putting a woman I care about, the woman carrying our child, into harm's way. And I've given her a free pass to romp all around Europe in hopes of finding her former supervisor.

What if he's not in Spain? What if this Terrence Malstrom finds her before she finds Alan? All these questions and more puzzle me, and I can't help but feel like we're way in over our heads at this point. I want to call the whole thing off, tell Sam it's too dangerous for my company to risk.

But I know she'd still go, with or without my support.

And I want to do everything I can to make sure she gets back home. Safe and sound.

I'm going to have to go with her if I want to do this right, no ifs, ands or buts about it.

I sigh, taking a deep breath as I inspect myself in the mirror.

I can do this.

I *have* to do this.

I leave the bathroom, making sure my suitcase is packed and shut tight as it can be. I pull my cell phone out of my pocket, dialing Samantha's number.

"Hey," she says. "You packed?"

"Yeah," I reply. "Ready to go. Just say the word, and we'll make sure our plane's cleared to land in Madrid. We can shove off whenever you need."

"Well, I'm ready to go if you are."

I take a deep breath. "Okay. Let's go, then. I'll swing over to the airport, bring Kennedy with me. We can come pick you up in Richmond, take the plane to a coastal city to re-fuel before the trip overseas. Bring a book, or something. It's going to be a long flight."

"You got it," Samantha beams. "I'll see you soon, okay?"

"Sure thing," I tell her.

When I hang up, I feel like I've just made the biggest choice I'll ever make in my entire life. And there's no going back from it now.

I call Kennedy, tell him the news. Sam and I are going to leave the country for an undisclosed amount of time, and we need a ride to the airport as quick as possible.

"I'll be there in two shakes of a rabbit's tail, boss," he says before hanging up.

I grab my suitcase, heading downstairs. I fill a glass of water in my sink, staring out my kitchen window. I don't know when I'll make it back home. But I know I won't be alone when I return.

I step outside, locking my front door behind me as I sit on the porch, waiting for Kennedy to arrive.

I guess it's now or never.

TWENTY
Samantha

I get the call from Alistair that the limo's waiting for me out-side, and I grab my packed bags as I throw on my tennis shoes. I'm not sure what kind of security a private plane has, but I'm fairly certain I'm not going to have to get a full-body scan before we take off.

I lock my front door behind me, scurrying on down to the shiny jet-black limo that's parked on the curb. As I hop in the back, I see that I'm alone in the car as Kennedy rolls down the partition window. I can see his barbed-wire tattoo painted across his forehead from here, his beard as fluffy as always. I want to burst out in laughter again when I remember how much frustration a little bit of ink had caused for Alistair.

"Kennedy," I ask. "Where's Alistair?"

The driver nods. "Right. He's back at the airport, where I'm going to take you. He's waiting for you on the plane."

"Are you coming with us? To Spain?"

Kennedy nods. "Our mutual acquaintance can't be without a driver. Plus I get to sightsee in Europe, so win-win, right?"

I shrug. "Can't complain, I suppose."

And just like that, Kennedy buckles up as the partition win-dow rolls closed. He re-starts the engine, pulling out into the street as we make our way to the airstrip where Alistair's wait-ing for us.

◆ ◆ ◆

When Kennedy pulls up to the airport, I can't help but look around in awe as I try to spot which of these planes belongs to Alistair Jensen. I see massive 737's scattered around at various terminals, so those can't be it. I see a few private planes, a few Cessnas. They're too small for Alistair, I know he'd get something much more luxurious.

The limo comes to a gentle stop in the middle of the airstrip, and I peer through the window to see the plane we're about to board.

It's exactly what I'd imagined.

A medium sized plane, I can see Alistair's spared no expense. The plane's nearly as big as a commercial airliner, a red stripe traced across the center with *Pemberton Computers* stenciled across in big white letters. His company's logo is printed up close to the cockpit, the dove drawn onto the branch as usual. The stairs are extended, stewardesses in ruby-red vests hike up and down the flight of stairs carrying bags and suitcases, boxes of supplies for our journey ahead.

I step out of the limo while Kennedy takes my bags from me. He hands them over to a flight attendant, dressed in the same white button-down shirt with the ruby red vest, just like all the other attendants I see scurrying about. It's a young woman, no older than me. I guess Alistair's rich enough to have his own flight attendants. That isn't news to me, but still surprising nevertheless.

"Are you all ready to go, ma'am?" the attendant asks me, her curly-blonde hair bouncing as she speaks.

"Of course," I say, utterly stunned by the luxuries I'm faced with. Private planes, private stewardesses, bringing his own driver overseas. Alistair manages to find all the ways I could possibly be surprised and *still* manages to top them.

"Follow me, then," the stewardess says, handing my bags to another attendant as she leads me up the stairs into the plane's cabin.

Stepping inside the cabin, I find that the interior's even more luxurious than anticipated. The walls are a pristine white, the floor a red carpet that screams luxury to anybody lucky enough to step inside. The seats are leather, expensive I presume. No pleather for Mr. Jensen's private plane. The seats are scattered around the cabin of the plane, giving occupants plenty of space to stretch out. Each seat has its own television, a flat screen hidden behind the tray table. It's luxury in portable form, to put it mildly.

And there he is. Alistair Jensen, sitting in one of the leather-backed seats, reading a magazine, looks like a SkyMall to me. He looks up at me, grinning as he tosses the magazine aside and stands up. We embrace, a tender hug that's cautious of the dangers ahead. But I know we'll have each other, and the embrace reminds me I won't be alone out there. For which I'm ever thankful.

"How was the ride up here?" Alistair asks me. "Sorry I wasn't there to pick you up. We needed to make sure the plane was in tip-top shape for refueling before we cross the Atlantic."

I nod, understanding. "And is it? In tip-top shape?"

Alistair grins, sitting back down in his seat as he pats the seat next to him. "Oh yeah. We're going to be just fine," he replies. "Come on, sit with me. I'll show you everything the plane has to offer."

I nod, beaming as I sit down next to him. Alistair's taken the window seat, but I much prefer sitting in the aisle either way. More room to stretch out.

"Check this out," Alistair says, pulling out the tray table from the seat in front of him. The table's no ordinary plastic, instead the whole thing looks to be made out of stainless steel. A small television screen sits exposed after the tray table's pulled out, and Alistair presses a few buttons along the bottom row of the screen, powering it on. "We've got every channel known to man, new releases, any movie you can possibly imagine."

I smile. "You told me to bring a book, so I did. But this is still nice," I reply. "Really. Actually, I don't think 'nice' begins to cover just how elegant this all is, Alistair. I'm glad we did this together. I don't know where I'd be without you."

Alistair chuckles. "You'd be flying coach, is where you'd be. Not anymore."

I lean back in my seat, grinning. "Not anymore."

A flight attendant, ruby-red vest and all, walks into the cabin of the plane, knocking on the wall to signal for Alistair's attention. "Sir?"

Alistair looks up, nodding.

"We're ready for takeoff when you say the word, Mr. Jensen."

Alistair shoots me a look. "You ready?"

"Ready."

He gives the thumbs-up to the attendant, and she turns as the flight of stairs begin to retract.

"*Wait!*" a voice cries out from the runway, and the attendant gasps as she re-lowers the staircase.

Kennedy with his barbed-wire face tattoo steps up to the cabin, a leather duffel-bag in one hand as he pants, grinning from ear to ear.

"You almost forgot about me, boss," he says as he throws the bag down on the floor, sitting down in one of the front-row seats of the cabin.

Alistair groans silently. He looks back over at me. "Kennedy's tagging along, by the way. I'll need someone to get us around when we're there."

"I know. He told me himself he was coming along."

Alistair sighs, groaning again to himself. "Really could do without the tattoo," he mutters.

I giggle. "You're *really* bothered by it, I can tell" I whisper to him.

Alistair shakes his head. "Whatever," he says. I see him flash a hint of a smile, so I know everything's going to be okay.

The cabin's stairs extend back up, sealing the cabin door shut as the stewardess turns the valve to pressurize the cabin.

The pilot's voice crackles over the speaker as the engine rumbles to life. "*Ladies and gentlemen, this is your captain speak-*

ing. We'll be flying from Richmond International to Pittsburgh, where we'll stop to refuel for the flight direct to Madrid. Please fasten your safety belts and prepare for takeoff."

I look over at Alistair, grinning from ear to ear. The plane begins its taxi to the runway, the engine rumbling the entire cabin.

"I'm glad we did this," I tell him.

He looks over at me, returning the smile.

The plane, now sitting at the end of the runway, roars to life as the pilot throws back the throttle. We shoot forward, the g-force pushing up against us as we soar down the runway.

"Me, too," he says.

The plane lifts up into the air, and we're off.

As the plane stabilizes, reaching its expected altitude of thirty-five thousand feet, Alistair and I begin to formulate our game plan for when we land in Madrid. It's tedious, boring work. Figuring out hotels, making sure all the company credit cards are approved for international purchases. But after a while, we're fully prepared to touch down in Europe. Only ten-plus hours to go.

"So," I say. "Why don't we just sit back, relax for a while? It's not like we're going to be there anytime soon."

Alistair shakes his head. "No. I need to be prepared, ready for anything. You've got years of experience under your belt, Samantha. I don't."

I nod, Alistair makes a good point. "Okay, then. Where should we start?"

"Your supervisor, Alan. Where was his last known location?"

I pull out a guidebook to Spain from my carry-on underneath the seat in front of us. I flip through the pages, scouring the guidebook for the map I'm looking for.

"There! Right here," I point out to Alistair. "It's a residential neighborhood, halfway between Madrid and Toledo. The current capital of the country and its historical capital. Makes sense, I guess."

"Why?"

"Because Terrence Malstrom works out of Madrid. The safehouse has to be in Toledo, I'm sure of it. You wouldn't put your safehouse down the road from your usual base of operations, it's not well-hidden enough. And you don't shit where you eat."

Alistair nods. "Makes sense to me. So, we're going to start in Toledo, then?"

I shake my head. "No, Madrid. Randall Friendly, Malstrom's right hand man, is being held in captivity in Madrid. We need to find a way to get to him, to speak to him. He might know a little bit more about Alan."

"Let's go over the whole plan," Alistair says. "One more time, just for posterity's sake."

I nod, in perfect agreement. "Got it. Let's start at the beginning, then."

After stopping in Pittsburgh, we settle back in for another take-off as the flight ahead of us stretches out across the Atlantic. It takes Alistair and I four-plus hours to go over the plan in its entirety, but afterwards I feel more prepared for the future than ever.

I gaze out the window, past Alistair as he naps. He's been out for a while, and I've left him to get his rest in the seat next to me while I watch old sitcoms on the TV just behind the tray table. It's dark outside, and I can see the stars are all shining bright over the clouds. Below, I can see the black darkness of the Atlantic Ocean, zooming below us as we make our way to Europe, still more than six hours of flight left to go.

I flick off the screen in front of me, embracing the roaring silence of the plane's engine as I grab a face-mask out of my pocket. I snuggle it on, placing it squarely over my eyes as I try to get some shut-eye myself.

It's a long trip, and I've got a minute to think things over.

Alistair and I have come so far since Paris. It's crazy to think about, but it's all true. The night of bliss together, falling apart. The reunion in Dubai, where Alistair shot me down in front of a business partner.

And then everything else after that. It's all been a blur, one that I've been more than happy to experience.

But still I worry. I worry about the baby, about their health and safety while we're traveling abroad. I worry about Alistair, putting him in danger where he doesn't need to be. And I'm worried about our future, most of all. Are we going to be able to face life together, after all this is over?

I have no idea. Truthfully.

As I drift off to sleep, I can't help but feel the past and present mixing, stirring up in the forefront of my mind. It's all a blur, and I fall asleep dreaming about Alistair. Only Alistair.

I couldn't dream about anyone else even if I tried.

TWENTY-ONE
Samantha

The hotel bar's practically empty this time of night, only a few scattered patrons dotted along the length of the old oak bar. Soft music's playing, a gentle piano accompanied by a woman's singing. She's singing something in French I don't recognize, but I don't really care. It's been a long enough day in the field already, the search for this Terrence Malstrom fellow weighing heavily on my mind. I deserve a break, I deserve a night off. And it's high time I started enjoying my surroundings a little bit more.

After all, if I'm going to be stuck in Paris for another week, I might as well have a little bit of fun while I'm here.

I order myself a glass of water from the bar, nothing fancy. The bartender nods, pouring fresh ice and water into the glass and slides it over to me. Having something to do with your hands is half the battle, and I watch as the condensation sweats to the outside of the glass. A droplet forms, and I wipe that away with one finger.

Only a handful of blocks away from the Eiffel Tower, this hotel's a hidden gem in the Parisian landscape. I know the CIA paid top dollar for me to be here, so I might as well enjoy *some* of the amenities. After all, if I didn't I'd consider this trip a waste of money, to some extent.

"Having fun over there?" a dark oaky voice asks me from down the length of the bar.

I look up, surprised. A man in a three-piece suit is staring me down, eyeing me as he grins. His face is tanned, rough stubble dotting a perfectly chiseled jawline. And those eyes, dark and brown like the richest coffee you'd ever get to taste.

I've seen this man before, I know that face. But I'm having trouble pinpointing it, and I start to wonder if this is someone I've met once before.

"I'm sorry, do I know you?" I ask the man in the suit. I can see he's sipping a drink, a crystalline glass resting comfortably in his hand.

"Maybe you do, maybe you don't," the man says, still grinning. He takes a sip of his drink, swirls the glass around as ice clinks up against the rim. I swear to *God* I know this guy. I definitely know who he is, and it's positively killing me. "Who am I to decide that for you?"

I laugh, my game thrown off by the man's sudden appearance of charm. "Well, if you told me if we've met before, that might jog my memory. That'd help."

"We haven't met before," he says. "Otherwise I'd remember it."

I smile, spinning in my chair to face the man sitting down the length of the bar.

"Well, how do I know you, then?"

"Guess." The man chuckles again, taking another sip of the drink.

I pause, scrubbing through my memories to see if I can pinpoint who this is.

"Are you famous?" I ask.

"Maybe. Depends on who you ask."

I'll take that as a yes. I try to remember every movie I've ever seen, every awards show, every music video, sports game. I'm still drawing a blank.

"Are you a movie star?" I ask. The man grins, shakes his head. That's not it, then. "What about a musician? Some alt-rock band I've never heard of."

The man bursts out into laughter, slapping his knee with delight as he cackles. "That's rich," he says. "Me, a rockstar. I'll remember you said that."

Jeez, who is this guy?

Maybe he's a nobody, somebody just *pretending* to be famous. But where would be the fun in all that?

I shrug. "I'm at a loss, then. Sorry. Drawing a blank."

The man returns the gesture, shrugging as the throws back the rest of his drink. "I'll make you a deal," he says. "You let me buy you a drink, and I tell you who I really am."

I look down at my glass of water. "Thanks," I reply, "but I'm not finished with this one yet. I appreciate the offer, though."

The man shrugs again. "Guess it'll just have to remain a mystery, then."

"Guess so," I reply.

I go back to my water, sitting in silence as the man in the suit flags down the bartender, pays his tab with a flourish of a metallic jet-black credit card. For a moment, I think that's it; the strangest interaction I've ever had while working out in the field finally coming to an anticlimactic close.

Suddenly, I remember. I know where I've seen that face before.

The man gets up out of his seat, walks over to the rack by the end of the bar as he grabs his coat. He throws it on, and I set aside my water as I stand up and race over to him. I see the man's eyebrows cock, and he looks down at me in surprise as I scurry over to him.

"I know who you are," I burst out. "I'm sorry. I couldn't let you leave without getting it off my chest."

The man grins. "So, who am I, then?"

"You're Alistair Jensen. Billionaire CEO of Pemberton Computers. You practically re-invented the personal computer. Oh my *God.* I can't believe I didn't recognize you right away."

"Congratulations," Alistair Jensen says. "You've done it. You've cracked the code." He raises his eyebrows at me, takes a sip of his drink casually. "Want a prize?"

I feel my face flush. "I-I don't think that's necessary—"

Alistair shrugs. "How about a drink on me, to celebrate?"

"Celebrate what?" I look up at him, curious.

He smiles. "Celebrate us meeting, of course."

I grin, but shake my head. "Thanks, but no thanks. I'm technically working, I couldn't..." I trail off, hoping Alistair takes the hint.

"Well, at least give me *your* name, first. You guessed mine, it's only fair I get to know yours."

My face is redder than a ripe tomato, but I oblige him anyways. "Samantha. Samantha Jacobson."

"Well, it was nice meeting you, Samantha Jacobson. Shame we couldn't get that drink together. And may I suggest one thing?"

I nod. "Sure."

"When you introduce yourself, reverse the order."

"Huh?"

Alistair grins. "Like James Bond—'Jacobson, Samantha Jacobson.' Makes you sound cooler," he chuckles.

"I'll have to try that out, then."

"I know a few other tricks you could try out, too."

My heart skips a beat, and I look up at Alistair. I grin, I can't help it. I'm pretty sure I want him. I just have to know if he wants me, too.

"Such as?" I ask.

"We've got all night," Alistair says with a wink. "Why don't you take a guess?"

The plane jostles, shaking me awake. Turbulence. I feel my head rattling as the plane's thrown about, ducking and bobbing under the atmospheric pressure outside. I tap the screen in front of me, checking out the real-time estimate for our journey's length. We're still flying high over the Atlantic, but we're closer than ever to reaching Spain.

I feel a hand reach out and touch mine. It's Alistair, sitting next to the window. He's awake, alert, just like me.

"You okay?" he asks.

I nod. "I'm fine, just…I was dreaming," I reply.

"Anything good?"

"The best memory of my entire life," I whisper, looking past Alistair and out the window beyond him. It's dark out, the night sky dotting the view with distant stars.

"Well, I can tell you're nervous," Alistair says.

"What, and you're not?" Even after years and years of flying, I still can't help but totally freak out when turbulence hits. It's not fun, not in the slightest. And I can't stop myself from worrying about a plane crash, or a part falling off the plane.

"No," Alistair says plainly. "Here, I'll show you."

He puts an arm around my shoulder, pulling me in close to him. It's a sweet gesture, and I smile at the token of appreciation.

"Look at the stewardess, just in front of us there," Alistair whispers to me as he pulls me in closer to him. I can peek through the seats, see the flight attendant at the end of the isle up ahead. She's calm as can be, a folding chair extended out of the wall for her to sit in as she reads a magazine. I can't believe how calm she is.

"How does *she* do it?" I whisper up to Alistair. Am I the *only one* on the plane freaking out? I can see Kennedy, a few seats up ahead. He's still fast asleep, passed out and snoring like nothing's even happening.

Alistair grins, holding me close. "I'll tell you the secret," he whispers. "Look at the flight attendant. You know I hired her from a major airline? She's flown thousands of miles, maybe millions. Probably enough to get you to the moon and back. She's been through so many bouts of turbulence, this is probably old hat to her. She knows when it's going to be bad."

"So?"

"So," Alistair continues, "when you're positive shit's hit the fan, look at the flight attendants. If they're freaking out, you better do so, too. But if they're calm? It's nothing more than routine to them."

I lean back in my seat as Alistair's arm returns to his armrest. The plane rocks, jostling me in my seat as I stare out the window. I can't believe I'd never noticed the stewardesses' calm before, not in all my years of flying. I know the road ahead's going to be rough, probably rougher than the turbulence we're experiencing right now. But with Alistair by my side, I know we're going to make it through to the end. No matter what.

I brace myself, preparing to ride out the turbulence myself. The plane rocks and throws us about, but Alistair and I stay buckled in, keeping our feet planted squarely on the cabin floor. It's almost too much to handle, but I keep looking up at the flight attendant. Every time, she's calm as can be. Cool as a cucumber.

After a few more bumps and shakes, the plane levels out, the turbulence behind us. The stewardess shuts her magazine, retracts the folding chair she'd been sitting on back into the wall as she gathers herself. I take a look at the real-time map on the screen in front of me, and I see we're flying over Portugal right now, less than an hour to go before we reach our destination.

There's a ding, the 'fasten safety belts' sign above illuminating as the loudspeakers in the cabin crackle on.

"Ladies and gentlemen, this is your captain speaking again. We're about to touch down in Madrid Barajas International, t-minus thirty minutes. Prepare for landing. Return all tray tables to their upright position, power down any electronic devices."

I guess it's showtime.

I see Kennedy shifting in his seat, stirring awake. He leans over his chair, peering back at us with that barbed-wire face tattoo of his.

He smiles, throws us a thumbs-up. Alistair reluctantly returns the gesture, grinning nervously.

I look over at the man seated next to me, the man I couldn't have done this without.

"You ready?" I ask. He nods, determined as ever.

We buckle our seatbelts, preparing for the plane to land.

TWENTY-TWO
Alistair

I feel the plane's landing gears extending below the cabin floor, the gentle familiar shake of the cabin signifying we're here.

I peer out the window, see the faint orange glow of Madrid outside. We're here, landing safely in one piece.

Now the *real* fun begins.

I check my wristwatch, I see it's still going off of East Coast time. I adjust my watch, eight hours ahead, silently motioning for Samantha to do the same on her wristwatch. Our phones'll update automatically, but for now I can see why we're so damn exhausted—it's the middle of the night in Madrid, we've just gotten the proverbial half-sleep you usually get on a plane. Now I know the feeling we're all experiencing: half-awake, half-asleep, jet-lagged and exhausted from flying for half a day.

The plane sinks down, the runway coming up to meet us as the landing gears finish retracting, extending out to meet the paved road. The plane touches down with a *thud,* and I feel the brakes skid as the pilot does his best to bring the plane to a standstill.

Looks like we've arrived, and not a moment too soon.

I look over at Samantha, suddenly worried about the baby. "How are you feeling?" I ask her, careful not to give my anxiety away too quick.

Sam smiles, rubs her stomach. "I'm okay," she says. "Just some butterflies in my stomach is all. They'll go away soon enough."

I nod as the plane finally comes to a halt, stopping at the

end of the runway. I'm nervous as hell, terrified for the journey ahead, but I'll never tell Samantha that. Not yet, at least.

We disembark the plane, Samantha, Kennedy and I grab our bags and step down the cabin stairs as the stewardesses and pilots thank us. I tip an imaginary cap to them, thanking my employees for getting us safely overseas.

The three of us quietly head inside the Barajas Airport, the tired silence keeping us from light conversation as we make our way to the currency-exchange counter just near receiving.

I exchange a fat stack of hundred dollar bills for the equivalence in Euro, handing most of the stack to Kennedy as his eyes light up in surprise.

"That's your pay for the trip," I tell him. "One month's salary. If we're here for longer, you'll get paid for longer. If we're done before the time you're paid for, consider it a bonus on me."

My tatted driver grins, rifling through the Euro as he counts the bills himself. "Anything you say, boss. Just tell me what you need me to do."

"Find a hotel, a car, lay low. Wait for our signal, we're going to need you soon enough."

"Roger that," Kennedy says. He stands next to us, grinning eagerly as we watch the passerby flock to and from their terminals all around us.

"Kennedy?" I ask.

"Yeah, boss?"

"You can head out now," I tell him. "It's fine. We'll be in touch."

"You got it," Kennedy says, picking up his bags and stuffing the wad of cash into his jacket pocket. He gives us a nod, heading off into the airport as he starts his own journey.

Samantha chuckles. "What're the odds of him never coming back, you think?"

I laugh. "Fifty-fifty," I reply. "He's a good kid. Impulsive. Stupid. But a good kid. And one hell of a driver, best I've ever had. He'll come through for us, don't worry. I'll take those chances any day of the week."

We exit the airport, ducking through receiving as we pass customers waiting on their bags at the terminal. We take an escalator up to the next floor, stepping out a series of plate-glass doors to reach a road crowded with busses and taxis.

I flag a cab down, and the vacancy sign up top flashes on. Samantha and I head over to the cab as the driver steps out to meet us, a portly man with a bushy white mustache.

"English?" I ask, and the cabbie nods. "Good. We're going to Gran Villa, our hotel's in the middle of the shopping district. Think you can get us there quick?"

The cabbie nods. "Right away, sir."

He helps Samantha load her bags into the trunk, and I toss mine in after hers. We hop in the back seat as the cabbie gets behind the wheel, resetting the meter.

A moment later he pulls off into the road, merging into traffic as we head into the heart of Madrid.

◆ ◆ ◆

The cab reaches Gran Villa, and Samantha and I step out once we've reached our hotel, the *Duplass*. Gran Villa, Madrid's most profitable and expensive neighborhood, reminds me a lot of Time's Square in New York City. There are glowing billboards everywhere, every restaurant and building in the area positively brilliant in their shine. The whole street looks like a Lite-Brite, stocked to the brim with colorful glowing LCD bulbs.

"Wow," Sam breathes. "I never expected it to be so pretty here."

I nod, grinning. "If we're going to stay here in Spain, might as well spend our time in luxury. As long as we can manage."

The cabbie pops the trunk open, and Sam and I grab our bags out of the back as I hand the Spanish driver a fifty. He thanks me, nodding as he returns to the driver's seat and re-starts the idling engine, pulling away a moment later.

Sam and I look around, taking in the view of Gran Villa for ourselves. Honestly, I'd be more than okay if we never left this place, but I know Sam's going to have to start a manhunt tomorrow. And that could take us *anywhere.*

"Should we head up, drop our stuff off?" Sam asks.

I nod. "Only if we get something to eat afterwards. I'm *starving,* flying really takes it out of me."

Sam grins. "Works for me. I'm hungry, too."

We head into the lobby of the *Duplass,* an elegantly-polished marble room with enough space to house a small militia. I make my way over to the polished-granite countertop, checking in with the receptionist as I look around, taking the sights in for myself. I can see the glow of Gran Villa behind me outside, hotel guests still pouring in and out of the *Duplass's* lobby. I check my watch, corrected to the time zone, and I see it's already one in the morning.

"Any good places to eat still open around here?" I ask the receptionist, a young woman with a tight-black bun sitting atop her head.

She laughs. "Of course, sir. Everything's open at this hour."

I shrug, nodding. I turns around, waving at Sam with the newly acquired room key. I pick up my bags, following closely behind Samantha as we head over to call the elevator upstairs.

Our room's on the seventh floor, high enough to see the majority of Gran Villa from our bedroom window. The lights shine bright even up here, and I worry we're not going to be able to get any sleep. But I shut the curtains for a moment, checking to see if the light'll shine through, and I can see the heavy curtains manage to block nearly all the light coming in from outside.

Samantha heads into the bathroom, washing her face as the sink runs. I unpack my bag, find something a little fancier to wear. I'd worn an old hoodie on the plane, something comfortable to rest in. But if we're going out, I'll want to be dressed to the nines. I put on a button-down white shirt, dress pants and polished leather shoes, an easy enough outfit to throw together.

Sam changes in the bathroom, emerging in a blouse, floral print —my personal favorite of hers, along with some khakis, and some flats that look like they'll be easy enough to walk in. We look like a real pair tonight, a couple of fancy tourists out for a night on the town. Look how far we've come; all the way from Paris and back. It's been a lifetime since I met the international agent in the Parisian bar, and I feel like we've been through an entire lifetime's worth of experiences already.

Nothing can stop us now, and I nod as Samantha motions to the door. We head out, ready for the evening ahead of us.

◆ ◆ ◆

We walk the length of the Gran Villa, taking in the sights and sounds as they whizz past us. I see countless glowing LCD billboards, advertising Off-Broadway shows, restaurants, clothing lines and *so much* more. I'd be in Heaven here, hanging out in Gran Villa for an indiscriminate amount of time. But I know the real reason I'm here; I'm to help Samantha out in her search for her missing supervisor. I pinch myself, keeping myself from getting too distracted from the overall task at hand. But tonight we're just walking, relaxing. The conversation is non-existent, a side-effect from our exhausting flight overseas. I'm sure things'll improve once we've gotten some food in us, and I know Sam's gong to be eating for two, so she'll need more time than usual. No matter. Anything to keep the baby healthy and happy is fair game in my book.

"See any place you're interested in?" I ask Samantha as we walk down the length of the sidewalk, crowded by pedestrians surrounding us as we saunter. I'm afraid to lose her in the crowd, but I know if *anyone* could find me quick it'd be a former field operative for the CIA. So I don't let myself get too worked up.

"I dunno," Sam says. "There's so many options. Heck, they've even got some old chain restaurants from back home." She points up ahead, and I laugh when I see the bright gold Greasy Heaven sign, a burger joint I'm all to familiar with back home.

"Oh god," I chuckle. I wouldn't dare eat somewhere I could find back home, so I keep looking around. I see pubs, tourist traps, restaurants coming in all shapes and sizes. Some places have outdoor seating, others are no bigger than holes-in-the-wall. There's a restaurant across the street that looks inconspicuous enough, with the outside wall made up of colorful tiles depicting old bullfighting rings.

"What about that one?" I point out, stopping Samantha in her tracks as she investigates the restaurant across the street.

She nods. "That'll work for me," she shrugs. We take a look around, there's a stoplight up ahead with a crosswalk for pedestrians, so we head that way. Once we've crossed the street, we push our way through the endless sea of city-goers as we head inside the restaurant. I didn't even bother catching the name of the place.

It's a small venue inside, with the colorful tile wall of the exterior matching the decor inside. There's just enough room for a full bar, a couple of tables and chairs in a lobby that leads into a kitchen, double-doors blocking the view from inside.

I'm familiar enough with European customs to know that customers usually seat themselves in all restaurants all over the continent, and Samantha and I duck over and nab a table that's halfway between the kitchen and the front door.

Sam takes a look around, surveying our surroundings. There's patrons lined up along the bar, ordering *tapas* from the bartender as they sip their drinks and talk amongst themselves. Servers pop in and out of the kitchen, carrying medium-sized plates over their heads as they deliver them to the bar and patrons sitting at tables. One of the servers stops by our table, a young man with slicked-back black hair under a hairnet. He takes our orders in a thick Spanish accent, fluent enough in English for us to order without any misunderstandings. Samantha orders a Spanish *tortilla,* an egg-casserole dish that's served with a hearty chunk of bread. I get myself the works; a sample platter full of olives, cheeses, breads and meats from all over the country.

Sam and I don't even have a chance to speak to each other before the jet-black haired server is back out with our food, already prepared before we'd started ordering. We cock our eyebrows in amazement at one another, digging into our respective plates.

"How's your food?" I ask Sam, and she nods eagerly, unable to take her eyes off the food. She's beyond digging in; she's practically devouring the *tortilla* in front of her. I've elected to do the same, heavily sampling each type of olive, bread and cheese in front of me.

Her plate's licked clean in just a few minutes flat, and Samantha leans back in her chair, rubbing her stomach. *"Perfecto,"* she giggles, and I chuckle as I finish off the rind of Iberico cheese I'd been working on.

"So, now what?" I ask.

Sam, still leaning back in her chair, blushes sweetly. "I've been meaning to tell you something, ever since we got off the plane."

"What's that?"

"I had a dream about us," she says.

"Oh? Any good?"

She's still grinning from ear to ear. "Yeah, it was good," she replies. "It was the night we met. Remember?"

"How could I forget?" I reply. Because God knows I couldn't ever forget her if I tried.

Sam smiles. "You remember what you said to me, back in Paris, the morning when you left? You said, 'this wasn't going to be the end of our story'. How'd you know?"

I feel *my* face flush. Normally that's just a line I use, something I used to tell girls I'd hooked up with that I'd contact them one day without exchanging phone numbers. Nothing more than a diversionary tactic, I blush as I take my napkin off my lap and dab my chin with it, buying myself time to think.

"I just knew," I smile back at Samantha, her grin something I'm unable to ignore. And I *did* mean what I said to her back in Paris, I just didn't know it was true back then. But I know it's true now, and that's all that matters. I've changed since then. I'm sure Sam understands.

"So you knew our story wasn't over in Paris?" Sam clarifies.

I nod sweetly.

"Then why'd you shoot me down, back in Dubai?"

I want to groan, cover my face with my hands. I thought we'd been over this before, but I know the travel's probably stressed Sam out quite a bit. I won't think too much of it, but I know I have to tread lightly here.

"I was busy, Samantha, I wasn't thinking straight. I had no idea you were coming back to see me, which I'm still a little confused as to how you found me in the first place."

"Friend in the CIA made an app," Sam replies flatly. "So, you had no idea I was coming, and you had no idea I'd gotten pregnant after our night together. But you still make pretend you can see the future. You just let everything happen to you, don't you?"

I have no idea what she's talking about.

"Sam, did I say something to upset you? Anything at all I can do to make you feel better? Because I feel like this is coming out of nowhere."

Sam takes her napkin, tosses it on the table. "You're right. I'm just being irrational. But I know how I feel, and right now I feel like I need to be alone, Alistair. I'm sure you'd know that by now, considering the fact you can see into the future."

I want to raise my voice in concern, worried about Samantha. But she moves to fast for me to process, standing up and storming out of the restaurant in a flash. I can't even stand up fast enough to follow her out by the time she's out the front door. I flag down our server, pay the bill as quick as I can with a flourish of my credit card. Once I've paid the bill, I run outside, trying to locate Samantha as my eyes dart around the crowded sidewalk.

But I can't see her anywhere.

I know there's a ninety-nine per cent chance she's heading back to the hotel. It's the only familiar location we've got under our belts, so I figure I might as well head back that way. I start the short walk back to the *Duplass*, keeping a careful eye out for Samantha in case she's still out and about.

Normally I'd be livid, furious that someone in my life is so eager to start conflicts all the time. Samantha and I have had our fair share of arguments, that's for certain. But I know she's pregnant, the hormones are probably flooding her brain with mixed messages. And she's already such a headstrong woman; you don't join the CIA and become a field agent if you're a lukewarm-milquetoast person. That's just reality, and I'm more than okay with it.

What I'm *not* okay with is Sam leaving me in the middle of a country I'd never been to, ditching me in the most crowded part of the entire country's capital. And she's *pregnant,* to boot. I'll forgive her for tonight, but I know we're going to have to talk about impulsiveness while we're traveling together. Just to air on the safe side, I'll still apologize when we find each other back at the hotel. I know I haven't been perfect to her, that's for certain. But I know I don't deserve to be treated this way, not when I've stuck out my neck for Sam time and time again, even going so far as to fly her out here on my company's dollar.

And there's still so many unknowns on our trip. What if this whole trial runs cold, what if this Terrence Malstrom's right hand man isn't in prison anymore? What if Sam can't find her supervisor? Can we head back to the USA defeated, without what we came here to find in the first place?

I'm afraid for the future, because I know I can't see it for the life of me.

I *wish* I was prescient. It'd save us a lot of time in the long run, regardless.

As I continue the long walk back to the Hotel *Duplass*, I can't help but worry about Samantha. I know she and I can face any obstacle together that comes our way, but what if we're separated when that happens? And what if I'm not as strong as I need to be?

But I know I'll never let her go, no matter the answer to my questions. I've given up a lot to be with Samantha; my bachelor lifestyle, my complete and utter devotion to my role as CEO of Pemberton Computers. And I'd give up even more just to make her happy.

All this and more plagues my thoughts as I walk, and I feel the weight of a thousand questions bearing down on me as I try to return back to the woman I know I love. Surrounded by all these people on the sidewalk, I've never felt more alone.

TWENTY-THREE
Samantha

I'm practically kicking myself on the long walk back to the hotel *Duplass*. I know I was being shitty, back at the restaurant, but you know what? So was Alistair. And I know his line back in Paris wasn't how he really felt at the time.

'*This isn't the end of our story,*' he'd said to me. And sure, he was right, but at what cost? And I know his words didn't ring true for him back in Dubai—hell, he'd forgotten who I was until he was forced to jog his memory and remember me for the first time since Paris.

Still, I should cut him some slack. Someone as busy as Alistair Jensen doesn't—*didn't*—have time to remember what was just another one-night-stand to him. He didn't know I was pregnant at the time, how could he? I'm the one being irrational for expecting him to be a mind-reader. That's unfair of me, and I know the next time I see Alistair in the hotel I'm going to have to apologize to him.

If I want to keep Alistair in my life, I'm going to have to drop the headstrong bullshit, and that's never been more true in my entire life. It's only landed me in hot water; in the office, back at home, with my friends and family, I've only managed to scare off people with my stern temperament. And I want nothing more for that to change, for that bullshit to end. Once and for all.

As I walk the length of Gran Villa back to our hotel, the streets are packed with people. Bright lights shine from billboards and advertisements, showing me a life I *could* have. But I want this life, the one I've got. With Alistair. And I'm about to throw it all away if I keep this BS up. The mood swings, the outbursts of anger. Alistair doesn't deserve someone as unhinged as me, that's for sure. And I don't deserve a guy as kind and sweet as him. He's been nothing but patient and understanding, and I've thrown all that back in his face every chance I get.

I need to get my shit together, *fast.* Otherwise I'm going to lose the one person I can't stand to live without.

To hell with it. I know the truth. I can admit it to myself.

I know I'm in love with Alistair Jensen.

No ifs, ands or buts about it.

I just hope he feels the same way about me. And after that last display of emotion on my part, I wouldn't be surprised if he never wanted to see me again. I'd feel terrible, sure, but I'd understand his motives.

Because I'm pretty sure he loves me, too.

And there's no denying the feelings that make us human.

I can see the bright-red cursive signage up ahead, I know I'm within walking distance of the Hotel *Duplass*, and I've never been more eager to crash into bed than I am in this very moment.

I need a vacation. A *real* vacation. I just hope Alistair likes me enough to come with me by then, otherwise I know I'll be in real deep shit.

Back in the hotel, I clean myself off with a hot shower and a fresh towel. Honestly, it's the best break there is on Planet Earth, and a hot shower's able to change your entire outlook on life if you let it. You can stand there, letting the warm run all over you as you ponder the nature of whatever issue you're currently facing.

And I know now more than ever. I owe Alistair an apology, big-time.

He's not back at the hotel by the time I emerge from the bathroom, drying myself off and wrapping the towel around my waist as it hangs from my chest. I rifle through my suitcase, digging out the pair of sweatpants and the tank top I'd brought along to Spain. I throw them on, getting as comfortable as possible as I flop down on the massive California-King sized bed in the middle of the room.

Are beds this size in Spain still called California King? Or is it something else entirely? I've got no idea, and I'm too tired to think about it. I flick on the TV, scrolling through the Spanish-speaking channels as I find something familiar to watch while I wait for Alistair to come back. I see Spanish equivalents of every channel back home: there's a Spanish-speaking channel focused on buying and maintaining real estate, news channels just like the talking head stations we have back home. It's funny to see how different things are here overseas, and at the same time, how similar everything is. I settle on a Spanish-language soap opera, flicking on English subtitles as I watch characters argue about where they were standing in line for the movie they're about to see. Universal stuff, that.

After a while, I hear a gentle knock at the door, and I realize I'd left out the 'Do Not Disturb' sign on the handle. I hop up, bounding over to the hotel room door as I fling it open.

Sure enough, there's Alistair on the other end, waiting for me. He's grinning optimistically, but I can see the look on his face just the same: I hurt him tonight, no getting around that. But he's still happy to see me, and Alistair wraps his arms around me as we embrace in the doorway.

"Everything okay?" he asks as I nuzzle my face into the crook of his arm. I nod, letting a sniffle escape me. I can't help it, I'm just that excited to see him after the rift between us tonight. I'm eager to put things right between the two of us, and I step back as I gesture for Alistair to come in.

"I'm really sorry, Alistair," I start as he works his way over to the bed, flopping down on top of the bedsheets. "For everything back at the restaurant. And everything before that, too. I know I'm a lot to handle."

Alistair sits up, propping his head against the backboard behind the bed as he watches the program I'd been checking out on TV. He nods, never once taking his eyes from the television.

"Alistair, I feel like shit. I don't know why I keep acting up like this, I really don't. All I know is I want it to stop."

He spares a glance over at me, temporarily taking his eyes off the television.

"Really?" he asks.

I nod. "Really. I know this outburst wasn't the first. I wish I could guarantee you it would be the last, but you've seen me getting upset more than I'd like to. Blame it on hormones, blame it on the stress of the job we're doing. I really don't know. All I know is that I'm sorry. I messed up. And you're the greatest guy in the world for coming back to me, even after everything I put you through."

Alistair looks over at me pensively. He thinks my words over carefully, I can see he's deep in thought. I fear the judgement he might bestow on me, but I know I'll deserve it.

"I understand, Sam," he says quietly.

"Really?"

He nods. "Yeah. Stacey was the same way, back when we were...you know. Expecting. It's normal. She lost her cool even more than you did, if you could believe it."

I feel a hint of a grin spreading across my face. "Seriously?"

Alistair nods again, gravely this time. "If you can recall she left me, not the other way around. I understand the outbursts, Sam. Every time, I understand. They're not coming from an irrational place. It's on me to be more understanding, more patient. You're going through a tough time. We both owe the other an apology, Sam, and I should tell you that I'm sorry, too."

I walk across the room, sitting down next to Alistair as his arms wrap around my shoulders tenderly. It's a loving embrace, one that's a much-needed welcome after such an emotional rollercoaster of an evening. I return the favor, wrapping my arms around Alistair as I press my face into the crook of his arm. I take a deep breath, taking in his scent and his aura as I try to calm myself down. Fortunately, it works, and by the time we're pulling back from the embrace I feel a hundred per cent myself again.

Alistair smiles down at me, and I smile up at those dark brown hazelnut eyes of his.

I know it'll never be the *perfect* time to tell him, but it's now or never. Before things heat up too fast, before we get too busy with our mission.

"I love you," I blurt out.

Alistair practically flinches, thrown entirely off-guard by my admission. I worry, no, I'm *terrified* he won't feel the same way. I can see the gears faintly turning in his head, and Alistair ponders my outburst as I stare up at him longingly. It's the longest five seconds of my entire life, to say the least, and I worry we're about to have a repeat of history like back in Dubai.

But that's not what happens.

"I love you, too, Samantha," Alistair replies.

We embrace one another again, this time Alistair pulls me in for a kiss. It's soft, tender, loving. The slowest we've ever shared, yet still the most meaningful as I feel the warmth of his love pressing up against me. He wraps his arms around me again, this time he holds my waist tight as I scoot closer to Alistair, my arms draped around his shoulders like ornaments on a tree.

This moment couldn't be more perfect.

Our embrace continues as we sink into one another, flopping back down on the bed as the kissing ramps up. The TV blares, the cars outside honk, and the chatter of pedestrians outside drown each other out in a mutual cacophony of sound.

I've never felt more wanted in my entire life.

No, loved.

I've never felt more loved in my entire life.

TWENTY-FOUR
Alistair

The next morning, Samantha and I head to the *Duplass*'s lobby for breakfast. The complimentary meal consists of bread, ham and cheese, some espresso served from an old coffee machine. It's good enough for us, and Samatha and I gather our plates and cups as we sit down at a secluded table on the opposite end of the lobby. Nobody'll overhear our conversation, not if we don't want them to. And besides, Sam and I have business to get down to.

I take a bite of bread, layering it with some Spanish ham and Iberico cheese.

"So, today's the day, huh?" I ask. Sam nods, her voice just barely above a low whisper.

"Yup. Today we're going to the Alcala-Metro Prison Complex, just a few blocks away from the US Embassy. You ready?"

I nod. "I've been practicing my lines in the mirror every chance I get."

Sam grins, takes a bite of cheese. "Good. You're going to have to stick to the script I gave you, only go off-topic if Randall Friendly does, too. He's Terrence Malstrom's right-hand man. He's going to have some tricks up his sleeve if you're not prepared for him."

"Don't worry, I am. What if Randall isn't there, what if he isn't available or they're already locked him up?"

"Then we move on to finding the safe house," Samantha says. "We have the neighborhood we're pretty sure Alan disappeared in, but Friendly can give us explicit confirmation. Plus, if you manage to find the address of the safe-house…"

"It's a win-win," I say, finishing her sentence. "I just wish you could come in there with me."

Samantha shakes her head. "No way. There could be American governmental agents in there; they may recognize me if I pop my head into the biggest prison in Madrid."

"They'll recognize me, too, though." I mean, come on, Sam. You think they'd recognize a CIA field agent, but *not* the billionaire CEO of Pemberton Computers? No way, José.

"They might," Sam concedes. "But they'll still let you in if you just stick to the script. It can't *not* work. Trust me, we've got this in the bag."

I nod, finishing the last bite of bread and cheese I've still got left on my plate. I wash it down with the last of my espresso, and I give Sam a determined nod when I'm finished. "So, when do we start?"

The Alcala-Metro Prison Complex is one intimidating building, I'll give it that. It's a giant concrete box, made to look as grey and menacing as possible. In my gut, I know that anyone who gets locked up here probably doesn't have much hope in getting out. But we're not here to spring this Friendly guy out.

We're here for information. Information that only Friendly can give us.

I grip the briefcase in my left hand tight, it's the only prop I'm going to need in my endeavor. Well, that, and a safety net. And speaking of…

I reach into my jacket breast pocket, pull out Samantha's cell phone as I rack my brain to remember the password she'd given me. I blink, scattering my thoughts as I leave the screen powered-off and lift the phone up to my face.

"Jellybeans," I mumble the password into the phone, putting it back in my pocket a moment later.

Let's just hope this works, or else we're really fucked here.

I collect myself, taking a deep breath as I head inside.

◆ ◆ ◆

The inside lobby of the prison complex looks like a courtroom, with darkened-oak columns extending up into the ceiling and a massive wood-grain counter that police offers work behind. They're scattering to and fro, coming in and filing papers before leaving out the door just behind the front desk. I approach the counter, briefcase in hand as I clear my throat for a police officer's attention.

"How can I help you, sir?" one officer asks me, a woman no older than Samantha. Her dark hair is tied up in a bun, and her uniform is clean and pressed, looking snazzier than her co-workers in that regard. I see the same look of determination that Sam usually wears, and I know this cop can smell through any bullshit I try to peddle her.

Well, here goes nothing.

"Yes, you may," I reply. "I'm here for Randall Friendly. American. I'm his lawyer. Just got in through our embassy."

The officer nods. "Here to see your client, then?"

I nod back. "That's correct."

"Name, please?"

"I just gave you his name."

"No, sir, I mean yours."

"Oh, right." I chuckle faintly, my nervousness already seeping through. I'm not Samantha Jacobson, I'm not apt to lie to officers of the state when it's for my own personal gain. But I know this is important to Sam, and I'm the only one who can pull this lawyer game off convincingly enough. "My name is

Alistair Jensen."

The officer pauses as she walks over to a computer sitting behind the front desk, and she plugs in my information, clacking away at the keyboard. The officer—I see *Cortez* printed on her name tag—pulls up some page and reads it over, looking back and forth between me and my computer.

"Mr…Jensen, you said?"

I nod. "Am I not in the system?" I already know the answer, of course, and I know this is where Sam's plan comes into play.

Officer Cortez sighs, shaking her head. "I'm afraid I won't be able to let you in, we don't have any contact or confirmation of your visit from the US Embassy."

I put on my best stern face I can. "Try calling them, please. Here. I have my office secretary's number, you can call her directly. She'll sort this mess out."

Officer Cortez stares at me blankly. "You got a card or something?"

I reach into my breast pocket, the same one housing Sam's cell phone, and I pull out the phony business card we'd printed just a few days prior. "Here," I say, handing Officer Cortez the card. "Try this. See if this clears things up."

Officer Cortez grabs a desk phone from under the counter, putting it in front of her as she dials the number on the card. Of course, what she *doesn't* know is who's going to answer.

Officer Cortez calls the number, and Samantha picks up on the other line, the number going directly to our hotel room in the *Duplass*.

"Yes, this is Officer Cortez of the—yes. Yes, he's right here, in front of me. No. It's not in my system, but we can—Oh. Sure. No, no, that works just fine. *Gracias, que tenga buen día.*"

Officer Cortez hangs up, looks over at me from across the counter.

"Looks like your secretary cleared everything up just fine," she says. "I didn't know we had an international businessman in our midst, my sincerest apologies. Follow me. I'll take you to Friendly's cell, you can talk to him there."

I grin sheepishly as I follow Officer Cortez, who steps out from behind the front counter and leads me through a set of double-doors just beyond the desk.

◆ ◆ ◆

Officer Cortez leads me past rows and rows of jail cells, men behind bars, some women locked up in cells. We pass by a few interrogation rooms, I can see the metal doors leading to the isolated rooms as well as other adjacent rooms featuring one-way mirrors to peer inside. I know we're going to be watched when I confront Randall Friendly. But there's no escaping that, and it's not like we're going to try to bust him out of incarceration. That's not why I'm here, and that's not the primary objective of our mission to begin with.

The Officer takes me past one interrogation cell, leading me into the adjacent room with a handful of other officers and a few men and women in suits. They look American to me, and their faces light up when I enter the room. The Spanish police officers remain seated, but one of the Americans in a suit—a young man, no older than twenty—rushes up to shake my hand.

"Alistair Jensen," the young man in the Pinkerton-grey suit beams. "I never thought I'd see someone like you *here.* And forgive me for being so forward, I'm just a huge fan of Pemberton's latest model on—"

"I suppose that makes two of us," I grin heartily, playing the situation out as best I can. Sam and I never prepared for this, but we've got countermeasures in place in case anyone starts asking questions.

"When did you become a lawyer?" the young man in the suit asks.

Questions *exactly* like that one.

"You know my net worth?" I ask. The young man nods.

"Then you'll know law school isn't putting me in debt," I chuckle. The young man looks like I'd just given him the meaning to life, and he sits back down next to the other Americans in grey suits. "What are you all doing here?" I ask.

The young man in the suit chimes in: " We were observing Friendly here, taking notes. Another officer just got done asking him some questions, too. You just happened to show up at the right time."

"Well, we're going to get privacy in there, right?" I turn to Officer Cortez, who responds to my question with a nod and a wink.

"Of course, sir," she replies, sparing a glance at the other officers and Americans in the room. They all snicker, and I know they don't *actually* intend to give us any privacy. No matter. I'm going to have to be quick about this either way.

"Can I go in, then?"

Officer Cortez nods. "I'll show you to the door," she says.

Randall Friendly sits peacefully inside the isolation room, hands clasped on top of a stainless-steel table his wrists are shackled to. His ankles are cuffed as well, and the right-hand-man to Terrence Malstrom spins about as Officer Cortez pushes open the heavy metal door.

"Randall? I'm Alistair Jensen, your lawyer."

Randall cocks an eyebrow. A lanky young man, he's scrawnier than I could have imagined him being. I expected him to be tall, muscular, threatening. Not this scrawny ruffled-hair kid I see in front of me. He's staring up at me with contempt, and I notice that he's probably younger than Samantha, even. "I didn't ask for any lawyer," he says, clearly confused.

"No, you didn't," I reply. "You know who I am?"

Randall shakes his head.

"I'm a billionaire," I tell him. "CEO of Pemberton Computers, you've probably heard of us. I took a personal interest in your case, and I wanted to come talk to you. Get some more information. That okay with you?"

Randall gestures to the metal chair across from him. "Take a seat," he says. "I ain't going anywhere."

I nod, obliging the prisoner as I sit down across from him, putting my briefcase down on the floor next to me. "So, anything you want to say to Officer Cortez before she leaves?" I ask, nodding at the officer standing behind Randall.

Randall turns around again. "Nah, she's good," he says. "Time for her to leave. Bye-bye, Officer Cortez," he says playfully, waving his fingers for childish emphasis.

Officer Cortez shoots me a look, *good luck,* it says. She rolls her eyes, pushing open the heavy metal door as she steps back outside.

Now we're alone. Time to get down to business.

I reach down, pulling up my briefcase as I set it down on the table between us.

"Hey, wait a second…" the prisoner says, trailing off. "I *do* recognize you! You're that businessman on TV that's always trying to sell me a new monitor—"

"Yeah. Glad you remembered," I say flatly. "That's not why I'm here, though. Like I said, I took a personal interest in your case. I'm here to get some more information before we can talk about extradition."

"Extradition? Like, sending me back home?"

"Yes. For a trial, but you'll be back home. That's correct."

I half-expected Randall to shut down, but instead he breathes a sigh of relief. "Okay, whatever you want to know, then. I'm done with Terrence, he's told me to fuck off one too many times. So here I am, asshole. Fucking off. You tell me what the government wants to know, and I'll help."

Of course, the US government doesn't know I'm here. They aren't sponsoring this, all of this is just an act. One that I'm terrified to blow my cover on.

"Okay," I say, thumbing open the latches on the briefcase and removing a stack of manilla file folders. "You tell me what I want to hear, I take this back stateside. Show it to a judge. See if we can get you on a plane back home."

All lies. But it's necessary, and I spare a nervous glance over to the one-way mirror. I know we're being watched, and I have to watch my step so we don't get caught in the middle of our daring operation. We've come too far for me to blow it now.

"I told the feds here everything I had on Terry. Why not get the information from them, save us all the headache?"

"Because I need to hear these things from *you,*" I say, lying through my teeth.

He sighs, exasperated. "What do you want to know, then?" Friendly asks, throwing his cuffed hands up for reference. "I'm *literally* a prisoner here."

I thumb open one of the manilla file folders, find a blank piece of paper as I click a pen, ready to write.

"You'd be prepared to testify against Terrence Malstrom in open court?"

"Yes," Randall replies.

Good. I'd be worried what to do if he said he wasn't, but Sam and I prepared for the former. It's common knowledge in the CIA that Malstrom's regime is crumbling overseas, this is just a disgruntled ex-employee eager to rat out his former boss. And we're going to run with that, because it's our only hope in finding Malstrom, and by extension, Samantha's missing supervisor.

"What would you say your relation to Terrence is?"

"I'm...I *was* his second in command," Randall says. "Not anymore. Like I said, I'll roll on him. No problem."

"You can give a federal judge insight as to what Terrence Malstrom was doing back in the US?"

"Yeah, all that. Crimes here, crimes there. Anywhere. I don't care."

"Okay," I reply. "We just want to clarify a few details. Can you do that for me?"

Randall nods. "What do you want from me?"

"We want this entire operation laid out. Any crimes that we may not have known about, any safe houses, anything at all. You know about his safe houses scattered around Europe? We'll start there."

Randall nods. "Oh yeah, he's a paranoid fuck. He's got a safe-house just a few hours away from here, one that I'm sure is still up-and-running."

"You think he's there, now?"

"Shit if I know," he says. "All I know is the feds didn't raid it when we got caught. I got brought in on some flimsy trumped-up charges. I don't think the feds found his house in Spain just yet."

"Where is it?"

"Just outside of Toledo," he says. "What, you want the ad-dress or something?"

I stare at him blankly. "Yes."

"Okay, fine. Give me a pen and paper, I'll write it down."

I slide the pen over to Friendly, a blank sheet of paper as well. He takes the pen, his shackled hands joined together as he strug-gles to write out the address to Malstrom's safe house.

"There," he says, sliding the paper back over to me. "Check that place out. I doubt your friends here checked it out."

I nod, folding the paper up as I stuff it into my breast pocket. "We'll be in touch, then. This is enough to start with for right now."

"You're going to get me out of here?"

I stand up, shutting my briefcase after stuffing the folders back inside. I grip my briefcase, prepared to give the fattest lie so far.

"Of course," I tell Randall. "I'm going to do everything I can to make this right."

And with that, I turn on my heel and knock on the metal door, eyeing the one-way mirror to my left. A moment later, the heavy door swings back as Officer Cortez escorts me outside.

"Got what you needed, then?" the officer asks. I nod in reply, making sure the sheet of paper in my breast pocket never leaves its place.

"I sure did," I tell the officer. "And I'd like to thank all of you for your hospitality. Really. I best be getting back to the embassy, I'm waiting for some correspondence back stateside."

Officer Cortez smiles politely. "I'll show you the way out, then."

◆ ◆ ◆

I step outside the prison complex gripping my briefcase tight. I was a nervous wreck in there, I can tell, and I worry I've just jeopardized the entire operation for Samantha before we've truly begun.

I reach into my breast pocket when I'm far enough away from the jail, and I inspect what Randall Friendly had written down for me.

It's just an address, one that I hope is real. 720 Avenida Marbella, planted in the suburbs just squarely outside Toledo. Looks like Sam was right about Malstrom's safe house. We just have to hope someone's there to give us some answers.

I reach back into the same breast pocket, pulling out Samantha's phone. Before I utter the password again, I give a short testimony to the device recording my every sound.

"This is Alistair," I say into the phone's receiver. "I've just left the Alcala-Metro Complex, having met with Randall Friendly. He gave me this address in relation to Terrence Malstrom's safe house: 720 Avenida Marbella. Signing off."

I clear my throat, utter the passcode to shut down the recording. "Jellybeans," I say into the mic.

I flick Samantha's phone on, type in her password she'd given me before.

I boot up the app she'd told me to check, *Recorder.* The app used the 'Jellybeans' passcode as a silent trigger to start a recording, and I see there's a twenty-five minute file that's just finished encoding.

I've recorded the entire testimony in secret.

I smile, shutting Samantha's phone down as I put it back into my pocket, heading out to the crowded Madrid sidewalk to catch a cab back to the hotel.

TWENTY-FIVE
Samantha

I'm a nervous wreck. No, scratch that—I'm utterly *terrified*. As I sit on the bed we'd rented in the *Duplass,* I feel like I'm on the verge of a complete nervous breakdown.

It's been half an hour since Alistair left for the Alcala-Metro Prison Complex, and I'm terrified I've just sent him to his doom. Asking Alistair to play lawyer like that could've really messed things up for us, but something in my gut tells me he's going to come through for us all the same.

Tracy sent me the *Recorder* app to spy on Alistair, and now we're using it together to spy on someone else. Ironic.

I scroll endlessly through the Spanish TV channels, never staying on one long enough to form an opinion. I scroll past cartoons, international house hunters, makeup and makeover shows, the works. Nothing is even remotely entertaining, and I feel the weight of each passing second as I nervously wait for Alistair to come back to the hotel.

An indiscriminate amount of time passes. I feel like I'm going mad here.

And then I hear a knock at the door.

I jump up out of bed, run to the hotel room door and fling it open. Alistair is standing out in the hallway, grinning from ear to ear.

I sigh, exasperated. "You know you don't have to knock, right? I mean, you paid for the room, after all."

Alistair shrugs, still grinning like a madman. "I know. I just thought you needed some rest. I didn't want to disturb you."

I hold the door open for him. "Come on in, I'm excited to hear about how it went."

"I think it went great," Alistair says as I close the door behind him. He sits down on the bed, kicking off his shoes. "Friendly gave me everything we needed and more."

"The recording work?"

He nods. "Took me a minute to remember the passcode, but yeah. I got it all down here." He reaches into his pocket, pulls out my cell phone as he hands it over to me. I flick it on, typing in the numeric password as I scroll to the *Recorder* app. I fire it on, checking the most recent recording. Sure enough, there's a twenty-five minute audio recording, geotagged at the Alcala-Metro Prison Complex.

I look up from my phone, beaming at Alistair.

"You did it," I say. He chuckles.

"Was there any doubt?"

No, there wasn't. But I still couldn't help my nervousness. Now that Alistair's back, safe and sound, I never want to send him out there alone again.

"And he wrote *this* down for me," Alistair says, reaching into his suit's breast pocket and fishing out a folded sheet of paper. He hands the paper to me, and I unfold it and read the address printed on top of it.

"You think he was telling the truth?" I ask.

Alistair shrugs. "I didn't see any reason for him to lie," he replies.

I nod, heading over to my suitcase as I dig through its contents. I fish out my headphones, a notebook, and a pen. I sit down on the bed next to Alistair, plugging my headphones in as I fire up the recording from the prison. I look up at Alistair.

"I'm going to transcribe the recording," I tell him. "This might take a minute, but it'll save our asses from going to court when this is all over. He admitted the address to you, right?"

"Yeah," Alistair says. "I didn't beat him up or anything. I made some fake promises, sure, but that isn't illegal, right?"

I smile. "Sure isn't. I'm going to get started on writing this out. We'll regroup in a little bit when I've got this done, okay?"

The billionaire sitting next to me on the bed smiles. "Sure. I'll go get a bite to eat. Want anything?"

I smile, shaking my head. "I'm good, but thanks."

Alistair hops up from the bed, putting his shoes back on. "I'll be back in a little bit, then."

He leaves the hotel room and I press *play* on the recording, getting ready to write down everything I hear.

◆ ◆ ◆

Half-an hour or so later, I hear the hotel door opening again as Alistair re-emerges into the room, a baguette ham-sandwich in hand as he munches on it. He tosses a second on the bed, which I snatch up and begin tearing into.

"How's it going?" he hollers as he enters.

I look up from my notebook, just having finished transcribing the interview he'd conducted with Friendly. "Just finished," I beam. "How was lunch?"

"Good enough," Alistair says. "Tell me what you found. If I missed anything back there."

I shake my head. "You did perfectly," I smile. "I couldn't have asked for a better lawyer impersonation if I paid an actor to do it myself."

"You looked into the address at all?"

I nod. "I pulled it up on some online maps. 720 Marbella is a real address just outside of Toledo. I guess we're going to have to pop by, pay them a visit."

"When?" Alistair asks.

I shrug. "Why not right now? Nothing's stopping us."

Alistair grins. "I'll call my driver, then. See if he managed to find us a car by now."

I feel myself holding my breath as Alistair calls Kennedy,

checking in with his driver. The conversation is short, brief, and Alistair smiles as he hangs up the phone.

"What's the news?"

"He's found a car," Alistair grins. "I knew he'd come through for us. He said he can be here in fifteen minutes. I told him we'll be ready by then."

"Let's get ready, then. We haven't got long."

Not even fifteen minutes later, Alistair gets a notification on his phone: Kennedy, his bearded and face-tattooed driver, is ready and waiting outside with an SUV as soon as we're ready to go. Alistair and I throw a bag together, tossing in our cell phones, a change of clothes in case we get stuck outside of town, some food for emergencies. Chargers, pens, notebooks. The works.

We head out of the hotel room and take the elevator downstairs, heading out the front doors of the *Duplass* as we look around for Kennedy's jet-black SUV he's rented.

And the car's parked right in front of the doors, the hazard lights blinking as Kennedy waits next to the car, grinning like a madman.

Alistair hands Kennedy his bag, pats his young driver on the shoulder. "I knew you could do it," he says as Kennedy beams. The driver loads our bags in the trunk, and we hop into the back seat as Kennedy gets behind the wheel.

"So, Toledo?" he leans back, his finger hovering over the GPS's buttons.

I nod, handing him the sheet of paper that Alistair'd given me. "We're going here," I tell him as he reads the address. "Avenida Marbella. Think you can get us there?"

Kennedy nods, punching the address into his GPS. "Says we should be there in a few hours," he leans back again. "I assume that's what *horas* means. I don't speak Spanish."

I nod, leaning back in my seat as I look over to Alistair. He nods, too, and we're all in agreement, then.

"Take us there," I tell the driver. "As quick as you can. We should make it there by sundown."

"You got it," Kennedy says.

He checks his shoulder and rear-view mirrors, signaling he's going to pull into traffic. A moment later, he does so, and we're on the road once again.

◆ ◆ ◆

The road to Toledo is long and dull, and I watch out Kennedy's SUV windows as the Madrid cityscape fades into brown, open fields surrounded by plantations and barnyards. It's funny, the USA looks *just* like this outside the major cities. I never thought we'd have all that much in common with Europe, but I figure everywhere really isn't that different from back home, when you get down to brass tacks. I'm already bored out of my mind, I've tried everything to alleviate it. I've tried doodling in the notebook I brought for field notes, I've tried to keep myself as busy as possible. But I *know* I should've brought a book with me.

Alistair's doing enough to keep himself entertained; he's staring out the window, taking in the Spanish countryside as he watches the countryside fly by in a blur.

"Hey," I say to Alistair, and he turns to face me, a warm smile stretched across his face.

"What's up?"

"I'm glad you came with me. This trip wouldn't have gone nearly as smooth without you."

"Hey, anything to help. Plus it'll help me sleep better at night, knowing I didn't send a pregnant woman to a jail in Madrid, asking for information. Too risky for you. I'm glad to share at least *some* of the burden here."

I beam. "You're too kind, Alistair."

"Only for you," he grins.

"So, nervous?"

"A little," Alistair replies. "Honestly, I'd never been more nervous in my entire life than I was back in that prison today. Really. Everything could have gone wrong back there, I could've been thrown into jail myself for impersonating a lawyer like that. What's going to happen when this is all over?"

I smile. "We go back to reality," I tell him snapping my fingers for emphasis. "Just like that. It'll be hard, sure, but that's what you get when you work out in the field."

"And the baby? What about them?"

"We'll cross that bridge when we get there," I say, looking down at my stomach. I've been pregnant—I've *known* I was pregnant—for the better part of a month. I'm not starting to show at the moment, but I know it's inevitable. It'll happen soon, and I hope we're back stateside by the time my belly starts expanding for real.

"As long as we cross the bridge together," Alistair says quietly. I smile at him as he looks back out the window, and I gaze past him. I see farmyards, barns, fenced-in corrals of horses and cows. Alistair looks back over to me. "I was starting to get worried back there. About what we want to do when this is over."

"With me, you'll never have to worry," I tell him.

He smiles, leans over and kisses me, a quick peck on the lips.

But the gesture still warms me up inside, and I feel truly accepted for the first time in a long time.

The road to Toledo stretches on endlessly ahead, and I feel myself growing more nervous with each passing second.

We're coming, Alan. Just hang on a little while longer.

I just hope this works.

I can see the historical walls of the ancient city up ahead, and Kennedy leans back in his seat to get our attention.

"Looks like we're here, guys," he says from the front. Alistair and I lean up, staring out the front windshield as we admire the old city for ourselves.

The ancient city is made up of grey-and-brown bricks, signifying the old age of the city. I don't know much about Spanish history, but I know Toledo used to be the capital. And this city looks like it was built for a king; a castle on a hill, surrounded by ancient walls and a city big enough for a large population.

It's amazing here, and I wish Alistair and I were here for personal reasons instead of my hare-brained schemes. It'd make for one heck of a vacation destination. We'd probably have a great time exploring Spain and its countryside, and I secretly pray that Alistair and I can make this experiment last between us when we get home. There's nobody else I'd love to go on vacation with besides him.

"How far out to Marbella Avenue?" I ask Kennedy, and the driver inspects his GPS as he stops at an intersection.

"T-minus ten minutes," he calls out from up front. "We'll be there sooner than you think. Roads out here are pretty empty."

"Don't park right in front of the safe house," I tell Kennedy. "Park us a block and a half or so away. We'll walk to the house from there."

Alistair leans up from the backseat, getting in a word with Kennedy. "You got your phone on you, right?"

"Of course, boss."

"Good. Keep it on you at all times. If I call you for any reason, pick up instantly. Don't say anything until I say something, just in case someone takes my phone. Okay?"

"You got it, Alistair," Kennedy says. I feel like we're entrusting too much to Kennedy at this point, but what other choice do we have? I know Alistair's ready to improvise, and just in case we get trapped in a pinch, we'll have Kennedy to call to bail us out. Or if we need to prove a point, sell a lie, then Kennedy can handle that, too.

Let's just hope it never comes to that.

Kennedy pulls the SUV around a corner, and we're suddenly in an old Toledo neighborhood, not dissimilar to the suburbia you'd find back home in the good old US of A. The houses are all terra-cotta beige, and they look like they've been copied and pasted over and over, each house on the block looking exactly identical to the one that came before it. I see a street sign just up ahead, and Kennedy pulls right into the Avenida Marbella, Marbella Avenue.

We watch as the numbers on the houses tick up. There's 415, 445, 495. A block up, we see the numbers skip up to the six-hundreds. 610, 650, 685.

And then we see the house, just up ahead. The number's printed on the mailbox, house number 720 is just a few car lengths away. There's a truck in the driveway, a vehicle that's oddly familiar to me. Kennedy stops the car when we tell him to, and he backs up as he aligns the car with one of the neighbor's front yards, keeping us within walking distance of the alleged safe house.

Kennedy stops the car, shutting down the engine as he looks back at us.

"We're here."

Alistair and I nod, and we hop out of the car, keeping our bags in the back seat and the trunk. We're only going to need ourselves at this point, and our plan's simple enough: we're going to knock on the front door and see where we go from there. That's it. Simple enough, right? There's a lot of room for something to go wrong, but with my experience as a field agent and Alistair's uncanny ability to improvise, I believe we're going to be just fine.

Alistair and I approach House 720. It looks just like all the other houses on the block, the only difference being this one is the one we're looking for. That, and there's a familiar-looking car in the driveway. It's an old rusted red pickup truck, a car that isn't unlike what my supervisor Alan drives back home. Maybe it's his, maybe he rented it while he was out on assignment. Whatever the reason, I know the red pickup truck's the sign we need to know that this is the place we've been searching for.

Alistair and I walk up the length of the driveway, bracing ourselves for anything that might come our way.

The front door is standard; a silver-plated bull with a massive nose-ring is shaped and placed in the center of the door, serving as a knocker.

Alistair shoots me a look, and I return with a nod.

Here goes nothing.

I reach out, grabbing the knocker as I pound it against the door. After that, everything goes silent. My world fades around me, and all that's important to me at the moment is who's going to answer that door.

And then it swings open.

A tired, disheveled man answers the door. His beard has gone white, his hair ruffled and matted. I'm terrified someone might be hiding somewhere, poised and ready with a gun. But I'd recognize that face anywhere, and I gasp when I finally piece together the familiar face that's just opened the door for us.

It's Alan. He's tired, disheveled, and he looks like he's worn out beyond belief.

And he's standing right in front of me.

TWENTY-SIX
Alistair

I watch as Sam gasps in horror at the face that's just opened the door for us. It takes me a moment, but I recognize the beard and those dead, tired eyes from the briefing folder Sam's shown me before.

"Alan?" Samantha gasps. The man standing in the doorway nods sadly, and I feel a twinge in my gut telling me that something's wrong.

"Alan, what are you doing here?" Sam asks, but she shakes her head before her former supervisor's had a chance to answer. "Doesn't matter. We need to get you out of here. Come with us, Alan, we've got a car—"

I see a glint of silver brushing past Alan's shoulder, and Sam's words go cold when she sees it, too.

It's a hand, not belonging to Alan. And it's holding a gun.

A familiar hiss slithers out from behind the former supervisor, a voice I'd heard before on the evening news countless times.

"So, you came to save your friend, huh? How noble."

And then Terrence Malstrom slithers out, stepping past Alan as he stands in the doorway. His face is etched in a permanent sneer, a scowl always spread across his scarred lips. His usually long white hair is buzzed short, possibly to avoid detection by lawmakers and police forces.

Terrence grips the gun tighter, keeping it held aloft for all to see.

And just like that, I know we're fucked.

Terrence waves the gun at us, gesturing for us to step inside.

"Why don't we all settle in, get comfortable? We'll have time for introductions inside. Come on, I don't want the neighbors watching your brains get blown out on the sidewalk."

Samantha shoots me a nervous glance, and I know she never accounted for anything like this happening to us. She looks back at Terrence, nervously nodding as she steps inside, following closely behind Alan as he retreats back into the house. Malstrom shoots me a wicked smile, and I'm sure he recognizes me, too. He waves the gun at me, and I step inside the house after them. I don't have any other choice, it looks like.

Yeah. We're so fucked.

Alan leads us into a sitting room, and Terrence scuttles into a nearby kitchenette, grabbing two more folding chairs from behind a kitchen table. The house is dark, musky. The old floral wallpaper is peeling, and I can see the windows on either side of the house are dusty and grimy after years of neglect. There's a wooden doorway leading out into a backyard, a short flight of stairs leading to a second floor above us. Alan sits down in a folding chair in the middle of the living room, and Terrence follows closely behind, setting the two chairs on opposite sides of Alan like ducks in a row.

"Go on, sit," he croons. Samantha shoots me another nervous glance, and I return the gesture as we sit down on opposite sides of Alan, lined up perfectly for this asshole as he waves the gun in our faces. He grabs a roll of duct tape, wrapping it around the three of us individually, strapping us to the chairs we're now trapped in.

"So, what are *we* doing here?" Malstrom sneers as he tosses the roll of tape aside, waving his gun around the room again.

Samantha looks over at me with wide eyes, and I know she's drawing a blank on what bullshit to feed him.

I clear my throat, and the man with the gun stares me down intensely as I begin to speak.

"We're here for him," I nod over to the man sitting on my right. I look over at him. "I don't believe we've been introduced. I'm Alistair," I say to Alan. The former supervisor stares past me, his dead eyes and blank stare leaving me nothing to work with.

Terrence laughs. "You came back for him? How rich. Tell them, Alan."

Alan looks over at Samantha, sitting to his right. "I don't want to leave, Samantha. Mr. Malstrom is taking good care of me here, honest."

Sam looks up at Terrence with disdain. "How about he tells us how he *really* feels, when you're not pointing a gun at us?"

He laughs again. "And where would be the fun in that? I've been holed up here for weeks, waiting for my pal Randall to come back to me. First your friend showed up, Mr. Alan here. We've had a pretty good time together, haven't we?"

Alan nods glumly, staring down at the floor as I feel my heart breaking for Samantha. It's probably killing her, seeing her old boss like this. I know it's not ideal, but I feel a twinge of celebration wash over me.

We found her supervisor when everybody else told Samantha it'd be impossible.

We succeeded.

We just have to live long enough to see that victory through to the end.

And I've got a plan.

"So, I suppose there's no way in hell you're going to let us go, then?" I ask. Malstrom cackles, shaking his head.

"Why would I? Now that I've got three friends to keep me company, I bet we're going to have a good time. We just have to wait for Randall Friendly, of all people. When he's back, we should be good to go."

I realize that Terrence probably doesn't know the status—or

the current whereabouts—of his former right-hand man. And I know that's something to work with.

"Who's that? Randall Friendly?"

Malstrom sneers. "He's just the most important figure in this entire operation. He's the man who's cooked my books, the guy with all the money in the operation. And he's missing. So we're going to wait for him until we find out what the *fuck* is going on."

I take a deep breath, sending out a silent prayer to whatever God might be listening in.

"Your partner, Randall?" I ask. Terrence nods. "I saw him. Today, actually."

"Bullshit."

"How else do you think we got here? He sent us here."

"Like hell he did. Why wouldn't he come with you, then?"

"Because he's locked up in Madrid," I reply flatly. "And that's the truth. Accept it or not, you're going to see your friend on the national news one of these nights when they finally try to press charges."

Malstrom scoffs, lowering his gun. "I don't believe you," he says matter-of-factly. "So there. What other lies are you going to try and feed me?"

"That's it," I tell him. "And it wasn't a lie. Hell, you can swing up to Madrid, check in on this Friendly guy for yourself if you want. He's in the Alcala-Metro Prison Complex, just a few blocks away from the US Embassy. Trust me, he's there."

"Prove it," the man with the gun says.

I nod at Samantha, and her eyes light up.

"I've got a recording," Sam says. "It's in my pocket. You'll have to take this tape off, but I can walk you through the steps. You'll hear his voice, see today's date. Trust me, it'll put every-thing at ease."

Terrence Malstrom ponders this for a moment, scratching his chin with the barrel of his gun. He weight his options, tap-ping his foot for emphasis.

"Fine," he says. "Let me go get a knife. And no funny business while I'm gone, got it?"

Samantha and I nod as Alan sits there blankly. The man with the gun wheels around, racing upstairs as quick as he can. When we hear a door upstairs open and shut, Samantha turns to face her former supervisor.

"Alan, we have to get you out of here, don't you see—"

"What are you doing here, Samantha?" he asks, staring blankly at the floor. His voice is hoarse, tired. He sounds drained, used-up and rolled-out like an old tube of toothpaste. I can tell he's defeated, just by the sound of his voice alone.

"I—*We* came here to rescue you," Samantha hisses. "I thought you'd be a little more grateful than that."

Alan shrugs, and he keep staring down at the floor.

A moment later, we hear a door slam shut upstairs as Terrence makes his way back down to us on the ground floor, a massive butcher knife in his hand.

"It's all I've got," Terrence mutters as he walks around behind Samantha. "Now, don't move. Otherwise the blade might slip. And we wouldn't want that, would we?"

Sam shakes her head gingerly. Malstrom brings the knife down, cutting into the tape that's kept her glued to her chair. He works the knife down, searing the rolls and rolls of duct tape as he works Samantha free.

And then in an instant, the tape flies off, falling to the ground unceremoniously. Samantha looks at me with wide eyes, and I know she's about to try something stupid.

Don't do it, I think. I try to send her the message telepathically, but something tells me that's not going to work. *Don't do it, Samantha.*

She's free. Samantha stretches out her arms, rubbing them to try and alleviate some of the pain that she'd been feeling after being strapped to chair. She pulls her phone out of her pocket, hands it over to Terrence Malstrom.

"Don't forget to have him boot up *Locater* first," I tell Sam, raising my eyebrows at her. "He'll have to use that to login to the mainframe first. Then you can show him the *Recorder* app you've got installed."

She nods, taking the hint as Terrence takes the phone from her. "He's right," Samantha says. "There's a process to logging in, and—"

"How stupid do you think I am?" he sneers, cutting her off. He shoots a dirty look at me. "*Fire up the* Locater *app?* So the feds can track us here? No fucking way. Show me how to get around it."

I shake my head. "They aren't going to track our location with that app," I tell him, lying through my teeth. I have to think fast to keep Samantha safe, and by extension, her supervisor. If we came all this way for him, I'm not going to let Terrence hurt him. "If the CIA really *did* track all its operatives, wouldn't they have come for Alan already?" I say, nodding to the hostage on my right.

Terrence pauses, holding Samantha's phone in his hands as he considers his options. He can believe us, go for the bait. Or he can freak out, throw Samantha's phone aside as he decides to kill us all.

It's just the four of us here. No guards, no goons with guns. Just us and him.

Easy enough, right?

"Fine," Malstrom says. "Show me how to use this. And no funny business," he says, shooting Samantha a dirty look.

"Okay," Sam says. "I'll just walk you through it. See the app on the home screen, *Locater?* Fire it up. You have to press the first button that says 'confirm location.' After that, you can back out, go over to the *Recorder* app. From there it'll show you everything you want to know."

"Easy enough," Terrence mumbles. He presses a few buttons on the phone's screen, tapping in and out of the menus Sam just walked him through.

If he's followed her directions, then the entire CIA knows that Samantha's checked in at her location. That, or the person who made the app knows. Either way, we aren't going to be mysterious blips on a radar—someone back home is going to know where we are now. And that can only be a good thing.

Terrence fires up the *Recorder* app, pressing a button on the screen as Randall Friendly's voice fills the room.

"All I know is the feds didn't raid it when we got caught. I got brought in on some flimsy trumped-up charges. I don't think the feds found his house in Spain just yet," and Terrence's eyes light up as he hears his friend's voice.

"Okay," Terrence says. "Now you've got my attention."

"You know I'm not trying to pull your leg, then, right?" I ask him. The man with the gun nods slowly.

"Good. Then listen closely to what I'm about to say. It's very important."

Terrence stares at me intently, hanging on my every word.

"Jellybeans," I say.

He cocks an eyebrow, perplexed.

"What?"

"You heard me," I say, sparing a nervous glance at Samantha. With any luck, *Recorder's* going to activate, recording every word that's said in this room from here on out. And we'll have all the evidence we need to nail Terrence Malstrom to the wall after we get out of here.

"Start talking," he growls, pulling his gun back up. "Or else shit's about to get real, fast."

I take a deep breath, stalling for as much time as I can.

"You're going to listen to what I have to say," I say slowly. "And then, when I've finished, you're going to untie us. And you're going to let the three of us walk out, unharmed."

Terrence cackles, the strongest laugh so far.

"We'll see about that," he says, cocking the gun. "How about this? You talk, and I decide when to blow your brains out. Deal?"

Gulp.

"Now, what were you saying?"

TWENTY-SEVEN
Samantha

It takes all my strength not to blurt out for Alistair to shut up, stop talking. I watch in horror as Alistair tries to bargain with Terrence Malstrom, the man who's held my supervisor here as a prisoner for weeks. I can't help but feel like we're going way off-script, but this was never in the plan to begin with. Honestly, I have no idea how we're going to get out of here. Seriously.

"Look," Alistair says. "We aren't sponsored by the CIA. We weren't sent here by the FBI. I can guarantee you nobody's missing us back home."

"Yeah? And why come here?" Terrence sneers.

I nod over at Alan. "We came back for him," I say. "That's it. It's a personal mission. Nobody put us up to it."

Malstrom sneers again, walking to the other corner of the room and picking up the roll of heavy-duty industrial tape. He walks around me, taping me to the chair once again as I sit, helpless.

"We aren't leaving here until we've got Alan here with us," Alistair continues. "We don't want you. We don't give a shit about you, in all honesty. We came for *him.*"

Terrence finishes taping me back up to my chair, severing the tape as he throws the roll aside once again. "And why would I believe you?"

"Because we're sitting here with a gun to our heads," Alistair says. "It'd be a real stupid time to start lying now. We've been nothing but honest with you since we got here, right?"

"Sure, if you want to call that *honesty*," Terrence says. "I call it bullshit. I think you've got a squad of cops waiting outside, ready to make their move as soon as I slip up."

I want to cut Alistair off, tell the man holding us hostage that he's got it all wrong, we only came here alone. But I know it'll just put us in more danger if he knows just how unprepared we were for this.

"The CIA is going to notice we're missing," Alistair says, wrapping his argument up. "And when they notice we're gone, they're going to come here. See where we went missing. If you don't let us go, there's just going to be more agents here, swarming your place before you've got a chance to even think about the future."

Terrence chuckles. "So, let me get this straight, then: you didn't come at the behest of the federal government. You came alone. No backup, no walkie-talkies on you from what I can tell. And you're telling *me* I have to let you go? How about this, instead—I kill all of you. And then I leave this place, find a new hiding spot while I wait for Randall. That all sound fair?"

No, it fucking doesn't. But I know Terrence Malstrom doesn't give a shit about what's really fair and what isn't.

It's all on us now.

And we're officially running out of time.

"You know who he is?" I ask Terrence, nodding at Alistair.

Terrence pauses for a moment, inspecting Alistair's face as he tries to piece together the celebrity he's got tied up in his living room. His eyes widen, and Malstrom starts to laugh.

"Holy shit, I can't *believe it!* We've got the next Bill Gates of the computer industry with us, Alistair Jensen! Jesus *fucking* Christ!" Terrence cackles, and that's when I know he's definitely heard of Alistair and his company before.

"You know how much money he has, then, right?" I continue.

He nods eagerly. "Oh boy, do I."

He walks over to Alistair, gets down on his haunches as he stares down the billionaire eye-to-eye.

"So, she's not bullshitting us? You're really *the* Alistair Jensen?"

Alistair looks up, and a gleam in his eyes flashes as he winks. "In the flesh," he grins.

Malstrom stands back up, hooting and hollering. "God *damn*, today's a good day! So, you must be rich enough for them to have an insurance policy *just* for you at Pemberton Computers, right?"

Alistair nods. "The works. Life insurance, hostage insurance —"

Terrence laughs. "You got an insurance plan for when someone like me puts a gun to your head? Oh, that's rich. Tell me about it."

Alistair nods, never skipping a beat. "Pemberton knows I'm valuable. And why wouldn't they? I'm the CEO. So yes, when someone such as yourself has me at gunpoint, the company has safeguards in place. We can discuss those figures, if you like."

He nods. "Oh, you better."

"Fine. The buyout's pretty big, I don't know how much it is. But we can call my agent, see what they're offering."

"Do it."

"You'll have to untape me, first. My phone's in my pocket, after all."

Malstrom groans, but picks up his butcher's knife again as he slashes the tape strapping Alistair to his chair. I see him rubbing his wrists, tender from the awkward position they'd been held in.

"Don't waste any of my time," Terrence growls. "Make the call. Fast."

Alistair doesn't hesitate, reaching into his suit jacket pocket as he fishes out his cell phone. He flicks the screen on, and I see him pressing a few buttons to pull up Kennedy's contact.

"Hurry up already," Terrence barks impatiently. Alistair hurries, dialing Kennedy's number and putting the phone on speaker.

"Yes, boss?" Kennedy picks up on the first ring. His voice is tinny, and the speakerphone's shitty quality makes it seem like Kennedy is much further away than he really is.

"Kennedy, I've got a gentleman here with me who's curious about the hostage insurance plan Pemberton Computers has out on me. Think you can walk him through it?"

"You got it, boss. They on speakerphone?"

"Yes, they can hear you."

"How's it going? I'm Kennedy, Mr. Jensen's personal assistant. I handle just about everything he needs me to handle—"

Terrence leans over Alistair's shoulder as I shoot a nervous glance over at Alan, who's still staring blankly down at the floor.

"Out with it," he blurts out, grabbing the phone out of Alistair's hands. "Tell me about the policy, or else you're going to have to cash it out early."

"You got it," Kennedy says, keeping his cool. Honestly, I'm seriously impressed with how well he's handling it so far. I guess we're about to see just how useful Kennedy really is. "It's a massive payout, four-point-five billion dollars. We can have it wire transferred to any bank account in the world of your choosing. No police, no international feds. You let our guy go, and the money's yours."

"So he doesn't need to come out with his friends, then?"

Kennedy has to think fast to get us out of here as well.

"Yes, actually, he does. The policy includes anyone else he might be held with. Alistair, are you alone there?" Kennedy asks, playing along with Terrence's game.

"No, I'm not alone," Alistair calls out.

"Well, there you go, then," Kennedy says. "He needs to be released with the other parties for us to consider wiring you the money."

"Why?"

"Because that's just how it is," Kennedy says. "And I'll have you know, too, this conversation *is* being recorded."

"I think you're full of shit," Terrence says. "What do you have to say about that?"

"Fine," Kennedy says. "Suit yourself."

And then Kennedy hangs up.

I feel my heart begin to race as Malstrom wheels around,

screaming into Alistair's face with a white-hot rage that makes me shake in my boots.

"What the *fuck were you thinking?*" he barks down at Alistair. "You realize what you've done?"

"My job," Alistair says flatly. "You heard our conditions. Now you get to choose. Because Pemberton Computers knows about you now. If myself or any of my compatriots here wind up dead, they're going to know who to blame. And they're going to know where that call came from."

"So, in other words, I kill you, I don't get the money?"

Alistair shakes his head, triumphant that he's just saved our collective asses.

"Well, you're going to have to do a lot better than that," Terrence says, cocking the gun in his hands for emphasis. "Because you're about to run out of time."

He puts the gun up to Alistair's head.

"You better start talking, billionaire," he says. "Otherwise it's about to get a hell of a lot messier in here. Fast."

Alistair closes his eyes as he thinks, and my mind begins to race as I consider all my options. I can try to wriggle out of the tape, burst out and get the gun from him. But I know that would take too long, he'd notice it before I'd be free enough to make a move.

And Alistair's run out of options, too. I can tell the life insurance policy was his last bet on us, and now we're really starting to run out of time.

"You've got five seconds to come up with a better plan," Terrence growls. "Or else I start blasting."

"Five…"

"Four…"

"Three…"

"Two…"

"One."

And then I hear a knock at the door.

Malstrom lowers the gun, sneering at Alistair as he holsters the weapon in his waistband.

"You sit tight," he says. "We wouldn't anything drastic to happen once I open the door, right?"

Alistair and I shake our heads. Alan stares down at the floor longingly.

Terrence stands back up and walks over to the front door. I can just barely make out what's going on up there; I can get only a brief glimpse at the front door.

He flings the door open.

And I see who's standing outside. I'd know that cheeky beard and forehead tattoo anywhere.

It's Kennedy.

TWENTY-EIGHT
Alistair

Holy shit. I can't believe my eyes.

My driver is trying to save us.

Kennedy is at the front door. I can see him from here, I can just barely catch a glimpse of the barbed-wire tattoo on his forehead. Terrence Malstrom holds the gun behind his back as he cranes his neck to see through the crack in the door.

"Yeah, what?" Terrence barks at Kennedy.

I can see my driver through the door's crack, I know he's feigning surprise just based on his tone alone.

"Yeah, I—I just wanted to —"

"Out with it already," he sneers.

"I live down the street," Kennedy lies. I feel my heart rate start to accelerate as I watch my driver lie to the man with the gun in the doorway. This can't be good. I'm terrified to know what's going to happen to us next, and I can't take my eyes away. "I heard some noise."

Kennedy catches a glance of me through the crook in Terrence arm, and his eyes widen as I nod for him to look back at the man in front of him. We don't want to blow our cover just yet, and Kennedy's walking on dangerously thin ice.

"You didn't hear any noise coming from here," Terrence says, and he starts to close the door on Kennedy.

"Wait—" Kennedy slides his foot in between the door and the frame, catching Terrence off guard. "I know the noise didn't come from here. I just wanted to come let you know it probably came from another house. I've called the police already, they're on their way. Just a heads up, okay, neighbor?"

"Fuck off," Malstrom barks. He kicks Kennedy's foot out from the doorway, slamming it shut in my driver's tatted face. He walks back into the room where we're held captive, pulling the gun out in front of him again.

"Now, where were we?" he asks playfully, thumbing the safety on his gun as he looks between Samantha, Alan and I with dangerous eyes. He raises the gun, pointing it directly at my forehead.

"Shame I wasn't getting any of that money," Terrence says. "I could've used it. Done some real good for the world. Oh, well. You know what they say—you can't always get what you want."

He presses the gun up against my forehead again.

"Might as well start cleaning up my mess," Terrence mutters.

I close my eyes, prepared for the worst.

We all tried our best. Sam, Kennedy and I did all we could.

But it wasn't enough. And that's just reality.

I count down the seconds, bracing myself for impact as I try to spend my last few moments thinking about Sam.

And how happy she's made me.

And how we could've had a good life together.

The cold metal pressed up against my forehead, I know this is it. This is the end.

And then I hear them.

They're faint, somewhere in the distance.

Sirens.

It's unmistakable.

I open my eyes hesitantly, sparing a glance over at Samantha and Alan. Alan's still doing his thing, staring at the floor with those dead eyes. Sam's eyes are wide as dinner plates, and she's looking out the windows to our left and right, looking around for a sign of the police that are apparently on their way. The man with the gun stands back up, peering out the windows to the front and backyards as he glances back at us with chagrin.

"Don't fucking move," he growls. He tucks the gun in his waistband, stepping out the front door as he slams it shut behind him.

And just like that, we're alone.

I look over at Sam, nervous and panicked. She's looking around the room, eyes darting to every surface and counter she can, trying to find an escape route. Anything to help us break free of these bonds, anything to help us escape while our captor's busy outside.

I start looking around the room, too, for any clear signs of an escape route. I see the butcher knife Malstrom used to cut us free, tossed aside to another corner of the living room. If I can pick myself up, scootch over there and lean over, I can grab the knife, use it to cut Sam free. Then we can get out of here.

I look over at Sam. *"Psst!"*

She looks over at me. Her eyes are still wide, I can tell she's in full-on panic mode. I nod over at the butcher knife, and her eyes dart in that direction. She looks back to me, nodding intently as she starts hopping in her seat.

I start hopping, too, and Samantha and I start inching our way across the living room. It's a good five, six feet over to the butcher knife, and we're going to have to move fast as lighting to get over there in time before Terrence comes back inside and sees us.

Just as Samantha and I are halfway to the butcher knife, I hear a knock at the window.

My heart races. Fuck.

I turn around slowly, looking out the window to the front yard, terrified it's our captor standing out there, watching our futile attempt at escape.

But the front window's empty.

I turn back around, peer out the backyard window.

Kennedy's standing outside, waving eagerly as he points at the door to our right. The backdoor.

I've never been so happy to see a face tattoo in my entire life.

I mouth *"unlocked"* to Kennedy as he looks over to the backdoor. A moment later he gets the hint. He scurries from the window, and a moment later, the back door opens wide as Kennedy stands in the doorway. He sees us tied up to the chairs, spies the butcher knife sitting on the floor in front of us. Kennedy dashes over, grabbing the knife as he cuts me free in an instant. He rushes over, cutting Samantha free a moment later. He hands Sam the knife, motions for her to free Alan as he rushes back over to me.

"You okay, boss?" he whispers as he places an arm on my shoulder. I rub my arms gingerly, getting the ache out of them after being sealed in place with duct tape for so long. I nod.

"We need to get the fuck out of here. *Now,*" he urges.

Kennedy looks back over to Sam, and she's nearly got Alan free of his bonds. Alan stands up after he's freed, looking back and forth between Kennedy, Sam and myself.

I look up at Alan. "You good?"

He nods, expressing some twinge of emotion for the first time since finding him.

"Kid with the tattoo's right," Alan says. "We need to move."

"Yeah, before that fucker finds out where I left my phone."

I cock an eyebrow, turning back to Kennedy. "What did you do?"

My driver with the barbed-wire face tattoo winks at me. "I used my phone, just like you told me, boss."

"What?"

Kennedy snickers. "I put on a video of sirens, put the phone under the windowsill. Come on, let's go. I'll get a replacement when we get stateside."

I can't fucking believe Kennedy did that. "Son, I'll buy you a replacement if we get out of here. Let's go."

Kennedy, Samantha and I look at Alan, who nods.

We run out the back door, ducking into our captor's backyard. It's sparse, with only dry crabgrass and a few shrubs doting the the fence separating the backyards between neighbors.

I nod over at the fence, and Kennedy scurries over to the fence as he hops on the shrubbery, getting ready to hoist us over the fence into the neighbor's backyard. Samantha and I shove Alan forward, and Kennedy helps hoist the old supervisor over the fence.

I look at Samantha. "You next."

She doesn't hesitate. She dashes over to the shrubs, and Kennedy cups his hands for her to stand on as he hoists her over the fence.

"Last but not least, boss," Kennedy says. I dash over to him as he cups his hands again, and I step up as Kennedy helps me hoist my bodyweight over the fence.

I land on my feet in the adjacent backyard, where Sam and Alan are waiting for us. Kennedy climbs over the fence a moment later, joining us in the backyard.

"Well, what are we waiting for?" I ask the group.

Kennedy nods. "Come on, we'll sneak over to the car. We can use the backyards as cover."

It's the best plan anyone's had so far. Kennedy leads us as we scurry over the fences, hoisting ourselves over the fences with my driver's assistance. We hop from backyard to backyard, Terrence Malstrom nowhere in sight as we rush behind the block of houses.

When we reach an elegant backyard with a gazebo and a man-made pond, Kennedy stops us.

"I'm parked out front," he says. He reaches into his pocket, fishes out his keys. "We'll make a dash for the car. I'll go first, make sure that fucker with the gun isn't waiting for us by the door. I'll honk when it's clear, and then I need you three to *run*. Cool?"

"What the fuck do you mean, *cool?* We don't have much of a choice here," Alan says, and I watch as Sam grins. Her supervisor is already donning his old personality once again, I can tell it's a relief to her already.

Kennedy grins. "You must be Alan," he says. "Glad to finally make your acquaintance—"

"*Go!*" the three of us shout.

Kennedy nods, crouching down as he inches through to the front yard. He looks left, he looks right, and then nods back at us. Coast is clear.

He inches toward the black SUV that's parked just on the curb, and I look over at Samantha nervously. I know this wasn't part of the plan, *none* of this was. But it's the best we've got. I flash Sam a nervous smile, and she returns the gesture with a thumbs-up.

I hear a car door slam. Then, silence.

The SUV's engine starts up a moment later, I can hear it from the backyard.

Kennedy honks the horn, and Samantha, Alan and I don't waste another second.

We sprint from the backyard, running to the SUV as Kennedy opens the passenger door for me. I fling myself inside, Samantha and Alan dive into the backseat as they slam the door shut behind them.

"Go!" I bark at Kennedy.

He doesn't wait for us to buckle up, instead, he puts the car in reverse and slams on the pedal.

The SUV shoots backwards, careening down the street as Kennedy wraps his arm around my seat, staring through the back window as he drives us down the street faster than I'd ever believed possible in reverse.

After passing a group of houses, Kennedy slams on the brakes, spinning the wheel about as the car careens around. It stops, a perfect 180-degree turn as Kennedy throws the clutch, putting the car in drive as he slams on the gas again.

And just like that, we're out of the neighborhood. Each second moves us further away from Terrence, and I breathe a sigh of relief as Kennedy slows the vehicle down outside of the neighborhood.

We're in the clear.

And I've never felt so alive in my entire life.

"So, I guess that's behind us," Kennedy says. He peers through the rear-view window, looking at Alan as he speaks. "So, where to?"

Alan chuckles. "Wherever these guys are headed, I'm going with them," he says. Sam grins, and I peer into the backseat as I watch her playfully elbow her old supervisor.

"So, what were you saying about me training for a desk job with Tracy? I'll never want to work out in the field again?"

Alan laughs. "I guess you just changed my mind."

As we sit peacefully at the traffic stop, life couldn't be better for us.

We escaped. And Terrence Malstrom is nowhere to be seen. Up ahead, I can see we're parked at a roundabout, waiting for traffic to clear so Kennedy can merge. The traffic's too heavy, too packed to make a move right now. But we're safe, in the clear, so I'm more than okay with waiting.

A car pulls up next to us, another jet-black SUV. For all I know, it's the exact same model that Kennedy's driving right now. I look past Kennedy, looking into the vehicle that's just pulled up next to us.

I don't recognize the driver, but I do recognize the man sitting in the passenger seat.

It's Terrence Malstrom.

He's waving at us, holding the gun he'd just threatened us with.

I turn, frantically tapping on Kennedy's shoulder.

"What is it, boss?"

"Drive!" I bark.

Kennedy doesn't hesitate, slamming down on the gas pedal as he starts driving us into oncoming traffic.

TWENTY-NINE
Samantha

The SUV flies forward, Kennedy throws us into traffic as cars swerve and honk to get out of our way. The SUV next to us, Terrence Malstrom sitting in the passenger seat, flies after us in a chase.

I've been in my fair share of car chases, but I'm not the one behind the wheel.

It's all up to Kennedy to get us out of here safely.

The driver weaves in and out of traffic, dodging incoming cars as he drives the opposite way of the roundabout. He pulls through the circle, twisting the wheel hard to the right as he careens down a side road.

And the other SUV is right behind us. They haven't lost a single inch along the roundabout, and Kennedy looks through the rear-view window, yelping as he slams on the gas again. The SUV's engine roars, and the car behind us does the same as I can see Terrence sneering at his driver to hurry up.

There's no way we make it out of this alive. I can't see any way for us to lose them.

So it's all in Kennedy's hands now.

Alistair's driver careens us down a busy city center, shops and tourist attractions racing by us in a blur as the SUV gains on us from behind.

It's close, and I watch from the rearview window as the SUV behind us gets a little *too* close to our bumper, slamming into it. We're pushed forward, and Kennedy steps on the gas harder as he yanks the wheel to the right, swerving down an alleyway.

The SUV behind us can't anticipate the movement in advance, and the car behind us flies forward as we duck into the alleyway. Kennedy doesn't waste a single moment, driving quickly down the alley as he pulls onto another crowded city street.

For a moment, it looks like we've lost Terrence's car to the traffic of the neighborhoods surrounding Toledo, but I'm not ready to breathe a sigh of relief just yet.

Alistair turns around in his seat, checking in with Alan and I. "You guys okay back there?"

I look over to my former supervisor. "Alan, you alright?"

Alan's staring out the window to his right, staring down the road.

"Alan?"

My old boss shakes his head.

"They're still coming," he says. He points, and I see the black SUV careening down the street, heading right for us.

"Kennedy?" Alan says quietly.

"Yes, boss?"

"Keep driving."

"You got it."

Kennedy slams on the gas pedal, cranking the wheel hard to the left as the engine roars. We spin in place with Kennedy swerving the car at a ninety-degree angle to get us moving down the street. The SUV close behind us, Kennedy looks into the rear-view mirror as he starts to panic himself.

"I don't think I can outrun these guys," he cries.

"You have to try," Alistair says. "Up ahead, see that bridge?"

"Yeah, I see it."

"Head to it. I've got an idea."

Kennedy nods, pushing harder on the gas pedal as he pushes us towards the bridge. I can see it through the front window, it's just a small bridge. But it's over a small creek, a crevasse big enough for a car to sink into.

"Slow down a little," Alistair says. "They're coming up on the right."

Kennedy nods, letting up on the gas pedal as Terrence's car

pulls up next to us, careening down the road faster than we'd been going initially.

The bridge is just up ahead, only wide enough for one car to fit through. There are no incoming cars, just the two of us racing down the street at a hundred-plus miles an hour.

The bridge is deadly close, we're only seconds away from ramming into the side.

There's no way both SUVs can fit on that bridge, and I sure hope Alistair and Kennedy have their route planned out.

"You see what I'm getting at?" Alistair asks his driver.

Kennedy nods.

"Wait for it," Alistair mutters.

The SUV next to us matches our speed, and the driver's side window rolls down as Terrence Malstrom leans out, holding the gun aloft as he points it at our car.

"*Now!*" Alistair cries out.

Kennedy slams on the brakes, slamming into the car next to us. The car next to us pushes hard to the right, unable to slow down. Malstrom's car moves slightly off-center as the SUV mounts the sidewalk.

"Brake!" Alistair cries out, and Kennedy obliges him.

His driver slams on the brakes, yanking on the emergency lever to stop the car in its tracks. Alan and I are thrown forward, our seatbelts the only measure stopping us from flying through the windshield. Alistair jerks forward, his forehead slamming down on the passenger counter in front of him.

But compared to the other SUV, we're lucky.

The other SUV, with Terrence still leaning out the window, flies forward with the driver aiming directly for the bridge. But they're moving too fast, too quick to turn at such a tight angle, and the opposing SUV slams into the railing of the bridge, sending the car flying upwards as it crashes down into the creek bed below.

It's all over in an instant.

Alan, Alistair, Kennedy and I stare at the wreckage, smoke emanating from under the hood of the overturned SUV. There's no movement, and Alistair looks back at us.

"You two alright?" he asks.

I look over at Alan, shrugging. "I'm fine. Alan?"

My supervisor looks back and forth between me and the wreckage up ahead.

"So, Samantha," Alan says. "Long time, no see, huh?"

◆ ◆ ◆

Kennedy avoids the police, driving us back to Madrid without a hitch. No Terrence Malstrom behind us, no goons chasing us in the rear-view mirror.

We're finally in the clear.

After the two-plus hour drive back to the nation's capital, Alistair heads into the *Duplass* to check us out of our room. Alan and I head across the street, the two of us utterly starving. After all, I'm eating for two, and Alan's been held captive by Malstrom for God knows how long.

We head into a local restaurant, an inconspicuous pub that serves us *tortillas* and tapas by the plate. Alan orders a beer, and I watch my old supervisor breathe a sigh of relief as he takes the longest sip he can.

He holds the beer out to me. "Drink?"

I laugh, shaking my head as I decline his offer. "Right," Alan says. "Forgot about the pregnancy bit. Sorry. Other things got in the way today."

"If that's what you want to call them," I say. "But however you want to frame it, we're in the clear. I don't think that Malstrom is going to walk away from that accident."

Alan shakes his head, digging into his plate of olives and cheese while we wait for the next round of tapas. "No, he probably won't walk away from that. I'll make some calls later, check in with Langley. We'll have him extradited in no time.

That scene is the smoking gun we needed to put this guy away: incapacitated, probably stuck in some Spanish hotel somewhere. That is, until the CIA gets to him. We'll make him talk."

I nod. It's been one hell of a journey, and I'm overeager to get back home. I'm ready for this to be over, and I'm sure Alan, Alistair and Kennedy all feel the same after the hellish nightmare today was.

"So, how'd you find me?" Alan asks. "How did you manage to come through when nobody else could?"

I shrug. "I wanted to find you," I tell him. "It's my job. And now it's done. Finished."

"Still interested in getting back out in the field?" Alan asks. "After…" he gestures to my stomach with a flourish of his fork as he chews his bite, "… all *that* is taken care of, I mean. You'll have a job in the field waiting for you. If you want it."

I look down at my stomach, wrapping my hands around my midsection.

"I think I'll take that desk job, actually," I reply. "Call me crazy, but I don't think I'd like to re-live today. Or any of my old days out in the field. I'm ready for a change."

Alan smiles. "We can have that arranged," he says.

Alan and I finish our meals, paying the bill with the waiter. We step outside, stretching our legs as we look across the street to the *Duplass*. We can see Kennedy busy loading the car with the last of our bags, Alistair handing them over as he stands out on the curb. Alan and I cross the street, watching out for the Gran Villa traffic as we make our way over to the SUV.

"You two ready?" Kennedy calls out as he slams the trunk down. "We've got a flight to catch."

Alistair walks around the length of the SUV, pulling me in for an embrace after he's made his way over to me. His hug is warm, inviting. I've never felt more comfortable.

"You know, I bet a *private* plane can afford to wait a few minutes," Alistair chuckles over to Kennedy. "What are they going to do, leave us behind?"

Kennedy shrugs, hops into the front seat. "Whatever you say, boss." Alan follows after him, giving me a warm smile as he hops into the backseat behind Kennedy.

Alistair looks down at me, his arms still wrapped tight around me.

"So," he says, grinning, "ready to get back home?"

I'll admit it. I've never been more eager to do so.

"Back to reality," I smile.

THIRTY
Alistair

The flight back home is long, yet triumphant. We load up in Barajas-International, Sam, Kennedy and I taking out seats in the cabin as the pilot prepares for liftoff.

I sit back in my seat as the plane zooms down the runway, lifting off a moment later. I shoot a glance over at Samantha, sitting next to the window seat as she watches the Spanish countryside disappearing below us.

"Hey," I say to her. She turns, looking right back at me with those stunning blue eyes of hers.

"Hey," she smiles back.

"I love you," I say.

She grins. "I love you too."

I look over at Kennedy, our life-saver. He's passed out in his seat already, legs propped up on the seats in front of him. Normally I'd wake him up, tell him to respect the property, but today he deserves a break. After all that magic driving of his, I know he deserves a rest.

I look over at Alan, sitting in the row across from Samantha and I. He's exhausted, tired. I can see he's on the verge of passing out, but he looks up and smiles at Samantha and I.

"Thank you," he says. I nod. That's all that needs to be said.

I flag down one of the stewardesses, asking her for an eye cover. She hands one to me, warm and pressed, and I put it over my eyes as I lean back in my seat.

We've got a long flight home. And I need some well-deserved shut-eye.

◆ ◆ ◆

When we land back in Langley, Virginia, Alan hops up and gets off the plane quick as can be. I don't blame him, personally. Guy's probably got a family who's been worried sick about him for the past few weeks. The sun's shining overhead, it's mid afternoon here in Virginia, and I'm sure Alan has a million and one things on his mind for when he finally returns home.

As Alan watches the staircase descend, he shoots Samantha and I one more glance. He gives a thumbs-up, smiling. A moment later, he descends the staircase, and that's all she wrote.

Alan's home. Safe and sound.

Our mission's complete.

I turn to Samantha, shake her gently. She's been asleep for a while now, and I'm fairly certain she managed to sleep through the entire landing process. Kennedy's up and about, stirring as he grabs his bags from the overhead container.

I stop my driver as he passes by me, grabbing his arm gently.

"Hey," I tell him. "Thanks. For everything back there. I don't know how I can repay you."

Kennedy smiles down at me, grinning with that god-awful barbed wire tattoo on his forehead. Somehow, I don't find the tattoo nearly as offensive as I once did.

"You can get me that replacement phone," Kennedy says. "For starters."

I laugh, almost forgetting my promise to my driver. "You'll get a new model in the mail," I tell him. "Top of the line, the best money can buy. As a thank you. And a raise, too. With driving skills as good as yours, I *know* I'm keeping you around."

"Thanks, boss," Kennedy says. He pats me on the shoulder, walking past me as he exits the plane.

It's just me and Samantha now. She's awake, stirring gently as she yawns and stretches. She looks over at me, grinning.

And I know I owe my life to her. This never would've happened without her, and I know I wouldn't be around if it wasn't for her guidance. She taught me how to improvise, how to lie good enough to save our collective asses. And she taught me how to trust. Without that trust, I don't think Kennedy could have saved our lives back in Toledo. She inspired me, plain as day. Always have an escape route, and never be afraid to stand up for what you believe in.

All in all, I'd say we had a pretty good trip together. Our *first* trip together.

Hopefully it isn't the last.

"Hey," Sam says, smacking her lips as she looks around the plane, disoriented. "We're home?"

I smile. "Yeah, Samantha. We're home."

When we get off the plane, Samantha and I can see a massive huddle of black SUV's, swarming around Alan as men and women in jet-black suits inspect him for injuries. I guess the cavalry did arrive, however late it seems.

Kennedy loads up our car, tossing our bags in the trunk as Sam and I hop in the backseat. The driver gets behind the wheel, punching in Sam's address in his GPS.

It's time to go home.

I look over at Samantha, beaming. "I couldn't have done this without you," I tell her.

"Are you kidding?" she says, elated. "*I* couldn't have done this without *you*. Let's not pretend that your own personal driver didn't just save our asses back there."

Kennedy grins from the front seat as he starts the engine up. "Amen, sister." My driver pulls us around, wheeling us off the tarmac and back into the ordinary traffic of the Virginian after-noon. The cars around the airport are bumper-to-bumper, and Sam and I sit as Kennedy tries to weave us through the traffic.

Sam looks down at her stomach, smiling as she places one hand over it.

"So," she says, grinning up at me. "What was it you said to me, back in Paris?"

I look back over at her, elated. "Our story wasn't done there."

"You were right. Not by a long shot," Sam says.

She looks down at her stomach, then back up to me.

"Ready for another mission?" she grins.

"Only if you'll have me on your team," I reply. "Raising a kid isn't all it's cracked up to be, I'm sure."

"Nothing would make me happier."

I lean over and kiss her. Short, sweet, to the point.

She's already made me the happiest man in the world.

THIRTY-ONE

Samantha
Seven-and-a-Half Months Later

I can feel it; it's the sensation the doctors have warned me about for months now. And now it's here, the pain washing over me in an instant as I stand in the kitchen, dropping a half-filled glass of water as it shatters on the tile.

"Everything okay in there?" Alistair cries out from my living room. He's been hanging out in there, watching a football game on TV for the past few hours.

I wince, grabbing my stomach as I double over in pain. My belly is massive, and I know there's a baby in there just ready to get out and start their life.

I know it's time.

"No," I call out. "Everything is *not* okay!"

Alistair rushes in from the living room, eyes wider than dinner plates. He sees me doubled over in pain, clutching my stomach. He takes my arm, leads me slowly away from the shattered glass all over the floor.

"It is time?" he asks as he leads me into our living room.

I nod, doing my best not to snap at Alistair. We've been living together here in Langley for the past seven months, and we've been preparing for this moment ever since we decided to move in together.

And now it's time. My water's definitely broken, I can feel it in my gut.

Alistair grips my shoulder tight. "Hang on one second. I'll call Kennedy. He's the only one who can get us to the hospital in record time."

Alistair rushes over to the couch, grabbing his phone off the coffee table as he dials his driver. He tells Kennedy to get over here, *now,* and his driver tells him he'll be over in five.

"Hang on Samantha," Alistair says as he hangs up. "Just hang on. We're going to get you to the hospital."

I nod, clutching my massive belly as I hunker over in pain.

I need this to be over. As quick as possible.

◆ ◆ ◆

Alistair helps me get loaded in the back seat of Kennedy's SUV, and a moment later we're racing down the road, speeding along to the county hospital. Kennedy ducks and weaves through the midday traffic as he races us to the hospital, my groaning emanating from the back seat as I cry out in pain.

I can feel the baby coming. He—*or* she, we still don't know the gender—is *ready to go.* Now.

Alistair gives me his hand, and I grip it tight. I can see him wincing, but right now I don't really give a shit. I'm in pain, baby. I'm sure he'll understand.

Kennedy slams on the brakes, and Alistair and I jerk forward as the SUV comes to a screeching halt in front of the county hospital.

We're already here, I guess.

Alistair rushes inside, grabbing me a wheelchair as Kennedy opens the backseat door, helping me out so I can stand on my own two feet. Kennedy holds me by my shoulders, stabilizing me as Alistair rushes back out with a wheelchair.

I plop down in the chair, wincing as I hold my stomach tight. Everything goes by so fast, I can hardly comprehend what's going on. Alistair rushes me inside, talks to a nurse inside the ER lobby. I'm pushed into a hallway by a team of nurses, Alistair nowhere to be seen. I can't comprehend it, it's all moving so fast.

A team of hands help me out of the wheelchair, pushing me onto a bed as I lay back, wincing and moaning in pain.

I just want this to be *over*.

I look up, and I can see a curtain being extended over my midsection.

"Hey! What's going on?" I call out.

An older doctor, mid-to-late fifties steps out from behind the curtain. He's calm, cool, collected. His wrinkled smile and salt-and-pepper hair give the impression that I'm in experienced hands, and the doctor smiles at me calmly.

"Samantha Jacobson? I'm Doctor James, I'll be taking care of you today. Looks like we're having a bit of a rough delivery, am I right?"

I nod. I never imagined it would hurt this bad.

Doctor James peers back behind the curtain as a team of nurses rush into the room. He looks back at me, grinning nervously.

"Anyone told you the good news yet? Or did you already know?"

"Know what?" I groan. I'm not ready for more bad news, I don't want Doctor James throwing a monkey wrench into the works this early.

He peers back behind the curtains again, then looks back to me, a grin spread wide across his face.

"Let me be the first to congratulate you, then. You're carrying twins, Samantha."

I wake up a few hours later, disoriented and confused. The window peering outside has turned from a glowing afternoon to the dead of night, and I take a moment to recollect my thoughts.

They're fuzzy, sparse, and the details are slow to come back to me. I'm alone in the room, there are no other beds beside me. Nobody's sitting waiting for me, nobody's standing by the door.

But I know I'm not alone in here.

I look down at my arms, and I gasp.

Two children. Babies. Newborns. A boy, wrapped up in blue blankets, and a girl, wrapped in pink.

I was carrying twins. Two happy, healthy twins.

I seriously can't believe this.

I see a familiar face poking through the door's window. It's Alistair, and I wave at him eagerly, careful not to lose my grip on either of the babies.

Our babies. Our children. Our family.

Alistair comes into the room, carefully and slowly as he approaches the bed. He's got an eager smile stretched across his face, and he grins down at the three of us from where he stands.

"So, have fun without me?"

I giggle, admiring the babes in my arms as I smile back up at Alistair.

"No, you came at the perfect time," I beam. "Just in time to hand these over to daddy. Here, be careful."

Alistair hunkers down, and I hand him the girl first. He takes her in his hands, and I can see faint tears stinging the corners of his eyes.

I hand him the boy, and Alistair takes both of them in his arms as he stands back up, cradling them.

He looks down at me, the tears flowing freely now.

"You did it, Sam," he whispers.

"No. *We* did it," I reply softly.

We sit there in silence for a moment, Alistair admiring his children bundled up in his arms.

"So, I guess we were pretty stupid not coming up with names, right?" he chuckles through the tears. And now I'm crying, too, It's a perfect moment, one that I know I'll never forget for as long as I live.

"How about we name them after someone?"

"Like who?" Alistair asks.

I shrug, grinning as I wipe away the tears from my cheek. "What about naming them after the person who saved our lives, back in Toledo?"

"You're not saying—"

I grin at our children. "Face Tattoo and Barbed Wire. I think it's fitting."

Alistair bursts out in laughter, careful not to drop the twins.

"How about something a little more subtle?" he asks.

I smile. "I think I have the perfect names for them, then."

EPILOGUE
Samantha
Five Years Later

"John! Jackie! Lunch is ready!"

I finish plating the PB&J sandwiches, scooping out a serving of Mac 'n' Cheese out onto their plates as well. I grab their silverware, napkins and glasses of water as I carry my balancing act into the dining room. I set their food down on the table, watching in surprise as the coverall-garbed twins rush into the room, sitting down at their places almost instantly.

I'm impressed with just how much they've grown already. Sure, they're both five, going on six years old. But they're both mature as all-heck, and their teachers in kindergarten have nothing but amazing things to say about them. And they're taking after their father well-enough; both of them are sporting their father's dark hair and hazelnut eyes.

"Alistair! Hungry?" I call upstairs.

"Be down in a second!"

I sit down at the table across from my kids, grinning as they dig into their food. John's getting bigger every day, and I know he's going to be a strong brother to Jackie when they're older. And Jackie's smart as a whip, and she's pretty funny, too. I'm so proud of them both, I can't help but beam as I watch them eat. Tracy and Louis usually have their hands full with babysitting, but today I wanted us to all spend time as a family. We'll all make it out to the Farmer's Market next weekend, I already promised Tracy we wouldn't miss it for the world.

"Moooom, don't stare at us!" Jackie smiles as she croons.

I shrug, putting my hands up defensively as I return the smile. "Hey, just making sure you two are eating. I'll leave you alone, I promise."

I stand up and watch as Alistair descends the staircase. He's dressed casually today, a collared polo shirt over sweatpants. Truly a man of class. He's been working from home this past year, and things couldn't be smoother for us. His work as a CEO only requires him to be on the phone for ten hours a week or so, and the rest of that time is all up to us.

We've got everything that we need.

Hell, we don't even have to worry about Terrence Malstrom anymore. He ended up getting captured a few years back, and now he's rotting in an American prison cell. Just how thing should be. He survived the wreck that Kennedy maneuvered him into, and the American people finally got justice for all the financial crimes and more that Terrence Malstrom committed.

"It's happening," Alistair grins as he stands in front of me, arms wrapping around my shoulders to bring me into an embrace.

I gasp as I wrap my arms around his waist. "Really?"

"Yup," Alistair says. "We're selling Pemberton Computers tomorrow. Pennies on the dollar, but it'll be enough for us to go off on for the rest of our lives. We can retire. Send those two to a good college as *soon* as they're accepted."

I snicker, looking back into the dining room as our twins devour their lunches. "Think Yale's going for early admission this year? I could swing a summer alone."

Alistair laughs. "I'm in if you are. And let's eat, too. I'm starved."

I pop back into the kitchen, grabbing mine and Alistair's plates from the countertop. Two PB&J's and some more Mac 'n' Cheese. Never hurt to eat like a kid for once, and I can't complain.

We sit down at the dining room table just as John and Jackie finish their lunches.

"Can we be excused?" John asks.

I nod. "Of course, sweetie."

The twins carry their plates into the kitchen, and I hear them rattle as they put their dishes in the sink for us to clean off later.

Alistair and I chow down, savoring the sandwiches and pasta. It all tastes just like when I was a kid, too. When I look up from my food, I can see Alistair grinning like a madman.

"What is it?" I ask.

He shrugs. "Nothing. Just a passing thought."

"No, tell me," I smile, reaching out to take Alistair's hand. His grip gently tightens around my fingers, and I've never felt more at home than I do right now.

"I always knew we'd end up here," Alistair grins. "Together."

He grips my hand tight, and I gaze across the table and stare into those piercing hazelnut eyes of his.

Somewhere, deep down, I know I did, too.

We finish eating, the future ahead of us brighter than I ever thought possible.

And I know, no matter what, we'll always be together.

We've still got plenty of road left ahead of us. Our story didn't end in Paris, and it's nowhere close to being finished.

Just the way I want it.

THE END

BOOKS BY THIS AUTHOR

Breaker's Bargain: A Small-Town Bad Boy Standalone

I'm his auctioned-off date for a charity fundraiser. But he's the last guy on Earth I'd ever want to spend an evening with...

Ryan Jaeger. He's the hothead around town, known for cat-calling and leering at any girl unlucky enough to pass him by. And the last guy I'd ever expect to see at a charity auction for the local hospital.

But there he is. He's been staking out the auction I'm participating in, preparing to bid on a date for the evening.

And I'm his only choice.

He outbids everyone else by a hundred, five hundred, a thousand dollars. Just to spend a few hours on a date with me while the fundraiser continues.

My heart is racing. But when Ryan greets me, the bad boy facade fades as I'm instantly pulled to him. His charm, his smile, those rugged muscles, hidden under that leather jacket of his. Those stunning baby blue eyes. I can't stop staring at him, and I know he's been checking me out, too.

When he offers me his arm, I'm surprised...but a little excited as well. Ryan's promised a date and a night to remember, and I'm

nervous to see what the bad boy has planned. I accept his invitation for a simple walk around town, eager to see what's in store for me.

I guess I'm along for the ride.

And to the highest bidder go the spoils.

"Breaker's Bargain" is a STEAMY 78k standalone with tons of angst, small-town charm, and enough romance to keep you reading until the very last page! No abuse, no cheating, and a HEA with no cliffhanger.

Heartbreaker's Contract: A Billionaire's Fake Fiancée Standalone

Five years together. A fake wedding, a fake divorce, a fake everything. But the paycheck he's offering is very real…

This was supposed to be my dream job. Personal assistant to Shane Lockwood. Yes, that Shane Lockwood. The billionaire cutthroat sports agent who's got a new supermodel on his arm every week and an endless list of world-famous athletes as his clients. But his career is stagnating, Shane tells me. And the only thing that can save it is a plan involving a publicized fake marriage to a fake fiancée.

The phony fiancée he has in mind?

Me.

When he hands me the contract detailing our agreement, our fingers touch, an electric heat pulsing down to my core. I can't stop staring at his dark, lustrous eyes, his broad shoulders and strong arms, his concealed muscles sculpted to perfection.

All he needs is my signature. This jerk will own my life for the next five years, but I'll be paid handsomely, making me richer than even my wildest dreams.

I sign.

The ink's still wet when I realize that I have no idea who the real Shane Lockwood is. That's something he keeps behind a cold steel wall--and doesn't let anyone inside.

When a crisis strikes our office, Shane makes me choose between two equally undesirable outcomes when we're forced to collect a client's unpaid debt. And now I've got to get his business and our wedding planning sorted out before the heartbreaker rips our contract in two.

But he's not the only one who can cut a deal. I know my way around the block, I can play his game too...and I just might have a shot at winning.

Heartbreaker's Contract is a STEAMY 55k Romance with a HEA and can be read as a standalone with no cliffhanger. Snag your copy today!

Billionaire's Secret: A Steamy And Suspenseful Standalone

I'll help keep his secret and cover up his crimes, but only if he gives me something in return...

I never thought this would happen to me.

Daniel Livingston, CEO and investor extraordinaire, is looking for a new personal assistant. Oh, yeah, that Daniel Livingston

—the ruggedly handsome billionaire who's always playing the stock market for a win.

And he wants me to come work for him.

When he offers me the job, I'm floored. I haven't been able to take my eyes off of him—those hidden muscles underneath his suit jacket just beg to be touched. His rugged charm excites me, and I can't stop staring into those stunning emerald-green eyes of his.

So when he tells me he's working for the Mob, I'm shocked beyond belief.

He's been given fifty million a week, invested to launder and make clean for the Mafia. And in return, Daniel gets to keep a massive slice of the pie all for himself.

And I don't know what to do.

I still want the job, sure. It's a tempting offer. Daniel Livingston is too good to pass up, but I never asked for this.
Now I have to choose between doing the right thing and making a butt-load of money. And it's more cash than I'd ever hope to make in my entire working life.

I guess the secret's out now.

Billionaire's Secret is a steamy 60k standalone with plenty of suspense, action, and enough romance to keep you reading until the very last page. This book contains intense action, no abuse, no cheating, with an HEA and no cliffhanger. Snag your copy today!

FOLLOW ME ON SOCIAL MEDIA!

You can follow me on social media to stay up-to-date with new releases, deleted chapters, fan content and more!

Instagram: @adrianapeckromance
Twitter: @Adriana_Peck_KU

www.ingramcontent.com/pod-product-compliance
Lightning Source LLC
Chambersburg PA
CBHW051147130726
47988CB00005B/2021